THE
Third
Son

DYAN LAYNE

ISBN: 978-1-7364765-4-3

Cover photography: Michelle Lancaster, @lanefotograf
Cover models: Lochie Carey, Anthony Patamisi, and India Woollard
Cover designer: Lori Jackson, Lori Jackson Design
Editing: Michelle Morgan, FictionEdit.com
Formatting: Stacey Blake, Champagne Book Design

This book contains subject matter which may be sensitive or triggering to some and is intended for mature audiences.

Playlist

TOOL | *Triad*
Kid Rock | *Cowboy*
Big & Rich | *Save a Horse (Ride a Cowboy)*
Mother Love Bone | *Come Bite The Apple*
Lil Nas X (feat. Billy Ray Cyrus) | *Old Town Road*
Machine Head | *NØ GØDS, NØ MASTERS*
Silversun Pickups | *Lazy Eye*
Yeah Yeah Yeahs | *Date With The Night*
Rivals | *Heathens*
Alexisonfire | *Born and Raised*
Unprocessed | *Haven*
Brooks & Dunn | *Boot Scootin' Boogie*
Blanco Brown (feat. Ciara) | *The Git Up (Remix)*
Jamie Bower | *Start the Fire*
Greg Puciato | *You Know I Do*
Crowder (feat. Tommee Profitt) | *Carol of the Bells*
Ghost | *I Believe*
In This Moment | *The Last Cowboy*
Mother Love Bone | *Gentle Groove*
The Weeknd | *What You Need*
Bad Omens | *Come Undone*
Sleep Token | *Alkaline*
Wolf Alice | *Don't Delete the Kisses*
Death Cab for Cutie | *I Will Possess Your Heart*
Blanco Brown | *Funky Tonk*
Bebe Rexha (feat. Florida Georgia Line) | *Meant to Be*
Ben Gallaher | *Still A Few Cowboys Left*
Ghost | *Jigolo Har Megiddo*
The Black Queen | *Secret Scream*
Sleep Token | *Jaws*
††† (Crosses) | *Bermuda Locket*

IAMX | *Simple Girl*
The Black Queen | *One Edge of Two*
††† (Crosses) | *The Epilogue*
Slipknot | *Vermilion Pt. 2*
Yeah Yeah Yeahs (feat. Perfume Genius) | *Spitting Off the Edge of the World*
Devon Cole | *Hey Cowboy*
Thirty Seconds To Mars | *A Beautiful Lie*
Sleep Token | *Aqua Regia*
Bad Omens | *Just Pretend*
First Aid Kit | *Rebel Heart*
Two Feet | *Play The Part*
Greg Puciato | *Heartfree*
Jamie Bower | *Paralyzed*
Sleep Token | *When the Bough Breaks*
Bad Omens | *Nowhere To Go*
Ghost | *Life Eternal*
Sleep Token | *The Offering*
††† (Crosses) | *Option*
Tommy Profitt (feat. Fleurie) | *I'll Be*
5 Seconds of Summer | *Best Years*
††† (Crosses) | *Bitches Brew*
HIM | *Gone With The Sin*
First to Eleven | *So Cold*
Jacob Lee | *Demons (Philosophical Sessions)*
Currents | *Kill the Ache*
Greg Puciato | *Evacuation*
Chase Rice (feat. Macy Maloy) | *Ride*
Ghost | *Call Me Little Sunshine*
MCC (Magna Carta Cartel) | *Silence*
Imminence | *Infectious*
Ghost | *Waiting For The Night*
††† (Crosses) | *Goodbye Horses*
Amy Lee | *Love Exists*
Thrice | *Beyond The Pines*

Author's Note

This book contains subject matter which may be sensitive or triggering to some readers and is intended for mature audiences.

I loved a cowboy once, but I let him go.
This one's for you, Randy.

There is no remedy for love but to love more.
—Henry David Thoreau

THE Third Son

One

Coming out of the bathroom, Arien stubbed her toe, close to taking a tumble over a stack of forgotten boxes in the hallway. "Ouch. Motherfu…"

She held onto her foot, hopping the rest of the way to her bedroom in the small townhouse apartment she shared with her mom. It was all packed up, cartons neatly labeled, identifying the contents inside. Bed stripped. Closet and drawers emptied.

It wasn't like she had a choice.

A moving van was parked outside.

Holding her towel closed, her back against the wall, Arien sat cross-legged on the bare mattress. She had exactly thirty minutes to put on some makeup and get dressed. It should only take her ten.

This is so not fucking fair.

She blew out a breath. A week ago, her room was pretty and her life wasn't packed away in cardboard boxes. That all changed when her mother and her boyfriend—if that's what you call a man in his forties—took her out with them to dinner.

And that alone should have told her something was up.

Jennifer Brogan had been dating Matthew Brooks for about six months now, but Arien didn't know him all that well. A real cowboy, her mother said. He had two sons and lived on some ranch up in Wyoming, an eight-hour drive from Denver. He'd come into town for business, and to see her mom, a few times a month.

He was the one to break the news to her. "Arien," he said with a smile, taking her mother's hand in his. "First off, I need you to know I love your mama very much. So much, that I've asked her to marry me."

She about choked on her green chili cheeseburger.

Her mom held up her left hand, waving the huge diamond glittering on her finger. "I said yes."

Okayyy.

Arien was seventeen, soon-to-be eighteen. She'd be going away to college at the end of summer anyway. Her mom deserved some happiness, right?

Swallowing down the cheeseburger, she put on a smile. "At least you won't have to change your monogram. When's the wedding?"

"Next week," her mother announced, biting her lip. "I'm pregnant."

"Three months already," Matthew said, like he was proud of the fact, patting his new fiancée on the shoulder. "I'm coming back with the boys. We'll get married and have you all moved in before Thanksgiving."

What? To Wyoming? Nope. Not happening.

"Wait. You want me to move, to change schools during my senior year?"

"I'm sorry, sweetie."

"You're going to love Brookside." Her soon-to-be stepfather

patted her on the hand. "We have a superior private school there. The ranch. The mountains. You can take lots of pictures."

"There's mountains right here."

Isn't thirty-six too old to have a baby anyway? Apparently not. And what happened to all those lectures her mother gave her about having sex, taking precautions, and all that stuff? Mom should've listened to her own advice. If she had, Arien wouldn't be going to a courthouse wedding to leave Denver, and the only life she'd ever known, behind.

Only for a little while.

True. She already had her acceptance letter to UC. She'd be back.

"Sweetie, are you ready yet?" her mother asked from downstairs. "Matt and the boys are here."

Dammit.

"Almost," she answered, plucking through her makeup bag.

Clearly a lie. She hadn't even begun.

Holding a compact mirror in one hand, Arien applied mascara with the other, the towel slipping away from her.

She couldn't say for sure what made her look up. A feeling she was being watched, maybe.

Two boys—no, these were not *boys*, they were hot-as-fuck men—stood smirking in her doorway.

"Who the hell are you?"

"I'm Tanner." The darker one smiled, and taking a step inside her room, he hitched a thumb behind him. "That's Kellan."

"And I'm naked." She snatched up the towel, covering herself.

Kellan snickered.

Tanner came closer. "Well now, that's a mighty fine hello, little sister."

You've got to be friggin' kidding me.

Her eyes darted between the inked brother looming right in front of her to the blond one leaning against the doorframe behind him. Both of them tall, gorgeous, and ripped, they were hardly the annoying prepubescent boys she'd presumed Matthew's sons to be. Not that she'd bothered to ask about them. And why hadn't she?

Too caught up in her *poor, poor me* shit, Arien had been too angry to care. In the space of a week she'd packed up her life, said goodbye to all her friends, and for what? So her mom could get married to some dude who knocked her up. Were these two "Save a Horse, Ride a Cowboy" poster boys supposed to be like a consolation prize or something?

"She's even prettier than her picture, ain't she, Kel?"

"Hmm." Kellan rubbed his finger back and forth over his upper lip. "I reckon."

"Do you mind?" Arien pulled the towel tighter. "Naked here."

With a chuckle, Tanner leaned down and kissed her cheek. "We don't mind at all."

The wedding went off without a hitch. Her mother in a short ivory dress and Matthew in a navy-blue suit, Arien and her new stepbrothers stood as witnesses to their parents' nuptials. It took all of five minutes. She took their photos on her Nikon Z50 she'd spent years saving up for. The Denver County Courthouse, a magnificent example of neoclassical grandeur, made for a gorgeous backdrop. Its three-story portico of columns, the wide staircase, and ironwork lanterns gave her some amazing shots.

Matthew tapped her on the shoulder. "Can I see, honey?"

"Oh, yes, of course." And she handed him her most prized possession.

"These are really good."

"Thanks."

He glanced at her. "There's only one thing wrong."

"What's that?"

He smiled. "There aren't any of you and the boys."

They went to Benzina, a trendy new Italian place nearby, after. Sadly, green chili cheeseburgers weren't on the menu, but the coconut macaroon panna cotta wedding cake came pretty darn close to making up for it.

Sandwiched between the two brothers, each nursed a beer on either side of her. Arien assumed then, they were at least old enough to drink legal. Or perhaps their dad simply allowed it? She glanced over to Tanner, since he seemed more approachable. "How old are you anyway?"

"Old enough." He winked. "I'll be twenty-two on Thursday."

"Your birthday's on Thanksgiving?"

"This year."

Appraising her from the corner of his eye, Kellan raised his beer to his lips, draining the glass.

"Are you older or younger?"

"Older," he clipped. Then Kellan addressed his father. "We leavin' tonight or waitin' 'til mornin'?"

"I figured we could load up the truck tonight, get a good night's sleep, then hit the road first thing in the morning." With a wink, Matthew threw an arm around his bride. "That okay with you, son?"

"Yeah, sure." Kellan glanced at his brother, the corner of his mouth ticking upward. "Suits us just fine."

Tonight. Tomorrow. What's the difference? She'd still be leaving in the end, so to Arien it didn't matter either way.

"I think I'm gonna have another piece of cake." Yeah, because sugar can fill up the hollow pit inside, at least for a little while. Not to mention, she had the feeling there probably wouldn't be desserts that came anything close to this where she was going.

"Arien," her mom began to protest, but Matthew covered her hand with his and stopped her.

"I love me a pretty girl with a hearty appetite." Kellan slapped a huge slice on her plate. "No need to be counting all those calories there. We'll be workin' 'em right off you, won't we, brother?"

"Do I look like a cowgirl to you?"

"Not yet." And he grinned.

Leaning into her ear, Tanner squeezed her knee beneath the table. "He's just trying to get a rise out of you."

Arien looked at Kellan, and giving him the most saccharine smile she could muster, lifted a forkful of cake to her mouth. "Mmm." She licked panna cotta filling from her lips. "So good."

"Eat up, baby cakes." His wicked gaze fixed on her. "We got things to do."

She stood with her mother in the living room, watching the new men in their lives cart boxes stacked three high down the stairs, as if they weighed nothing at all. Being these boys probably threw bales of hay around all day long, moving their stuff must be an easy breezy walk in the park. Admittedly, Arien wasn't exactly sure what cowboys, ranchers, or whatever they called themselves did. Except for what she'd seen on TV, and even that wasn't very much.

Her mattress went out the front door. "Mom, they can't take that. Where am I supposed to sleep?"

"The pullout sofa isn't going anywhere—not until Goodwill picks it up tomorrow."

"Okay, what about them?"

"Recliners?" Jennifer shrugged, then pulled her into her side. "It's one night, Arien. Just make do. Tomorrow you'll be in your beautiful new room, in a big, beautiful house, breathing the fresh mountain air."

"Great."

"Listen, sweetheart, I know this is a huge adjustment for you." Her mom squeezed her tight. "It is for me, too, but Matt is so good and the boys are nice, young men…we have a family now, baby. Life is going to be wonderful, you'll see."

Biting her lip so she wouldn't cry, Arien nodded. She'd never seen her mom this happy, and dammit, she deserved to be. So, she was going to suck it up and put a smile on her face. For Mom. It was only nine months out of her life, right?

An hour later, with the truck loaded up and their parents tucked away upstairs, the boys kicked back in front of the TV.

Kellan aimlessly scrolled through the channels. Tanner patted the empty space between them. Armed with her pillow and a blanket, Arien took it.

"What are we gonna watch?" Making herself comfortable, she folded the old, lumpy pillow in half and tucked it under her arm.

His gaze remaining on the screen, Kellan shrugged a shoulder and passed her the remote. "Pick somethin.'"

"Fine, Hallmark Christmas movie it is."

Kellan snatched the pillow from her, playfully swatting her with it. "See if I ever let you have the remote again."

"Hey," Arien squealed, looking from one brother to the other. She couldn't help but compare the two. Their subtle similarities. The stark differences. Her fingertips brushed the dirty-blond strands that had fallen into his brown eyes. "You must take after your mom."

"Guess so." His gaze returning to the TV, Kellan tossed the pillow to her lap.

Tanner leaned in against her shoulder. "She died when he was just a baby."

"Oh, God. I'm so sorry, Kellan." Arien took his hand and squeezed it. His calloused thumb, sandpaper on petal-soft skin, slowly traced the pulse at her wrist. She turned her head toward Tanner. "Wait a minute…"

"Kellan and me don't have the same mama."

"Oh, you're half-brothers then."

"Brothers." His thumb stopped moving. Kellan didn't look at her when he said it, "End of story."

"Where we come from…" Tanner slung his arm around her shoulder. "…there's no such thing as half, little sister."

"Okay, you're close. I get it." Resuming their movement, Kellan skimmed his fingers along the back of her hand. "Where's your mom, Tanner? Did she and your dad get divorced?"

"No."

"Oh, they were never married?"

"They were married."

"She's dead." Kellan turned the TV off. "Buried in the family plot next to mine."

"Fuck." Her hand flew to her mouth.

"I was three days old." Tanner hugged her to him closer. "Weak heart, they figured, bein' that's what took his mom too."

"Why would that matter?"

"Because they were sisters," Kellan said, matter-of-factly. "I say we get some sleep. We've got a long drive and a truck to unload tomorrow."

Scrunched together, the three of them made themselves fit on the pullout sofa. Kellan faced one way, and Tanner the other, while Arien stared up at the ceiling. She thought of two little boys growing up without a mother. Two sisters lying side by side in the ground. The man who had been married to them both. How tragically sad.

Something woke her. Tanner softly snored behind her, his tattooed arm thrown across her middle. It was heavy.

She gasped.

Moonlight illuminated the piercing eyes that studied her.

Kellan held a finger to her lips. "Shhh."

Two

Raising his arms high above his head, Tanner stretched his limbs at the back of the U-Haul and inhaled a lungful of city air. It lacked the scent of clear spring water, wild meadows, and earth. Undertones of pine. Ozone. Denver was an all right city, he supposed, but it wasn't the evergreen forests, the place he called home.

His new stepsister was sad to be leaving here, he was sure. Tanner was just as certain she would fall in love with Brookside, the ranch, the majestic wilderness that surrounded it.

And us.

To have Arien love him. Kellan. Their family. Well, as far as he was concerned, that was the most important thing of all.

Their blood might not run in her veins, but just as the land would seep into her skin, they'd steal their way inside her heart and brand their names upon her soul. Yeah, he'd make sure of it.

Tanner was working in the horse barn that day in May, laying fresh straw in the foaling stall, when his dad came home from one of his business trips going on about this pretty blonde waitress he'd met. He and his brother snickered under their breath, not thinking much of it at the time.

But the trips became more frequent and he didn't stop talking about her.

"Wait 'til I get my hands on you, Jennifer." Leaning against the paddock fence, his dad whispered into the phone, "Just the sound of your voice gets me hard, baby."

Yeah, you still got it, old man.

Even if he was his father, Tanner had to admit Matthew Brooks was a handsome dude for forty-four. Virile and fit. It was in their genes. Hell, on the rare occasions Dad went out with them to Jackson, the ladies threw themselves at him.

"You fucking her, Dad?" Course, Kellan had to already know the answer to that.

"Mind your mouth, son." But as he pushed off the fence, his voice wasn't at all stern. The look he gave them was enough, though. "Jennifer is…different. Special. She's the one…"

"How do you know?"

"Because I know." Matthew winked. "That woman is just what I need, what this family needs." He paused, the corner of his mouth quirking up. "And she has a daughter."

Tanner was all ears. Dropping his work gloves, Kellan sat on the bale of hay beside him. "Oh, yeah?"

"Her name's Arien." With a brief nod, he clicked his tongue. "Pretty little thing. Seventeen. Blonde like her mama."

"You've met her?" Kellan asked.

"A couple times." His father reached into his back pocket to pull out his wallet. "And I got a picture of her too."

Blue background. Obviously a school photo. Expressive eyes.

Lush lips. A dimple in her chin. Arien wasn't just pretty, she was beautiful.

His brother took the picture from their father's fingers. "How'd you get that?"

"I asked Jennifer if I could have it." A hand on each of them, Matthew got down on his haunches. "So you both could see her."

Kellan slipped the photo into his pocket. "And is this woman…this Jennifer is gonna pick up and leave Denver for you?"

"She will."

"What makes you so sure?"

Their father smirked. "I put a baby in her belly."

"You love her?" Tanner needed to know. It wouldn't turn out well, if he didn't.

"Yes, son, I do."

Taking another deep breath, Tanner rubbed the kink from his neck and closed up the U-Haul. As soon as everyone got their asses out of the apartment, they could go home. He went back inside. "Y'all coming or what?"

Sprawled on the sofa, twiddling his thumbs, Kellan shrugged.

"The girls will be down in a minute." Dad lowered his voice. "Now, remember what I told you. Arien's not exactly tickled to be leaving the only home she's ever known. She's strong-willed, independent like her mother, because she's had to be."

The notion didn't intimidate him. Quite the opposite, in fact. Tanner found it an attractive quality. Every woman in his family was spirited and strong. Grams. Aunt Kim. Emily.

"Until yesterday, the only family they ever had was each other. So we need to show them how a man loves and cares for his own. Understood?"

Kellan cleared his throat. Jennifer and Arien were coming down the stairs.

She carried one of those plastic laundry baskets. It was filled to the rim, the old pillow she'd cuddled with last night lying on top. A backpack dangled from the crook of her arm. Relieving her of the items, Tanner took them out to the U-Haul, placing them on the passenger-side floorboard. She'd be riding with him and Kellan.

His brother came up beside him. They watched Dad give Jennifer a hand into the dually. Kissing her cheek, Matthew buckled her in and closed the door.

"I'll take the first leg," Kellan offered, plucking the keys from his fingers.

Arien moved in closer, placing her hand in Tanner's. He gave it a squeeze. "All set?"

She looked ready to cry. Biting her lip, she nodded.

"C'mon, my girly." He gave her a boost up into the front seat of the truck and she moved toward the middle. Sliding in beside her, he curled his arm around her shoulders. "We got you now. It's gonna be okay."

In an effort to hide her tears, she turned her head, burying her face in his hoodie. Arien didn't make a sound, but he could tell she was crying. Her hand on his chest lightly trembled.

Tanner glanced to his brother with a single nod.

Kellan turned the key in the ignition.

And with his fingers combing her silky-soft hair, they drove north out of the city.

Her body curled into his, the way she fit beneath his arm, felt so good. He liked that she turned to him for comfort. Tanner could only imagine what Arien must be feeling. It would tear him up to have to leave Brookside, but then everything and everyone he loved was there. Denver was just a place. They were hers now, and with time, she would see that.

Almost an hour went by before Arien raised her head. With a stuttering breath, she rubbed her eyes. "Was I sleeping?"

"Yeah." Tanner chuckled, ruffling her hair.

"Are we in Wyoming yet?"

"Not yet." Kellan stretched his arm out behind her on the bench seat. "Just passed Fort Collins."

"I didn't mean to fall asleep on you." She shifted to sit back up, the softness of her body leaving him. "I'm not usually such a crybaby, I swear."

"You're allowed." Tanner rested his arm on her shoulder. "We'll show you around the ranch tomorrow—give you the grand tour, won't we, Kel?"

"You ride, baby cakes?" Kellan's fingers slipped into her hair.

"Ride?"

"A horse."

"Uh, yeah." Head bobbing, Arien pursed her pouty lips. "I've been on a trail ride a few times. Does that count?"

Hardly. Sitting saddle on a pony for an hour-long walk through the woods ain't ridin'. Not really. With a snicker, Tanner and his brother exchanged a glance.

"Guess I'll be teachin' you." Kellan winked. "Got a good mount for her, brother?"

Me.

"Buttercup or Daisy would do well, I think." Running his thumb along her jaw, Arien smiled up at him. "Gentle and strong, but fast—so you can keep up with us. Well-behaved too."

"Do you have a lot of horses?"

"Yeah, I suppose we do."

Flush darkening her cheekbones, she gave her head a little shake. "That was a stupid question. It's a ranch. Course you do."

"Tanner's the horse guy." Kellan grinned, putting his hand back on the steering wheel. "He breeds 'em. Trains 'em too."

"Yeah? Like for racing?"

"No, those are thoroughbreds. We have sport and draft horses. Friesian, Shire, and American Quarter mostly."

"Wild mustangs too," his brother added. "Tanner has this habit of findin' stray foals and bringin' 'em home."

"Are you like *The Horse Whisperer* or something?"

His breath locked in his lungs. It was the way Arien looked at him. Sunlight dancing in her big hazel eyes. Sparkling green. Flecks of amber honey and cognac. "Something like that."

They crossed the state line into Wyoming.

"Welcome home." His head dipped to her ear and he whispered, "I'm keeping you."

"Hope the weather holds," Kellan said as he folded himself into the passenger side of the U-Haul. "Dad and Jennifer are a good hour ahead of us."

They'd stopped at a roadside bar and grill in Sweetwater Station. He and Arien would have been okay with McDonald's, but Kellan didn't do fast food. Like ever. He could be a pain in the ass like that. Though, truth be told, Tanner wasn't a fan of it, either.

Arien sipped on a pumpkin spice latte. He'd never seen anyone get so excited over coffee. She darn near squealed when she saw it on the menu. "How much longer 'til we get there?"

"Three hours, give or take." Tanner squeezed her knee and started up the truck.

"More like four if we hit snow." Kellan tapped her on the thigh. "Let me try some of that."

She handed him the paper cup. Sniffing it first, he shrugged and took a sip. "God, that's awful. How in the hell do you drink this shit?"

"How in the hell can you not like it?" Arien countered. Taking her coffee back, she drank some. "Mmm, so good. I don't suppose you've got a Starbucks in Brookside."

"Nope." Kellan snickered. "But Jackson's only an hour, hour and a half away."

"There's a coffee house in Dubois," Tanner offered. "That's the closest town."

"Just a forty-five-minute drive."

"We'll be passing through it." He gave her knee a squeeze again. "We can stop and get you another one, if you'd like."

"Yeah." And she smiled, her pretty eyes gazing up at him from a thicket of black lashes. "I would."

"You're gonna like Dubois. Lots of artsy people—writers, artists, photographers, musicians—live there."

"Really?"

Kellan rolled his eyes. "Only one way to drink coffee, and that's strong and black." He leaned over, and lifting the pillow off the top of Arien's laundry basket, began rummaging through it. "What's this?"

"My portfolio for school." She looked over at the album in Kellan's hands, her smile somewhat wistful, and sighed. "Photography club."

"Mind if I have a look?"

"Not at all."

Traveling the scenic byway he'd driven countless times before, Tanner couldn't see the photos his brother was looking at. The pages slowly flipped, Kellan studying each one. Seeing the world Arien had left behind, through her lens, likely told him more about her than she could possibly imagine.

"You took all these?"

"Yeah."

"You have an eye." He paused for a long moment. "They're good."

"Thanks."

Tanner could hear the smile in Arien's voice. Was she blushing? Her lashes fluttering? Did she look up at Kellan the way she'd looked at him?

"Who's this guy?" A brisk, sardonic laugh followed. "Your boyfriend?"

"I wish. I've had this sorta crush on him since middle school, ya know? And when does he finally get the *cojones* to ask me out?"

Brow raised, he glanced over her head to his brother. Their eyes locking, Kellan winked.

"My last day of school, that's when."

"Ya snooze, ya lose," Tanner told her, grinning to himself. They had her and no one else could get to her now. "His loss."

"I'm sure I'll be seeing him this fall at UC. Maybe I'll let him have another shot."

"UC, huh?" Kellan's thumb rubbed over the image on his lap, as if he was attempting to erase it. "Making plans to leave us already?"

"That was always the plan. I have my acceptance letter, so I'll be going back to Denver in August."

Not if we can help it, little sister.

"What for?" he asked. Arien looked at him like he'd uttered a foreign language. "What I mean is, what's your major gonna be?"

"Fine arts." Her lips turned up then. "I'll be studying photography mostly."

"Looks like you already know how to take pretty pictures." Kellan tossed the album back into the basket. "Don't see why you have to go away to college for that."

"Because I want to."

Folding his arms across his chest, Kellan tipped his head back and closed his eyes. He stayed that way the rest of the drive home, even when they stopped in Dubois to get Arien another one of those overpriced coffees she loved. But Tanner knew his brother wasn't sleeping.

It was dark by the time he punched the code into the gate. Matthew and Jennifer were waiting on the porch as they pulled in. Kellan jumped out of the truck and went right around to the back, the cargo door opening before he could turn off the ignition. Running to her mother, Arien followed him out.

Tanner joined his brother, who was already unloading boxes. "She's perfect. I want her."

"I wouldn't get your hopes up." Kellan tossed him a box,

not looking at him. "You heard her. End of summer and she'll be gone."

"The way I see it, that gives us plenty of time to make her want to stay, brother."

"Maybe."

"A lot can happen in nine months, Kel."

He tossed him another box and the corner of his mouth slowly lifted.

Three

Sitting at the kitchen island, Kellan rested his elbows on black granite, drinking a second cup of coffee while he waited on Arien. Tanner was out in the stables, getting the horses ready for their ride. He hadn't seen his dad or Jennifer yet this morning, but considering they'd shared their first night at home together as newlyweds, he figured they were sleeping in.

Course, he hadn't slept much at all. After unloading the truck and eating a quick supper, Kellan went right upstairs to his room across the hall from Arien's. He peeked in on her through the open crack in her door. She sat on the king-sized brass bed, organizing her clothes in neat, folded stacks. Every now and then, she'd stop what she was doing to gaze into the fire, or take in the room Grams and Aunt Kim did up for her. No doubt it was larger than the entire second floor of the little townhouse apartment they'd moved her out of.

Without a sound, he turned away, slipping inside his room. Not bothering to close his door, but then he never did, Kellan stripped off his clothes and walked buck naked to the shower in the Jack-and-Jill bathroom he shared with his brother. Even with the thought of Arien, not twenty feet away, he was too tired to jerk himself off. He thought about it, though.

When's your birthday, baby cakes?

He was going to have to find out. She was seventeen, which made her off-limits—for now. Kellan hoped it was sooner, rather than later. They still wouldn't be able to fuck then, damn rules, but anything else was allowed. He'd teach her, show Arien all sorts of other things.

She could take his dick in her hand and stroke him in the shower when he was too tired, when the muscles in his arms burned after working all day. She'd soap up his balls, his ass, twisting her finger up inside him. *Fuck, yeah. You're gonna be a good girl for me, aren't you?* Then he'd push himself past those pouty lips and fuck her throat.

"Choke on this fat dick," Kellan murmured to the stone shower walls. Aroused now, he wasn't so tired anymore.

Had she ever sucked cock before? Fuck, he doubted she'd even touched one. As soon as she turned eighteen, he'd teach her how to give pleasure, and she'd get plenty of practice.

He'd teach her to take it, too.

At the thought of laying her down right here on the shower floor, he jerked himself harder. Spreading those thighs wide, he'd get his tongue all the way up her cunt and nibble on that clit at the same time. Slide a finger or two in her ass and she'd be seeing stars.

That's just for starters, my good fucking girl.

Yeah, he had so much to teach her, so much to prepare her for.

Did she ever touch herself? Make herself come? He could show her how. Kellan could picture Arien sitting on the bed like the very first time he saw her. Naked and so fucking beautiful. Fingering her pretty pink pussy at his instruction. Rubbing her swollen clit. *Jesus*. And for that, he didn't have to wait until her birthday, now did he? Watching ain't touching. Arien could take her fingers from her pussy and put them in his mouth. Then he could taste her.

He'd let her watch him too. Feed her his cum from his fingers.

Yeah, they could learn a lot about each other without touching.

And so much more once they could.

At midnight, Kellan lay naked in bed, hands clasped behind his head, counting the wood beams in the ceiling. Sleep wouldn't come and it was all her fault.

"That was always the plan."

Her lights were off, but the door across the hall was still ajar. A faint glow from the fireplace emanated through the crack.

"Fuck UC and fuck your plan."

Arien leaving here sure wasn't a part of his.

"A lot can happen in nine months, Kel."

It could. But until he trusted her to stay, maybe it was best he didn't let himself get too close to her.

Glancing at the clock on the microwave, Kellan drained his cup. Tanner told her to be ready at nine, and it was five minutes past, dammit. *Inconsiderate.* Did she think he was going to wait around for her to grace him with her presence? Arien needed to learn everyone else's time was just as valuable as hers.

Tapping his fingers on the granite, he debated whether he was going to pour himself a third cup of coffee or just go on without her, when she strolled into the kitchen like she had all the time in the world. "Morning."

"Don't like bein' kept waitin', Arien. You're late."

"Am not." She reached for a mug. "It's only quarter after."

"You want some of that, you're drinking it on the way." He slammed a Thermos next to her on the counter. "Tanner's in the barn already, and you and me? We're gonna have us a little riding lesson first."

"Lesson?" Arien scurried out the door after him. "How hard can riding a horse be?"

"You think you just hop on and yell 'giddy-up'?" Glancing over his shoulder at her, Kellan scoffed, "We've got half a million acres here, girly. Ain't taking a walk through the woods."

"Jeez." Hooking her arm through his, she caught up to him. "I guess someone's not a morning person."

Trust me, baby cakes, one day you're gonna find out.

"I'll have you know I've been workin' since five, Sleeping Beauty." He stopped cold, scanning her from head to toe. Blonde hair twisted into one of those fancy braids down her back, loose strands blowing in her face. Cable-knit sweater beneath her jacket. Faded jeans and a pair of old sneakers. "Where's your damn boots?"

Arien stared down at the well-worn Ariats on his feet. "Sorry, I don't have any like those, and I'm not ruining a cute pair. I mean, what if I step in horse shit?"

"C'mon." Laughing, he grabbed her by the hand and led her to the paddock where Gunner waited for them.

Kellan whistled and the horse trotted over.

She tipped her head back, staring up at the majestic Friesian. "You expect me to get on that?"

"Yup," he replied, rubbing the horse's muzzle. "Meet Gunner."

"He's beautiful." Arien tentatively reached her hand out to touch him. "And big."

"Almost seventeen hands." Kellan gave her an apple. "Go on. Make friends."

Taking a step back, he watched his horse gently take the of-fering from her palm, an astonished giggle bubbling up from her throat. Gunner chomped on his treat. Timidly, Arien gave him a pat. "Hey there, boy."

"See? Nothin' to be scared of." Kellan stroked the animal's flank. "C'mon now, up you go."

"Not scared," she shrieked as he gave her a boost up onto the horse.

"Coulda fooled me." He chuckled to himself. "Take your foot out of that stirrup and hold on."

Kellan swung into the saddle behind Arien, pulling her snug against him. "There. Now, sit back in the saddle and kinda slouch that cute little butt of yours." He took the reins. "First thing, always loop your reins over the horse. This way, if you drop 'em, they won't fall to the ground."

She did it exactly as he showed her. "Like this?"

"Just like that," he said, and giving Gunner a nudge, the horse moved forward. "Let your lower body move with the horse while you keep the upper half still."

Kinda like fucking.

"Got it."

"Thattagirl." He looped an arm around her waist.

Arien steered Gunner counterclockwise around the paddock, relaxing into the easy rhythm of his gait. "This isn't so hard."

Squeezing his legs into the horse's sides, Kellan signaled him with a click. Gunner sped into a trot, Arien's ass bouncing up and down in the saddle. "Yeah, like that. Move with him."

As they circled the field, she leaned forward a little, her crotch pressing into the pommel, the movement obviously stimulating her. He could hear the catch of her breath, see the flush in her cheeks. Gripping Arien tighter, Kellan urged his horse even faster.

Feels good, don't it, baby cakes?

Teeth sinking into her lower lip, a whimper of sound escaped her with every exchange of air. He held her, his thumb sweeping up and down her abdomen, muscles rippling in waves beneath his fingertips. Kellan angled his head.

He wanted to see her green eyes glaze.

He wanted to slide his hand inside her jeans.

But he couldn't.

What the fuck just happened?

Catching her breath, Arien inhaled deeply through her nose. Of course, she wasn't an idiot. She knew exactly what happened to her, she just hadn't expected it. And with Kellan flush up against her ass, she wasn't quite sure if straddling a saddle was entirely to blame for the mess in her underwear.

She tried to keep it from happening, tried to stay quiet, but lost that battle in the end. At least she'd managed not to scream. Arien only prayed her stepbrother hadn't noticed. How embarrassing would that be?

If Kellan could tell, he was playing it cool. His thumb lazily strummed over her sweater, rocking behind her in the saddle like nothing happened. But then she didn't know him nearly well enough to read him.

A horse whinnied. The distinct clip-clop of hooves coming from the barn had Arien glancing over her shoulder. Tanner sat astride a gorgeous horse, black with a white blaze and stockings, leading another alongside him.

"Whoa." Kellan took the reins. "There's your ride."

His smile a mile wide, Tanner rode into the paddock. He jumped off his horse and strode over to Arien. "She's for you."

Golden coat, its mane and tail white, the mare gazed at her from the post with the softest brown eyes. And instantly, Arien's heart melted.

"Daisy's yours now." Tanner reached up for her.

"Really?" She slid from the saddle into his arms. "She's mine?"

"Yup." Lowering her feet to the ground, he wrapped his arm around her waist. "And I'm gonna show you how to take care of her."

"Hello, sweet girl," she cooed, running her fingers through the forelock of Daisy's mane. "Do all the horses have names?"

"Sure do." Tanner squeezed her to his side, patting the horse's flank. "This guy here is Tux."

Arien lifted her gaze to striking eyes of celadon. A lopsided, boyish grin. He was as much of an unknown as his brother, yet somehow he put her at ease.

"What about the cows?" She giggled.

"Yeah, we call 'em Dinner," Kellan answered with a roll of his eyes. "Can we go now? I still got work to do and it's lookin' like snow."

"He always such a cranky-butt?" Arien asked as she placed her foot in the stirrup.

"Kel's a moody fucker." Tanner gave his brother the side-eye. "Ignore it."

What was up with him? Unlike his brother, Kellan didn't come off as being the friendliest guy anyway, but he'd been acting strange—cold almost—since they got here yesterday. Well, except during their ride when she…yeah. But then everything felt strange. Waking up in an unfamiliar room. This place. It could be she was just overanalyzing things, right?

Maybe. Or could be he just doesn't like you.

They left the paddock together. Kellan was silent, leaving Tanner to do all the talking. "This is private land. The ranch, the town, all of it. Has been for almost two hundred years." He pointed somewhere off to his right. "The highway is that way. Brookside is behind a gate at the end of a five-mile drive. It's easy to miss the turn-off if you don't know it's there. There's no sign. Google Maps don't work up here. Anyone who mistakenly goes down our road would think it's a gate to a private residence, not a whole dang town."

"Wait." Arien threw him a look. "No Google?"

"Don't worry." Tanner chuckled. "Cell service can be spotty, but the internet is all right."

Surrounded by evergreen forests and jagged ridge lines, they followed a stream to a clear alpine lake. Mountain peaks, reminding her of medieval castle turrets, mirrored its smooth surface. Arien wished she'd had the foresight to bring her camera along.

Kellan dismounted at the water's edge and took a seat on a log. "The Sheepeaters called this home long before we were ever here."

"The Shoshone," Tanner explained, joining his brother. "This is Brooks Lake. Most of the time, we have it all to ourselves—lots of trout. There's a cascade falls downstream, closer to town. And see that three-headed mountain?"

Gazing up, she nodded.

"That's Brooks Mountain."

Her eyes flicked between the brothers. "It's named after you?"

"Not officially, but yeah." The corner of his mouth ticking up, Tanner's arm came around her.

"You must be pretty important around here then—the big shits."

His dark eyes narrowing, Kellan turned his head from the water to look at her. "Ain't like that. There's no bullshit hierarchy in Brookside. Our family was one of the founding families to settle on this land, same as the other families here. We built the ranch, is all."

'*Okay*,' she silently mouthed, pursing her lips.

Tanner drew her closer. "Come August we can watch the Perseid meteor showers—it's better than the Fourth of July, I promise you."

I'll be gone by then. But she didn't say it.

Kellan moved his hand to rest beside hers on the log. "Where's your dad, Arien?"

"Well now, that's a good question." And usually, it was a question she didn't care to answer whenever the subject of her sperm donor was brought up. Considering they were family now, for better or worse, it didn't seem rude that he asked. "Couldn't tell you, but then I don't even know who he is."

"What?" His hand sliding over hers, their fingers entwined.

"My mom and her friends went on a ski trip to Aspen their senior year of high school. It was spring break and they ended up at a party some college guys were throwing in their hotel room. Mom got drunk. Frat boy knocked her up." Arien shrugged, her voice trailing off. "She can't even remember his name."

"Damn." Squeezing her waist, Tanner laid his head on her shoulder. "What about your grandparents?"

"Mom's dad kicked her out when she wouldn't get an abortion."

"No other family?"

She shook her head.

"You have us. We're your family now," Kellan reminded her. "When's your birthday?"

"January twenty-first." Arien looked up at him, and noticing tiny slivers of green in his chocolate-brown eyes, she smiled. "When's yours?"

"August…" He smirked. "…thirty-first."

"You're a Virgo. That explains it." She sniggered. "You never did tell me how old you are."

"Twenty-two."

Tanner lifted his head.

"Oh…wait a minute." *What the fuck? That can't be right.* "You're only three months apart?"

"Yeah."

"And your mothers were sisters?"

"Yeah."

So, Matthew Brooks knocked up two sisters at pretty much the same time. Marries one, she dies, then he marries the other?

And then she died too.

That was all sorts of fucked up no matter how Arien looked at it.

"I've got to get back." Kellan stood and retrieved Gunner. His foot in the stirrup, he paused to look at her. "There's bears in these mountains. Never walk alone."

Suddenly, she was so confused. "Tanner?"

"Told you he can be a moody fucker," he said, tucking a strand of hair behind her ear. "How about we go back? I'll teach you how to untack Daisy, then we can go into town and I'll show you around."

"Yeah, okay."

His fingers slowly skimmed her cheek. "I'm so happy you're here."

Four

Tanner slammed the bathroom door shut.

Damn you, Kellan.

He wasn't sure what the hell his brother was thinking, but if he kept on with his bullshit, he was going to fuck everything up. And then what?

Fortunately, Arien didn't say anything about it during their ride back to the house. She was so smitten with Daisy, and soaking up everything he was teaching her like a sponge, she didn't question him in the barn either. Still, he could just imagine the thoughts spinning in her pretty little head.

"You're only three months apart?"

Surely, she'd ask him more about that on the way to town. He hoped not. It's not like it was a secret or anything, but Arien wasn't acquainted with their ways. What did she know of loving? Nothing, besides the love that exists between a mother and daughter. Friends, maybe. If anything, there'd been such an absence of it in her life, Tanner feared the sacred concept would be difficult for her to understand.

He found her in the kitchen with Jennifer and his father, dressed for their outing in a pale-gold sweater that reached mid-thigh, leggings, and over-the-knee boots. Arien leaned over the island, long blonde layers framing her face, a mug in her hands. The three of them appeared to be having an amiable exchange. He released a breath. Tension draining from his shoulders, Tanner joined them.

"Jennifer made hot cocoa." His dad waved a can of whipped cream. "Want some?"

"Uh, no, thanks." Tanner squeezed Arien's shoulder. "Takin' my pretty girl here to town. Gonna show her off."

She glanced up, cheeks turning pink, looking at him in that way he'd come to love, and smiled.

Letting his hand slide down to her waist, he squeezed her hip and winked.

"Arien was just telling us all about the horse you gave her." Holding onto Dad's arm with both hands, Jennifer was beaming. "So darn sweet of you, Tanner."

"Daisy's a good choice for her, son." Matthew kissed his wife on the cheek. "Make sure you two are back in time for supper. Grams'll be here."

"And Auntie Kim?"

"You know it." His head bobbed with a chuckle. "Emily too. Maybe she'll have Billy with her since they'll all be goin' to school together."

Holding Arien close to his side, Tanner walked her over to his truck and opened the door. She angled her head to look up at him. "Who's Emily?"

"Your new cousin." He smiled, buckling her in. "And your new best friend."

"Oh." She watched him climb into the driver's seat. "And who's Billy?"

"Her, uh…boyfriend." Tanner started up the truck. "Emily's the same age as you. Until we get you a car, I reckon you'll be gettin' a ride to school with her."

"I don't need a car." Chewing on the corner of her lip, Arien looked down at her lap.

"Sure, you do." He laced his fingers with hers. "Bet you get one for your birthday. Me and Kellan got our trucks last year."

Arien glanced over at his brother's RAM parked there next to his. Their father got them matching TRXs, Kellan's red and his blue, like they were still five, when Grams used to dress them in identical outfits for school.

"For your birthdays?"

"Yeah." Turning his head, he leaned over, barely an inch of space separating them. "I s'pose you wanna ask me about that."

"No."

"No?"

"Your dad was the same age as you when you were born, right?"

"Yeah, 'bout that."

"And guys your age are…you know."

He sniggered. "Got us all figured out, huh?"

"Hardly." Fingertips grazed his cheek. "But I am the girl who was conceived at a drunken frat party, remember? Anyway, who am I to judge?"

With a subtle dip of his chin, Tanner covered her hand with his, holding her fingers to his face. She was so close he could kiss her. He wanted to. But he didn't.

Ten minutes into their drive, Arien turned away from the scenery she'd been staring at out the window. "How far is town?"

"We're almost there."

Both hands waved circles in the air. "All of this is ranch land?"

"Yup." Tanner threw her a grin.

"It's hard to put half a million acres into perspective."

"Have you ever been to New York City?"

Arien shook her head. "No."

He'd never been to the Big Apple either, not that he had any real desire to go. "How about Disney World?"

"Once, when I was eight."

His dad and Aunt Kim had taken him, Kellan, and Emily there on a family trip after his uncles were killed in Afghanistan. She was only four at the time.

"Well, the Disney property is almost twice the size of Manhattan. Imagine twenty-one Disney Worlds put together and there you have it. Eight hundred and forty square miles tucked between two national parks and two national forests."

"That's mind boggling," she exclaimed, fingers at her temples. "And you own it all."

"Everyone in Brookside has an equal share of everything. That's the way it's always been."

"Oh, like a co-op?"

"Yeah, you could call it that, I guess." He pulled into an empty spot that fronted the quaint shops on Main Street. "See, back then people had to come together to build a community that could sustain itself and survive. They did, and we're still doing it."

Not only did Brookside survive, it flourished and grew. They heeded the words of a sage mountain man and prosperity, that continued to this day, had been granted to all of them.

Opening the passenger door, Tanner took her by the hand. "Everyone has a say and everyone does their part. Doctor, teacher, working the ranch, running a store. Doesn't matter. Equal share."

"Didn't they try that in Russia?"

"That's communism, pretty girl. Not the same thing here." He chuckled, holding her to his side as they walked.

"Explain it to me then."

"It's simple. Here, sit with me." Taking a seat on a bench,

Tanner held her hand in his lap. "This is gonna require a little history lesson."

Huddled against him, he watched her take in the idyllic surroundings. Gas lampposts. Colorful awnings and storefront windows on buildings that had stood for more than a century. Towering pines. The Absaroka peaks.

In this place, where everyone knows everyone, Arien turned heads. Catching a glimpse of the daughter of Matthew's new wife, townsfolk tipped their heads in greeting, whispering amongst each other as they passed.

Hazel eyes glanced up at him. "I'm listening."

"The mountain men came first. It was 1841 when the first wagon train pioneered the Oregon Trail all the way to the Pacific Northwest. Then the Mormons traveled to Utah in 1847. It was about that same time, the Brooks family went west too. The plan was California, but they didn't make it that far. Their journey ended here in Wyoming. None of this was the United States then. Hell, it wasn't even a territory yet. But they, and the other families who left the trail with them, pooled their resources and worked together to make a life here."

Maybe she loved history as much as he did, or more so his telling of it. He liked to think it was the latter. Regardless, with her gaze riveted on him, he knew he had her attention.

"In 1862, Congress passed the Homestead Act and everyone got a hundred and sixty acres of free land. The original settlers, then their children, and every person who came of age thereafter, staked their claim—until 1906 anyway. They combined all of that land and here we are."

"Half a million acres."

"That's right." He gently tapped her on the nose. "And every person who lives here either came from or married into one of those families. Understand now?"

"Kind of. Explains why you aren't the big shits, I guess."

"Can't live on cows alone." Pulling Arien up from the bench

to walk with him, Tanner chuckled. "It's pretty isolated up here, in case you haven't noticed. We've always had to provide for ourselves. So the doctor and the farmer, the rancher and the teacher, the shopkeeper, everyone…"

"…does their part. Equal share." Pausing her footsteps, she looked up at him with a smirk, hair dancing around her face in the cold wind.

"Good girl." He tucked a wayward strand behind her ear. "You *were* listening."

"So the doctor is fine getting the same share as the farmer?"

"We all gotta eat."

"Well, yeah. I see your point, and while that might work in a perfect world…"

Tanner was well-aware how things worked on the other side of the gate. The world out there wasn't Eden and never would be. But they were different and the life they shared here was a beautiful and wondrous gift.

"Brookside must be as perfect as it gets then." He resumed walking. "Because it works."

⛰

Opening her eyes, the rough-hewn beams above her slowly came into focus. It was early, morning mist swirling outside her window, like the inside of a cloud. Well, they were nine thousand feet in the sky, so maybe it was.

She should get out of bed. Help her mom with the turkey— make that turkeys—apparently one wasn't enough around here, but then she'd seen firsthand just how much food her stepbrothers could eat. It was warm beneath the covers, though, so she was loath to leave them. Even the dog, cozy by the fire, his paws in the air, didn't stir.

Crazy dog. How do you sleep like that?

Snuggling into the soft goose-down, Arien scanned her sumptuous bedroom. Rustic, but feminine, simple, yet luxurious—at least to her—she could imagine photographing it for a magazine. Textured walls washed in a pretty sage green. A blush faux-fur throw at the foot of her bed. Pillows covered in velvets, linens, and silks. The stone surrounding the fireplace extended to a corner reading nook. It was the eclectic mix of elements, textiles, and colors that created the gorgeous aesthetic.

Never mind being torn away from Denver, she should be happy to be living here, right? And for the most part she was. Her stepfather was more than good to her, and he sure loved her mom a whole lot. Melinda Brooks—who insisted Arien call her Grams like everyone else did—and Matthew's sister, Kim, and her daughter, Emily, had been especially warm, welcoming her into the fold. By the time they finished with supper on Sunday, it felt as if she'd been around them her entire life. And her stepbrothers. She should be thanking her lucky stars they weren't total assholes.

Okay, Kellan could be a prick sometimes. That boy ran hot and cold. So darn confusing. One minute he'd be glaring at her, all steely and sullen, then the next, especially if he thought she wasn't looking, it was something else entirely. His dark eyes would grow darker, features softening, as he studied her.

And Tanner? He was wrong. Tough-guy exterior with his bulging biceps and a sleeve of tattoos, that boy was six feet of beautiful sweetness. Gentle bear hugs and forehead kisses. *He* was her new best friend, not Emily. And today was his birthday.

Arien wasn't sure what to get him. She'd gone back to town with Matthew and her mom, perusing the upscale shops on Main Street, which was strange in and of itself. Brookside wasn't Aspen or Telluride—or even Jackson Hole. All their customers lived here, right? This was a ranching town, for fuck's sake, yet all the stores seemed to cater to expensive tastes.

It was then she took a closer look at the town, and the people around her. Everyone appeared to be exceptionally content and extraordinarily beautiful, from the oldest man to the youngest child.

The vehicles parked along the square were all showy and new. Not an old Ford pickup in sight.

So odd.

And if that wasn't weird enough, no money exchanged hands. No cash registers. No credit cards swiped. Nothing. She got Tanner's gift and the clerk all but laughed at her when she pulled out her card to pay for it.

"We'll put this on your account, young lady."

"I don't have an account."

"You're Matthew's daughter, aren't you?"

"Stepdaughter."

"Then you have an account."

After shopping, Matthew took them to lunch and it was the same thing. No check. They simply ate their food, and when they got up to leave, her stepfather just waved goodbye as he ushered them out the door.

She was overanalyzing again, wasn't she? Yes, they did some things differently here, and so what? Maybe it wasn't what she was accustomed to, but she'd get used to their ways eventually. Still, she couldn't shake the notion that something was off here, she just couldn't quite put her finger on what.

Arien pulled the covers off, and the dog, realizing she was awake, jumped into bed with her. "Did you have a nice snooze, Sunday?"

Or was this one Monday? Five border collies lived on the ranch. Each one named for a day of the week, with the exception of Thursday and Saturday. *I wonder who came up with that?* Before she could give him a scratch, his ears perked up. Jumping back down, he ran out the door. "Well, good morning to you, too."

As much as Arien hadn't wanted to get out of bed, after her shower she couldn't wait to start the day. She loved all things pumpkin spice, so Thanksgiving was one of her favorite holidays. Since she'd be helping out in the kitchen, she dressed for comfort more than anything. Leggings and a cotton bralette trimmed with lace under an oversized pullover.

Slipping her feet into a pair of cute knit booties, the clamor of her stepbrothers returning from their chores could be heard from across the hall. Grabbing Tanner's birthday present, she opened her bedroom door.

And Kellan hadn't closed his.

Turn around, Arien.

But she couldn't.

His back was to her. Frozen in place, she just stood there, slack-jawed, watching him push denim down his thighs, a gift bag for Tanner dangling in her fingers.

Kellan shucked off his jeans, kicking them to a chair. He wore nothing underneath. *Sweet Jesus.* He was beautiful. Stretching his arms over his head, he resembled a living, breathing statue. Rock hard, but at the same time, fluid.

Now, Arien. Turn the fuck around.

She didn't, but he did.

Molten-chocolate eyes stared into hers, his gaze heavy-lidded and sultry. It was as if he knew all along she'd been watching him. Liked it even. Taking a step toward her, Kellan leaned against the doorframe. And still, she didn't move.

Whatever you do, Arien, do not look down.

She looked.

He sniggered, gripping himself in his hand.

Mesmerized by the sight of it, Arien watched him fill.

Something pulled deep inside her belly. How would it feel to have Kellan inside her? God, why was she even wondering?

As if he could read her thoughts, his tongue swept across his bottom lip. Kellan smirked, and fisting his cock, he stepped away, heading for the shower.

Holy fucking hell, what's wrong with me?

It took her a minute. Arien stood there, her gaze on the hallway door to the bathroom the boys shared, imagining what Kellan was doing in there. She inhaled deep and let it go, knocking at the door on the other side of it.

"Happy birthday," she exclaimed, giving Tanner a hug. "I wanted to give you your present before I go downstairs to help Mom."

He hugged her back, her feet lifting off the ground. "You didn't have to do that."

"I wanted to." Smiling up at him, Arien put the shiny gift bag in his hand. "I'm sorry, it isn't much."

"Thank you." He smiled, backing away from the door. "Come in."

His room was as large as hers. Same wooden beams in the ceiling; textured walls a warm cream; velvet linens of soft denim blue. A painting of Tux hung above the fireplace. She walked over to the expanse of windows and looked out at the vast landscape. "We got more snow."

"Yeah," Tanner said from behind her. "You won't be seeing the grass again anytime soon."

"What about the cows?"

"What about them?"

She turned toward him. "What will they eat?"

"Hay." Chuckling, he patted the empty space beside him. "What is it you think we do every morning?"

"I dunno." Arien shrugged. She sat down on the bed. "Ranch stuff."

"You should come out with us and find out." Draping his arm across her shoulders, he pulled her closer. "And Daisy misses you. We could go for a ride."

His brow raised, the corners of his mouth kicked up. Tanner had the most amazing smile, and he showed it to her often. Kellan hardly ever smiled at all.

She reached for him, combing his still-damp hair from his face. "Yeah, I'd like that."

His gaze locked on hers, green eyes drinking her in, he dropped his hand from her shoulder to squeeze her waist. Maybe seeing his brother naked had her all flustered, because she was looking at Tanner differently now.

Arien slowly pulled her hand from his hair, fingertips sweeping down his cheek. Lowering her lashes, she took in the swift rise and fall of his chest. She bit her lip, not allowing her eyes to wander below the waistband of his jeans.

"I would too." With a gentle nudge of his finger, he lifted her chin. "Do you want me to open my present?"

"Oh, yes." She nodded. "Please do."

Tanner took his gift out of the shiny, little bag. Chewing on her fingernail, Arien watched him tear away the tissue paper.

"I didn't know what else to get you."

A framed selfie of the three of them, sitting together on a log at Brooks Lake. She didn't have the foresight to bring her camera that day, but she had brought her phone.

"Look at us." He smacked a kiss to her lips. "I love this."

"Got one for your dad—Kellan, too." Glancing to the door that went to the bathroom he shared with his brother, Arien sniggered. "He'll probably burn it."

"No, he won't." Tanner got up, standing the framed photo on his dresser. "Why would you say that?"

"I don't think he likes me very much." Brushing a piece of lint from her leggings, she stood with a shrug.

"Oh, he likes you."

"How do you know?"

"He's my brother. Trust me, I know." Tanner wrapped his arms around her. "It matters to you, doesn't it?"

"What?"

"Kellan."

"We live together. Course, it matters."

"I like you, pretty girl." He kissed her forehead, his lips lingering on her skin. "A lot."

"You do?"

Tanner smiled. "Yeah."

"I'm glad." Lifting onto her tiptoes, Arien kissed Tanner's cheek. "Because I like you too."

They parted. She glanced at the door once more.

It was open.

And there, a towel wrapped low around his hips, Kellan stood leaning against the frame.

Five

Savory deliciousness wafted throughout the kitchen. Turkey number two roasted in the oven. Cranberries simmered on the stove. Arien breathed it in deep. Her mother, queasy with morning sickness, left to lie down for a while, leaving her and Grams to carry on without her.

For a woman who had to be in her sixties, Melinda Brooks was the epitome of timeless beauty. Porcelain skin. Not one strand of gray in her butter-blonde curls. Ever cheerful, she smiled so much her twinkling blue eyes crinkled at the corners.

"How've you been settling in, honey?" she asked, gathering ingredients to make the pies. "Big adjustment for you, I know."

"Yeah, everything's good…" Arien took the cranberry sauce off the stove, setting it aside to cool. "…just different, you know?"

"Mmhm, sure do. I remember the first time Paul brought me up here to meet his family. We came for spring break—it was calving season."

"You're not originally from here?" Grabbing her mug of lukewarm coffee from the counter, she went over to Grams, leaning onto the island with her elbows. "I thought pretty much everybody was."

"Nope, born and raised in California. I met Paul Brooks my freshman year at UC Davis. He was a senior. Swept me right off my feet, that man did. Cowboys have that way about 'em." She stared off into the fire roaring in the living room, wistfully smiling, then gave her head a little shake. "Can you fill this measuring cup with ice water for me?"

"Sure."

"That's the trick to making a good crust—cold butter and ice water. Don't you forget I taught you that."

Arien giggled. "I won't." She pressed the cup into her hand.

"Anyway, I fell in love with him quick and hard. Met the folks. His brother, Garrett—he was quite a sweet-talker too, let me tell you." Cutting the butter into cubes, she sighed. "That was in March. Paul graduated in May and we got married in June. Matthew came along a year later."

Kellan came into the kitchen. He poured himself a cup of coffee and leaned onto the counter. His back to them, he scrolled through his phone.

"You gave up college?"

"Just for a little while." The food processor pulsed. "Finished my degree over in Jackson by the time Kimberly was born. Your mom tells me you're planning on going to college back in Denver come fall."

Kellan tossed his phone to the counter. Turning around, he folded his arms across his chest and shot her a glare.

Arien ignored him. "I am."

"Good for you, honey. Don't ever lose sight of your dreams. When I was your age, I dreamt of being a teacher and having a family of my own. All my dreams came true—the Brooks men here made sure of it. They understood how important it was to me."

"You're a teacher?"

"Right here in town." Grams squeezed her hand and gave a chuckle. "Don't worry, dearie. I teach the primary grades, not high school." Pausing, her eyes flicked over to her grandson. "And just remember that dreams, like plans, can change. There are other colleges you can go to if you decide you'd rather stay close to home."

But Denver is home.

Or at least it was.

Kellan left the kitchen without a word. Grams taught her how to roll out dough, and together they made the pies—three apple and three pumpkin. Arien was playing Tetris, trying to fit everything in the fridge, when her mom returned from her nap, and Kim, along with Emily, came waltzing through the door.

"I picked up a birthday cake at Maizie's for Tanner," Kim announced. She made room for the bakery box on the counter. "Got him his favorite. I know we've got desserts out the wazoo, but I couldn't let my nephew blow out candles on a pie just because it's Thanksgiving."

"Hey there, cousin." Arms laden with covered dishes, Emily smacked a kiss to her cheek. "Sides and the ham. Where do you want 'em?"

"Umm…" *Anywhere but the fridge?*

Grams pulled turkey number two out of the oven. "Take it to the sideboard, Emily. We're about done here, or we will be as soon as your uncle carves this bird. Are Billy and Jake coming?"

Walking in with his brother, Tanner took the turkey from her. "Here, I got it, Grandma."

"Yeah, they'll be by later." Emily looked back over her shoulder as she left the kitchen.

"Who's Jake?"

Tanner and Kellan turned to her, both speaking at once. "Billy's brother."

"Her boyfriend."

Okayyy.

Arien was seated between them at dinner, Kellan on her left and Tanner to her right. They didn't say grace or anything like that, but once Grams poured each of them a glass of spiked apple cider—well, except for her mom, even she and Emily got one— her stepfather stood.

Matthew cleared his throat. "Y'all know, nothin' means more to me than our family." Looking at her mother, his feelings written on his face, he said, "Thank you, Jennifer, for our new baby and for bringing beautiful Arien to us. Never thought I'd be lucky enough to be a dad again. But most of all, thank you for loving me like you do."

Tanner squeezed her hand beneath the table.

Kellan's fingers skimmed along her thigh.

Matthew's attention turned to his sons. "*We* have been favored. There is much to be thankful for."

Glasses went up.

Arien tasted the wine-infused cider. Kellan drained his in one swallow. He leaned over, his voice whispering low in her ear, "Drink up now. I think you're gonna need it."

He might be right about that.

She was stuffed, and judging by the looks of them, so was everyone else. Sprawled on rich, warm leather in front of the fire, the football game was on, yet no one seemed to be watching it. A knock at the door came. Emily jumped up, chestnut hair flowing behind her as she ran from the room to answer it.

Grams chuckled. "Gee, I wonder who that could be?"

Arien's stepcousin returned, a man on each arm. One of them appeared to be about their age and the other somewhat older— early to mid-twenties, maybe. *Holy moly.* Both had long black hair, thick and straight, down to their chests. Chiseled jawlines. Dark, almond eyes.

Emily took them to meet Jennifer first, who suddenly looked like she was ready to toss her cookies again. Her fingers fidgeting, the older one patted her shoulder, while Matthew stroked her hair. Speaking softly, Arien couldn't make out what they were saying.

"Here we go." Kellan moved her down to the end of the sofa with him and threw an arm around her. "Gonna wish you took that second glass of cider when I offered it."

Tanner's gaze snapped to his brother, and fingers plowing through his hair, he scooted over as Emily and her arm candy came toward them.

"This is my cousin, Arien."

"Hi. Billy Gantry." Shaking her hand, the younger one nodded to the man on the other side of him. "And my brother…"

"Jake." He tipped his chin, his gaze traveling between her and her stepbrothers. "Pleasure to meet you, Arien."

The trio took the space they'd made for them, Emily sandwiched between the two. Interspersed with shouts at the football players on TV, the men in the room debated the merits of going for a winter breeding this year. *Good grief.* Billy sat there, talking and playing with Emily's hair. He'd stop to kiss her neck, while his brother held her hand. Leaning against him, her cousin kissed Jake on the cheek. He simply smiled, interlacing their fingers.

Shifting herself closer to Kellan's ear, Arien asked, jokingly, "Which one's her boyfriend again?"

He licked his lips, fingers pressing into her nape, but he didn't answer.

She didn't want to be rude, but she couldn't keep from watching them. Their behavior just struck her as so peculiar. But what did she know? Maybe Emily held Jake in high regard, is all. It was possible. Reasoning with herself, she considered it the most likely explanation. Billy didn't seem to mind his girlfriend's obvious affection for his brother, and it's not like Jake was encouraging her. He did appear to like it, though.

At halftime, Emily extricated herself from the Gantry brothers, and ruffling Tanner's hair, squeezed in between them. "Happy birthday, Cuzzy."

"Thanks," he said, scooting over to give her room.

"Hey, Kel. Why you lookin' so sulky over there, babes?"

Reaching past Arien's shoulder, he play-swatted her. "Shut up, Ems."

"I thought having you around would sweeten him up some, but I guess not." Giggling, Emily stuck her tongue out at him. "Do you have everything you need to start school on Monday? We could go to Jackson this weekend, if you want. I think a girls' day is called for here."

Kellan rolled his eyes.

"I brought all my school stuff with me from Denver, but yeah, sounds like fun." It would be an opportunity for her to get to know Emily better, and for that reason alone, Arien was all for it.

"Yes, and it's so pretty there, all decorated for Christmas."

Reaching over her to tap Kellan's shoulder, Tanner got up from the sofa. "Pops is here."

Kel gave her knee a squeeze and followed his brother.

"Uh-oh."

Arien followed Emily's gaze. The man stood with her stepfather, a package in his hand. He was older, with graying blondish hair, slicked back and thinning on top, a mustache and goatee.

"Who's that?"

"John Jacoby," Billy answered, moving over. "Their grandfather."

"Uh-oh? I don't get it."

"He doesn't come around much," Emily answered, snuggling against her boyfriend. "To the ranch, I mean. He lives in town. Adores those boys, so Kellan and Tanner see him all the time. But he steers clear of my uncle."

"Why?"

"Hard feelings, I guess." Pursing her lips, she shrugged. "I overheard Grams and my mom talking. He blames Uncle Matty for the deaths of his daughters."

"That's ridiculous. Wasn't it a weak heart from childbirth or something?"

"So they say." Emily gave her a pointed look. "Don't know the reasons, but there's bad blood between 'em. You can feel it. And my guess is he didn't come out here just to give Tanner a birthday present."

"Why else then?"

"To get a look at his grandsons' new mama." Gazing across the room, she bit her lip. "You."

"Me?"

"I think they're coming over here," Billy warned.

For fuck's sake, did she really have to be subjected to this? Arien was not about to get sized up by some old guy, who was already studying her like a mold specimen growing in a petri dish.

Kellan reached her first. "Pops wants to meet you." Taking her by the hand, he pulled her up from the sofa.

"Arien. A beautiful name for a beautiful girl." The old man kissed both her cheeks. "It means 'most pure.'"

"It's a *Lord of the Rings* character," she said.

He looked at her oddly, tilting his head from side to side.

"Tolkien. Yeah, um, thank you," she added.

Tanner stood on one side of her, Kellan the other. Their grandfather gazed at the framed photo she'd given her stepfather just that morning and a smile, it almost seemed sad, rose on his face. He turned to Matthew, his chin trembling, and subtly bobbed his head. "You've broken tradition, yet you have been greatly favored. A new wife, a baby—the third child. And a lovely daughter."

"Yes, I know how blessed I am, how fortunate we all are."

"For the sake of my grandsons, may you continue to be." He turned, embracing Kellan, then Tanner. "Happy birthday, my boy."

And he left.

Arien's heart squeezed. Surely his grandsons' birthdays were a painful reminder of what happened to his daughters.

Wait a minute.

"You've broken tradition? What did he mean?"

Matthew exhaled. "Let's go sit down, Arien."

Sunday followed her into the bedroom. Arien softly closed her door, while the dog took his place in front of the fire. Her mind still reeling, she took a shower to try and clear her head. It didn't work.

"Me and your mama discussed how to explain our ways to you. Planned to sit with you tonight and do just that. I know you're probably wondering how it is Kellan and Tanner are so close in age, especially their mothers being sisters and all."

They were all here. Emily was rubbing her arm and Tanner squeezed her hand so hard she thought he might break it.

"Our customs, how we live, the reason we prosper, goes all the way back to when Brookside was founded. I think you've already figured out we don't do things the same here, and here…" He paused. "…marriage is between a man and two sisters or a woman and two brothers."

"Huh?"

"Our unions are triads. There is a universal power in three. The nature of the world is tripartite—heavens, waters, and earth." Taking her other hand, Jake got down on his haunches in front of her. "As are human beings—mind, body, spirit. The triad is the whole, you see. It is all. Everything. The beginning, middle, and end."

Kellan watched her from across the room.

"Anthropologists call two brothers married to the same wife, fraternal polyandry, and two sisters married to the same husband, sororal polygyny. We call it the trinity, and to us, it is sacred."

What in the actual fuck?

Dumbfounded, she shook her head. "You can't do that. It's not legal."

"Not out there, no." Her stepfather came forward. "The elder sibling is on the marriage license at the courthouse…"

With his usual smirk on his face, Kellan slid his hand down the front of his jeans and winked.

"…but what we do inside our gate, how we live inside our homes, is no one else's concern."

"You were married to them both at the same time." She said it mostly to herself.

"Yes."

Looking at Emily, Arien pointed to Jake. "He's your boyfriend too?"

"Yes and no."

Jake gently turned her face back toward him. "We're to be married when Emily and my brother come of age."

"I'm a junior." Billy shrugged. "So not this summer, but next."

They had to be kidding. She'd never heard anything so absurd in her life. Arien's gaze flicked amongst their faces. This was no joke.

A burst of laughter sputtered out from behind her hand. "That's so fucked up. I'm sorry, but y'all are crazy."

"Arien!"

She rolled her eyes at her mother.

Tanner looked at her like she'd kicked his new puppy and let her go. Of course, Kellan was seething. His dark eyes narrowed into slits and he opened his mouth to say something, but with a shake of his head, Matthew stopped him. Only Grams showed Arien any compassion at all. But then she had to understand. She was an outsider once, yet she chose to marry into their fucked-up way of life.

Grams gave her shoulder a comforting squeeze. "I'll just go get Tanner's cake from the kitchen."

Wrapping herself in a cozy throw, Arien watched the snow gently fall outside the window. Thinking back to their Stepford-perfect town, she'd known something was off. All those beautiful people, yet not one couple strolled together holding hands. *Me and Tanner. Mom and Matthew.* She should've noticed that. But then who would expect the crazy-ass *Sister Wives* shit going on here?

Was this some weird religion? A cult? A strange secret society? *You've seen too many movies, Arien.*

Regardless, it didn't have anything to do with her anyway. They could do whatever the hell they wanted in their big houses behind that goddamned gate, come August she'd be gone. The sad thing was, Arien was starting to like it here. To feel like she had a real family. To feel like this was home.

And then there was Tanner. Her new best friend. Kellan. He *was* a cranky-butt, always trying to get a rise out of her, but still, she'd come to care for them both. Whether she wanted to admit it or not, to lose them would be the saddest thing of all.

There was a soft tap on her door. Composing herself, she swiped at her eyes. Tanner came in and took a seat beside her at the window. He was silent for a few moments. Wrapping an arm around her, he pulled her close, and together they just watched the snow fall.

"I'm sorry."

Not sure what to say, Arien laid her head against his shoulder.

"Talk to me, pretty girl." Fingers combed her hair. "I need to know what you're feelin.'"

"I don't know."

"I can't have you hatin' me." Tanner lifted her onto his lap. "Please, don't judge us for something you don't understand yet."

"Are you and Kellan going to share a wife?"

"Yes."

She nodded once. Emotion stinging the tip of her nose, a sardonic laugh escaped. "Who's the lucky girl?"

He didn't answer.

But those green eyes of his, silvery and shining, spoke volumes.

With the cozy throw wrapped tighter about her, Arien stepped out onto the balcony. White and bright, the snowy landscape glowed with the tint of a movie screen. Silence isn't quiet—her heart thundered, the stream trickled, a horse nickered, and the wingbeat of an owl thumped as it swooped into the night.

Six

It was strange to think only a week ago, she'd been surrounded by boxes in their little apartment back in Denver. Her nostalgia for it already fading, Arien pondered. Maybe home really wasn't a place, but rather a feeling. And it was that feeling she couldn't let go of.

No one was in the kitchen when Arien came down the stairs and poured herself a cup of coffee. Mid-morning, the boys should be back from chores by now. After last night, she didn't doubt they were making themselves scarce. Avoiding her. She was actually quite surprised when Emily texted she was coming by to pick her up to go to Jackson.

One sip of coffee had her near sputtering. Arien spat it into the sink. Bitter and burnt, it must've been left to warm in the pot

for hours now. She made a fresh one. Not for herself so much—
there was a precious Starbucks in Jackson—but for when Tanner
and Kellan got home. So focused on the task, she didn't hear Emily
come in.

"Boo."

Coffee grounds went flying. "Shit, you scared me."

"Didn't mean to." Emily giggled, sweeping up the mess. "Where
is everybody?"

"Dunno. Staying far away from me, I guess."

"Doubt that." She tsked, giving her long, dark waves a shake.
"Maybe giving you a little space. Some time to process, yeah?"

"That could be, I suppose." Arien half shrugged, pressing the
start button on the coffee maker.

"It is, trust me," Emily assured her, and pushed her out the
door. "C'mon, we can talk in the car."

She drove a convertible. The top was up, being it was only
twenty-seven degrees. Still, it wasn't the type of vehicle Arien assumed Emily would have. A Jeep, maybe, but not a little two-seater.

"Uncle Matty didn't mean for it to go down like that, you
know," Emily started chattering once they turned onto the highway.
"He and the boys—your mama too—have been frettin' over how to
tell you. That's why they had me invite Jake over. He's really good
at explaining things. I'm sure you've got lots of questions, though."

She did, although she was almost afraid to hear the answers.
"I don't even know where to start."

"Just ask me whatever comes to mind. We can go from there."

"Is this some kind of kooky religion you're in?" Chewing on the
side of her thumb, Arien turned in her seat. "I'm sorry, I shouldn't
have said it like that, but all I can think of is that *Keep Sweet* documentary I saw on Netflix."

"God, no. I read about them—horrible. Very disturbing. I
wouldn't even call that fundamentalist group a religion, though
people use God and the Bible to commit all sorts of atrocities, don't
they?" Biting her lip, Emily paused for a moment, then reached

over the console for Arien's hand. "I know the trinity would sound strange to most outsiders—fucked up, as you said. But is it, really? Three people who choose to share a life together, to love each other—I don't think so. It only seems that way because it's not traditional to you, but it is for us. Anyway, to answer your question, no religion. Some folks go to church in Dubois, but you won't find one in Brookside."

"So, no cult then, either."

Emily snorted. "There's no leader here. No shaman. We're a community where everyone has an equal voice. Share the work, share the wealth."

"That's pretty much what Kellan and Tanner said. Secret society?"

"We don't hide our existence, you know."

Right, just the extra spouse.

"I don't understand." Arien rubbed her head. "What is it then?"

"An ideology. A way of life that works for us, and has for almost two hundred years. We're kind of superstitious about it, honestly." Emily squeezed her hand, then let it go. "Jake can explain it better than I can. He's like the community historian. Many generations ago, his great-grandfather, Levi Gantry, and the two sisters he married, were at the origin of it all."

They reached the end of the highway, the Tetons just ahead. Thirty miles to the north lie Yellowstone. Emily turned south toward Jackson, while Arien's thoughts seemed to be going in a million different directions. She still wasn't sure what to make of everything.

"So, your mom has two husbands?"

"Had. She's a widow now." Emily's breath released in a sigh. "My fathers were both killed on duty in Afghanistan when I was three."

Jesus. "I'm so sorry. I didn't know."

And now she felt like shit for even asking. Of all the things her stepbrothers failed to mention. Then again, they'd forgotten to mention a lot of things, hadn't they? God only knows what else they hadn't told her.

"Thanks. I don't remember them very much, and what I do is probably from photos and videos we have." Emily glanced at her with a shrug. "I get little flashes sometimes, you know?"

Rubbing her lips together, Arien nodded. "You're really going to marry Billy *and* Jake?"

"Hell yes, and I cannot wait." Fingers squeezing the steering wheel, she lit up. Her exuberance so obvious. "I'm so happy, sometimes I think I'm dying because I love them so much."

"How do you know?"

"You just do. In a single moment. Months and years of small gestures. You want to share even the most insignificant things about your day with them and you want to know theirs too. They're always in your thoughts. I know that might sound dumb, but it's true." Her giggle melting into a dreamy sigh, Emily asked her, "Haven't you ever been in love?"

"No."

Innocent crushes, yes. Infatuation. But she'd never been so consumed it felt like she was dying. Arien couldn't begin to imagine what that might feel like.

"When it happens, trust me, you'll know."

Tanner and Kellan came to mind, although she couldn't say exactly why. "And you love them both the same?"

"Not the same—they're two different people, you know? But equally."

"Not sure I get it, but I'm gonna have to take your word for it. You sound so sure…"

"I am absolutely sure, Arien, with everything in me. I love Billy and Jake, mind, heart, and soul. The trinity is sacred, and it's for life—beginning, middle, end—remember?"

"Yeah." Arien sniggered. Sounded like a bunch of mumbo jumbo to her, but who was she to judge? "I still think y'all are crazy, but you do you, boo."

"Not crazy, just different." Emily parked the car and smacked a kiss to Arien's cheek. "And you'll come to love us for it."

Supercharged after indulging herself with not one, but three venti quad-shot lattes while she was in Jackson, Arien bounded through the door. She could see everyone, including her stepbrothers, at the kitchen table, plates piled high with Thanksgiving leftovers.

"Arien, sweetie, are you going to eat?" Jennifer called out. "We're doing hot turkey sandwiches with gravy and all the fixings."

"Yeah, okay." Shopping bags weighing heavy on her arm, she lugged them toward the stairs. "Give me five minutes."

After spending the day with Emily, and determining she was pretty normal, as long as she overlooked the fact that at seventeen her cousin was engaged to not one man, but two, Arien decided to take an impartial point of view. She didn't see herself as a judgmental person, and refused to associate with those who were. Maybe she didn't understand their ways, and perhaps she never would, but nevertheless, they were her family and at least deserved respect.

Arien sailed into the kitchen, and taking her seat between her stepbrothers, began filling her plate. "Smells even better than it did yesterday."

"Yeah, well after today I don't want to see turkey again until next year." Kellan shoveled a spoonful of mashed potatoes in his mouth. "Grilling us some T-bones for dinner tomorrow."

"It's a tad chilly for a barbecue, don't you think?" Arien chuckled with a shake of her head.

"Maybe where you come from, girly, but you ain't in Kansas anymore." A jab. She knew it. Dismissing her, he engaged his father. "Speaking of steaks, when's Lenny coming? It's time to fill the freezer for winter."

"I'll give him a call in the morning."

"Who's Lenny?" she asked, but Kellan ignored her.

Tanner put his fork down. "The butcher."

"*…we call 'em Dinner.*"

"You're gonna hurt a cow?" Just the thought made her want to cry.

"Nah." Kellan smirked, his nostrils flaring. "I'll be quick about it. Won't feel a thing."

Arien pushed her plate away. "I'm not hungry anymore."

"Chrissakes." Throwing down his napkin, Kellan abruptly stood. "Where the fuck do you think steak comes from?"

She blanched.

He was angry, and Arien knew it wasn't over a cow.

"Pretty sure she knows, Kel."

At least Tanner didn't hate her.

"I will not have you usin' that language at the dinner table," Matthew admonished his son. "Now apologize."

"Sorry." And he stalked off.

"Did you have a nice day with Emily, sweetie?" Her mom looked rather uncomfortable after the outburst.

"I did." It was her turn now. "We talked a lot, and um…well, I just want to say I'm sorry for what I said last night."

"C'mere." Her stepfather stood. She stepped into his arms and he hugged her. "I'm sorry, Arien. Hope you know that."

"I know."

"I'll always be lookin' out for you." Taking a step back, Matthew brushed the hair from her eyes. "You got Kellan's feathers all ruffled, but that just goes to show you he cares."

And somehow she'd made a mess of things with him. She had to fix it.

Arien peeked out her bedroom door. His light was off, but the embers in the fire cast a warm glow. He was still awake. Arien tiptoed across the hall. Kellan lay there, his arm behind his head, staring up at the ceiling.

"I want to talk to you. Can I come in?"

"Suit yourself."

Stepping into his room was like entering the dragon's lair, and now that she was in it, Arien was unsure how to approach him. Gingerly, she sat down on the edge of the bed. He didn't move. His gaze remaining on the ceiling, Kellan wouldn't even look at her.

"I...um, reacted badly, but in my defense I was so not prepared to hear that. I mean, c'mon, put yourself in my shoes. Still, I was wrong. For calling y'all crazy." *Maybe you are though, a little bit.* Arien went to touch his cheek, but before she could, he grabbed her wrist. "I'm trying to say I'm sorry, Kellan."

He put her hand down on the mattress. "Okay, you said it."

"Yeah." She got up, and halfway across the room, turned back around. "And just for the record, you're an asshole. I know where the fuck a steak comes from. Doesn't mean I can't feel bad for the cow, though."

She didn't make it to the door.

Kellan was behind her in a flash. His arm a vise around her middle, he held her against him. "I'm an asshole?"

"Yup." Her fingers gripped the unmovable limb. "That's what I said."

With the smooth skin of his hard chest pressed into her back, that pull she felt in her belly whenever they touched returned. Arien struggled, not to get away, but to feel more of him. And fuck all if he didn't know it.

"Go on." His head dipped to her ear. "I like it."

"Asshole."

"I am."

Pulling on her hair, Kellan bared her neck, lips skating over the sensitive skin. His strong grip loosening, he slid a hand beneath her T-shirt. Fingertips trailing across her stomach, her pulse skittered. Arien felt his dick, hard beneath his sweats, press into her.

She whimpered.

He groaned.

His breath fanned her face, and just when she thought he might kiss her, Kellan pushed her away instead. "Get to bed."

"What?"

"You heard me. Go on."

Arien went, but paused at his doorway. "You really are an as-shole, you know that?"

"Yeah."

She didn't look back.

"I know."

Seven

Built in the 1800s as a bunkhouse for the ranch hands, Brookside School was a three-story wooden structure, just a short walk from the shops on Main Street. Picturesque and updated, while retaining its original charm, it overlooked the trout-filled stream that trickled down the mountain and through the valley.

From preschool through high school, three hundred students were enrolled here. The primary grades, along with a kitchen and dining hall, were located on the first floor, the middle grades on the second, and high school on the third. Matthew sure hadn't exaggerated. The curriculum, individualized and avant-garde, was not only top-notch, it was engaging, and except for the less-than-welcoming reception from some of her classmates, Arien liked it here.

Not that she took it personally. After all, she wasn't just the new kid, she was an outsider.

Emily and Billy introduced her to Shiloh Lewis and her boyfriend, Griffin Archer. Both of them seniors, with the date of their wedding approaching, it was all they ever talked about. *How about a graduation party? Something. Anyone? ANYONE? Sheesh.* Still, they were nice to her, and she was happy to be included in their little friend group, even as the unattached fifth wheel.

On their way to the first-floor dining hall for lunch, Grams poked her head out her classroom door, waving Arien over. "I wanted to check on you. Everything going okay, honey?"

"Yeah." She kissed her cheek. "Not too bad for my first week."

"And at home?"

Arien responded with a brisk laugh, "Kellan hates me, but other than that it's great."

He'd gone cold. Ever since that night in his room, the only time he spoke to her, or even acknowledged her presence, was at the dinner table. In front of their parents, everything between them appeared fine. If Tanner was around, he tolerated her. Otherwise, he avoided her like the plague.

"Oh, honey." Grams wrapped her up in a great, big hug. "Believe me when I say this, that boy does not hate you. Quite the opposite, in fact."

Pffft.

"It's okay. I don't need Kellan to like me." She took a step back. "I tried to apologize, but he's made his feelings quite clear."

"Give him some time, Arien," Grams spoke on a sigh, combing her fingers through Arien's hair.

"I better go." Nodding, she hitched a thumb behind her. "They're waiting on me."

"All right, dear. Have a good lunch."

Last one through the food line, everyone was already eating when Arien made it to their table. Shocker of all shockers, Shiloh was going on about something other than her wedding, as she set down her tray and took a seat next to Emily. After skipping breakfast this morning, she was starving. Arien's focus was the cheeseburger on her plate, not the conversation.

She'd just taken the first juicy, delicious bite, her mouth full, when Shiloh tapped her on the shoulder. "You're going, aren't you, Arien?"

Jesus, can I just chew my food here?

Emily answered with a wink, "Tanner's bringing her."

Almost choking, she swallowed. "What? Bringing me where?"

"The bonfire party tonight."

"Did you say *party?*"

"Sure did." And tossing her blonde beach waves, Shiloh grinned. "We have to make our own fun around here. It's a good time, I promise."

Having dreaded the thought of spending another evening reading a book with Kellan looming from across the hall, her Friday night was starting to look a whole heck of a lot better. The girls sitting at the next table stopped their whispering to glare at her.

Arien smiled at them.

"Can't wait."

"C'mon, little sister!" Tanner shouted from downstairs. "Time's a wastin.'"

"Five minutes."

Not that it should matter, but her makeup, hair, clothes—everything—had to be on point tonight. If those bitchy girls thought they were going to stare her down, she was going to give them something to look at. Arien pulled the fleece-lined leggings on over her lace-trimmed thermal underwear. Checking her reflection in the mirror, she smoothed the fabric over her tummy. Sadly, the cold Wyoming winters necessitated wearing several layers.

She was struggling to get her foot inside a thigh-high boot when Tanner peeked inside her door. "It's been ten."

"Almost…" She pulled harder. "…done."

"Need help with that?"

"Maybe."

"Here." He pushed while Arien pulled. She fell back on the bed, Tanner landing on top of her.

Both of them laughing, he lifted himself up, his hands on either side of her head. Green eyes gazed into hers. His lips so close she could almost taste them. They stayed like that for a moment, her heart beating rapidly beneath him.

"You're so pretty," he whispered, fingering her hair. "Let's go."

Arien followed him down the stairs. Tanner wrapped her up snug in a heavy knit scarf and placed the matching beanie on her head. "Gotta bundle you up."

A snowmobile was parked outside. "I figured we'd be taking the truck."

"Why would we do that?" Scooping her off her feet, Tanner lifted her onto the sled. "This way's more fun."

Gliding across the powdery snow, she held onto him. Pressed against his back, her arms wrapped tightly around his waist, Arien breathed in the crystal air. Subtle, yet visceral, the dark and smoky, muted scent of winter tickled her nose. Sweet sap, evergreen needles, and manly musk.

Even with all the bulky layers, her body molded to his, and in spite of the cold, especially the biting wind as they whizzed through the trees, she felt warm. Sheltered. Safe. Smiles from the inside, fuzzy socks, a gently burning fire. That was Tanner. Tender and sweet, he was that familiar feeling she wanted to hold onto forever.

Leaning with him as he navigated the trail, his hand came down to hold hers.

And she found herself wishing for things that could never be.

On the far side of the ranch, past Brooks Lake and close to the edge of town, sat a big, old, red barn. A bonfire blazed in front of it, sparking embers shooting up into the black velvet sky. People came in and out. Congregating around the fire. Drinking. Dancing. Kissing.

Lots of kissing.

She recognized some of the faces from school. "Who are all these people? The entire junior and senior class must be here."

"Probably are." Helping her off the sled, Tanner chuckled. "Everyone fifteen through twenty-five is more than likely here. Unless they're hitched. Those folks got better things to do at home."

Huh? Ohhh.

"And this'll be the last party 'til spring, I reckon."

"Why?" Arien wondered out loud, slathering some balm on her lips.

"Winter, pretty girl." He curled his arm around her. "We'll have a good eight feet of snow dumped on us before it's through."

Keeping Arien close to his side, Tanner led her toward the barn. Everyone stopped to say hello to him. But not her. The guys would tip their chins in acknowledgment, nothing more. And she could have been in the dining hall at school, considering the looks she got from the girls.

Emily, Billy, and Jake stood waiting, drinks in hand, by the open barn doors. Griffin, with Shiloh pinned to the wall, making out beside them. That didn't shock her anymore. PDAs were commonplace and those two were always going at it.

"Hey, Cuzzy." Emily, who was leaning back against Jake, pulled Tanner in for a smack to the lips. Not that Arien was spared the same attention. "Hey, babes."

"Emily." She giggled, wiping the slobber from her mouth.

Tanner rolled his gorgeous eyes, but he was grinning. "You drunk already, Ems?"

"Nooo."

"She's cut off," Jake asserted. His arm coming around her front, he kissed the top of her head. "How're you doing, Arien?"

"Better than the last time you saw me."

Tanner squeezed her side. "I'm gonna get us some hot chocolate, okay?"

"Hot chocolate?" Scrunching up her face, Emily blew a raspberry into the air. "Party pooper."

"That sounds perfect." Arien rubbed her hands together. "It's cold out here."

"Tanner'll keep you warm, won't you, Cuzzy?" she called out to his retreating backside.

"God, Emily." Heat rising to her cheeks at the thought, she brought her hands to her face. "Everyone can hear you."

"And?"

"And they'll think—"

"They already think it." Emily pulled her in close. "Why do you think the girls are all bitches and the boys keep their distance from you?"

Arien flicked her gaze from Billy to Jake. "I'm the new girl?"

"No." Her dark waves moved from side to side. "See, the girls wish they could be you and the guys wish they could have you. They know you belong to Kellan and Tanner."

"That's crazy." She burst out laughing. "I don't belong to anyone."

Jake raised his brow.

"I know, not the best word choice." Pursing her lips, Arien exhaled out her nose. "Look, no offense intended, but I'm not getting married any time in the near future, and I'm certainly not planning on having two guys, my stepbrothers at that, share me like a Kit Kat bar. Seriously, how does that even work?"

Billy elbowed her and winked. "Oh, trust me, it works."

"Doesn't matter anyway. I'm leaving for school at the end of the summer."

Tanner returned with the hot chocolate. Leaning down, he kissed her cheek and whispered in her ear, "I put some Bailey's in it, shhh."

Looking over at them, Emily just smirked.

And the music from the barn grew louder.

Lined with bales of hay to sit on, the large open space was dimly lit by the warm glow of lanterns and Christmas lights strung from the rafters. In the front were a couple of rickety-looking tables with bottles of booze on them, stalls in the back, and stairs to a loft.

Sharing a seat with Tanner, Arien glanced around. It almost could have been a dance in her old high school gymnasium. Except they were in a barn. And it was dark, charged with an energy she didn't have a name for.

She recognized a girl from school dancing with two boys. One held her from behind, while the other kissed her as they swayed. Paired off in twos and threes, some took advantage of discreet, shadowed corners, touching and kissing on a blanket of hay. And most didn't seem to care who saw what they were doing.

To the left of her, Emily straddled Billy's lap, his hands in her sweater, squeezing her breasts as he kissed her. Jake leaned back against the wall behind them, like a chaperone, looking on, seemingly unaffected. *Weird.* To her right, Shiloh and Griffin continued with a make-out fest of their own. Arien would have sworn Shiloh and Griffin were doing it, if they didn't have all their clothes on.

Following her gaze, Tanner squeezed her hand. She turned away, her eyes meeting his, and cleared her throat. "For fuck's sake." Arien lowered her voice to a whisper. "He's dry hump…"

He sniggered, whispering back, "He's not gonna fuck her."

She giggled. "Not here anyway."

"Not at all. 'Til the wedding at least," Tanner added, tipping back a bottle of beer. "They should take that shit to the back, though."

Nope, nope, nope. Not asking.

"If they're making you uncomfortable, we can take a walk… dance or somethin'"

"Did you forget I go to school with them?" Arien tittered, rolling her eyes. "I'm getting used to it. Kind of. I'll take you up on a dance, though."

It was a slow song. Some country ballad she'd never heard before, since she rarely listened to that stuff. Growing up, she jammed along to what Jennifer had playing on the radio. Top 40. Grunge and metal. Even a little Sinatra sometimes. But not this. Tanner pressed one hand to the small of her back, holding her palm on his chest with the other. Loving the way she fit with him, Arien let out a little sigh. Twinkling lights reflected in his eyes. A lopsided smile appearing, his forehead dropped to hers.

"You're a good dancer."

"Why, thank you." And he twirled her to prove she wasn't wrong. "Grams always said the ladies love it. Taught me and Kel from the time we was little, dancin' in the kitchen while she cooked supper."

"I can't picture his cranky ass dancing," she said with a giggle.

"Heh." His nose brushed along hers. "You'd be surprised."

"Where is he, anyway?"

"Around here somewhere, I reckon."

Kellan's absence wasn't lost on her. Arien wasn't sure whether or not she was disappointed or relieved he wasn't here. On the one hand, she wouldn't have to endure his broody presence, the other only cemented in her mind what she'd already been thinking. He was doing his damnedest to stay far the hell away from her.

And it hurt.

By the time they came off the dance floor, the suck-face spectacle apparently over with, someone had rearranged the hay bales perpendicular to the wall. Facing each other, Emily, Jake, and Billy occupied one side, while Griffin and Shiloh sat on the other. Made conversing easier, she supposed.

He came out of one of the stalls. And he wasn't alone. His hand on her throat, Kellan backed the girl into a wall and kissed her. Voracious and hungry-like, the show he was putting on made Griffin's and Billy's look tame. It all made sense to her now, and the energy she felt here had a name.

Whoever the disheveled girl was, she obviously enjoyed his

attention. Fingers sank into his tight faded jeans. She held onto his ass, rubbing her rail-thin body up against his dick. Blonde hair down to her waist. A cowboy hat on her head. Arien assumed she was beautiful, it seemed like everyone in Brookside was, but with his mouth all over hers she couldn't say for certain.

Shaking her head, Emily stealthily passed her a flask. *Fuck it.* Arien tossed it back until the burn became too much.

If Tanner saw, he was pretending not to notice. Nudging him, she tipped her chin in their direction. "Is it her?"

"Huh?"

"That's her, isn't it?" She didn't want it to be true, but what other explanation could there be? "The girl y'all are gonna marry."

"What?" He began to laugh. "No."

"That's Cassie." Shiloh rolled her eyes. "My sister."

Emily leaned into her ear. "She's a couple years older than us. Was in high school with him...and, you know."

"Not following."

"They used to fool around, kissin' and stuff—nothin' more than that. Kellan has a brother and Cassie has a sister. They've always known they'd never end up together."

Wait a minute.

Her gaze flicked over to Griffin. He shrugged. "We're not married yet. She can't let me touch her, so I don't mind her messin' around some 'til then."

Fucking bizarre.

"I don't understand."

"Rules, Arien. Nineteen." He hitched a thumb behind him then pointed at himself. "Seventeen. But come my birthday, all bets are off."

"Seriously?" She turned to Emily. "Eighteen is the fucking magic number?"

"That would be three," she replied, biting on her lip with a shrug. "But yeah."

"Let me see if I've got this straight." With a shake of her head,

Arien held her chin in her hand. "Does that mean when you turn eighteen and Billy turns seventeen…"

"What do you think I kiss her so much for?" Billy chimed in, laying a smooch on his girlfriend's mouth. "It's gonna be a long year. Got to get as many in while I still can."

Jake's lips turned up into a smirk.

"Oh, hell." Leaning over to conceal her laughter, she reached into Emily's pocket for the flask. "I think I'm gonna need that back."

She didn't hide it. Taking a long swallow, Arien ignored the burn.

"Making a conscious choice, knowing who and what you truly desire, having free rein over your future. All of those things are important, Arien." Leaning over Emily and his brother, Jake took the flask from her hand. "The repercussions of the decisions we make are lifelong. You have to be of age to make them."

Wow.

"Guess you've been waiting for Emily a long time, huh?"

"We have our whole lives together." Taking her cousin's hand, Jake kissed it. "She's worth it. I can wait."

"Well, I can't." With a wink, Emily grinned.

Arien glanced up at Tanner, then followed his gaze across the barn. Kellan stood there, his arm casually slung over Cassie's shoulder, but it was Arien he was staring at. She looked away.

"So, any other rules?" Not that she really wanted to know, but it was the first thing that came to mind. Anything to keep her eyes from wandering back to her stepbrother.

Shiloh piped up. "Um, girls stay pure until the wedding, not that we don't do other stuff, because obviously we do. Just no fucking."

Nope, I shouldn't have asked.

Turning to Tanner, her jaw dropped. "And the boys, do they save themselves too?"

At least he had the decency to blush.

"Hell no, and why would you want them to? They better know

what they're doin'. Who wants a fumbly-bumbly under the covers, if you get my meaning. I heard some of the boys get plenty of practice with the ski bunnies in Jackson."

"Not me." Griffin grabbed her face and kissed her.

Billy shrugged. "Me neither."

Tanner and Jake remained silent.

Arien spoke under her breath, "Sounds like an antiquated double standard to me."

"Maybe, but see us girls, we bond when we fuck, whereas boys can easily compartmentalize it." Nodding as she spoke, it was written all over her face. Shiloh actually believed it.

She snorted. "That's ridiculous."

"Unless you've already done it, how do you know?"

Touché.

Six pairs of eyes were on her.

"Guess I don't."

Kellan never did come and sit with them. As if the kissing wasn't enough, now he was showing off his "Boot Scootin' Boogie" skills. *Puh-leeze.* She was getting a headache from rolling her eyes so much. Or maybe it was the Fireball she'd consumed from Emily's flask. Apparently Grams taught them well. Arien had to admit, he looked hella good out there. Not that she'd ever tell him.

It was getting late. She was about to ask Tanner if it was almost time to go, when she heard the opening bars of a more-than-familiar tune. Kellan and a bunch of guys stripped off their shirts, all of them ripped and gorgeous and flaunting their six-packs, two-stepping like they were in a TikTok video.

"Oh, my fucking God." Arien was laughing so hard she was crying. "I can't. I. Just. Can't."

"Told ya so." Tanner sniggered.

"What's next? The Hokey Pokey? Macarena?" she asked, swiping the tears from her eyes. "Can we go home now?"

"No."

It wasn't Tanner who answered. Arien glanced up and there was Kellan, breathing all heavy, wiping off the sweat from his chest.

"My turn to watch you." He smirked. "C'mon, city girl. Let's see what you've got."

Still giggling, thanks to the Fireball in her bloodstream, she looked over at Shiloh, and crooking her finger, whispered in her ear.

Cassie took over the spot next to Griffin. "That her?"

Arien pulled Emily in close and stood. "More than you could ever handle, cowboy."

Then she walked right on over to the dude in charge of the music, Emily and Shiloh following behind her, and handed him her phone. "Hi there, I'm Arien. Kellan's stepsister. We're gonna switch things up a bit, if you don't mind. Song's queued up."

"You got it." He chuckled. "Give'm hell, sweetheart."

"Let's show 'em, my girlies," she crooned, strutting out to the middle of the floor.

I got your cowgirl boogie right here, asshole.

Ciara's remix of "The Git Up" began to play. And all those years of dance classes paid off. She could get low and wind it up slow a million times hotter than Shiloh's skinny-ass sister without even trying. His mouth hanging open, Kellan couldn't take his eyes off her. Fucker didn't know what hit him.

Giddy-up, big brother. That'll teach you not to underestimate me.

And when the song was over, with that smirk on his face, Kellan approached her. He extended his hand. "C'mon."

Arien didn't say anything for a moment. Then glancing up, she sweetly smiled and said, "Sorry, that's the only barn dance I know."

Later that night, after they were home and the Fireball had worn off, Arien sat back against the headboard, her knees drawn to her chest, sniffling and staring into the fire. She didn't turn her head when he crept into her room.

"What's the matter?"

"Nothing." The word came just above a whisper.

"Bullshit."

"I don't think I belong here, Tanner."

Holy shit…look, there's a fireplace in my freaking bedroom, for chrissakes.

"Yes, you do." Slipping into the bed beside her, he held her. "I like holding you."

"See? That's the problem. I like it too."

His fingers combed through her hair. "I don't see how that's a problem."

"I can't…"

"Is it Kellan?"

Pursing her lips to the side, Arien scrunched her shoulders. "I don't know."

"You were jealous seeing him kissin' on Cassie."

She snickered. "They were doing a lot more than kissing."

"Didn't mean anything. They were just blowin' off steam, is all. It's not like they were fucking."

Course not. That's against the rules. She wanted to laugh.

"So why weren't you kissing on anyone? Don't you need to blow off some steam, too?"

Drawing her closer, Tanner's lips skimmed her neck. "Only girl I want to be kissing on is you."

"But you can't."

"No, I can't. And Kellan can't, neither." He tilted her chin up, forcing her to look at him. "I can hold you, though. Tell you how I'm gonna kiss you. And how I'm gonna touch you. And taste you."

"How are you gonna do that?" Closing her eyes, she smiled.

"I'm gonna kiss you everywhere, pretty girl."

He placed her hand between her legs.

Fuck.

And he burred, low in her ear, "That's how."

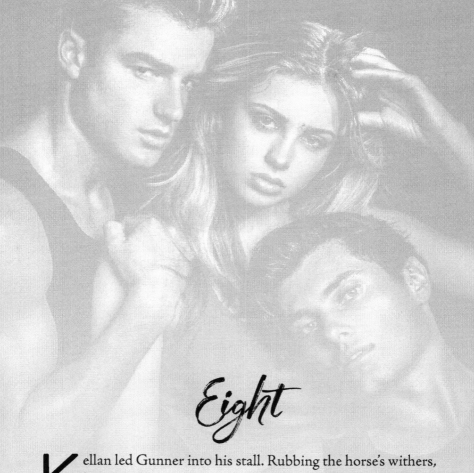

Eight

Kellan led Gunner into his stall. Rubbing the horse's withers, he treated him to an apple. He'd gotten him as a young colt when he was sixteen, and they'd been inseparable ever since. Their bond inexplicable, he felt closer to the animal than he did with most people.

With the exception of his family, he wasn't much of a people person anyhow—that was Tanner. And that's how he'd always been. Was just his nature. Kellan didn't see that as a fault within himself or something that needed to be fixed. He just wasn't very good at pretending.

Not that he didn't get on with folks. He did. Kellan could carry a conversation for a short while, but he didn't enjoy them unless they served a purpose. It seemed to him people tended to talk without thinking. He preferred to listen, think, and consider before he spoke, so his words were deliberate, chosen, and few.

Daisy neighed from the next stall. He went over to give the mare a pat. "You lonely? Missing our girl?"

"She ain't. Arien comes by every day after school to give her a good brushing." His brother's head popped up from the crossties where he was picking Tux's hooves. "She babies that horse. Caught her braidin' Daisy's mane the other day."

"Chrissakes." Kellan snickered. "She needs to be exercisin' her, not puttin' her in silly braids."

"Have you asked her to ride with you?"

He didn't bother to answer. Huffing out a breath, Kellan gazed up at the exposed-wood beams. Tanner knew he'd done no such thing. And what would be the point? Being around her more than he had to be would just make it harder later.

"Might try talkin' to her, brother, 'cause that was a real dick move, even for you."

"What?" He knew where this was going. Exasperated already, Kellan offered Arien's horse a handful of oats.

"Cassie."

"Yeah, okay." He turned around to meet his brother's stare. "Don't think she cares and I don't need to talk to her."

"You're wrong there. I think you do," Tanner countered, un-hitching Tux from the crossties. Damn fool was in love with her already. He could see it all over his face.

"Got nothin' to say to her." Brushing oat residue from his hands, Kellan shook his head with a smirk. "Heard enough."

"What the fuck you talkin' about, Kel?"

"At the bonfire. She didn't see me, but I was listenin'." Propped against the door to Tux's stall, he kicked at some straw on the floor. "Arien got her pretty little panties twisted, makin' sure everybody knew she wasn't about to have her stepbrothers sharing her like some candy bar..." Gripping Tanner's shoulder, he exhaled. "...and she ain't stayin.'"

Sorry, brother.

"Arien doesn't understand yet. All the more reason you need to talk to her."

And say what? If Arien was of the mindset that their ways weren't right, just because they were different, it wasn't up to him, or anyone else, to convince her. *More love is more, baby cakes. It's that simple.* She'd have to see the truth of it, learn the goodness of it, for herself.

"All she ever talks about is leavin'. Get your head out of the clouds, Tanner. She's just gonna break that big ole heart of yours."

"You're wrong, Kellan." Adamant, his brother stood toe to toe with him.

This once, he hoped he was. "Reckon we'll see."

He'd been struck by Arien the moment he first held her picture. The vision tangible at last, right there between his fingertips, this powerful current surged throughout his body. There was no denying it. His father had been right all along.

"Couldn't help but overhear," Matthew said, wiping the grime off his hands as he came out of the tack room. "And let me tell you, son, your brother ain't wrong. You've got to be her friend before you can expect to be anything else."

Hooking his thumbs on the belt loops of his jeans, Kellan shrugged. He should at least try, he supposed.

A hand on each shoulder, his father looked him square in the eye, proclaiming with a single nod, "You and Tanner have been generously favored. It's just as I saw it, Kellan. Arien's home is here. She's not goin' anywhere."

He went out the back door, Tuesday faithfully following him through the snow. Flurries gently fell, but it didn't feel all that cold, so he didn't bother zipping up his coat. He'd left Tanner and his dad in front of the TV watching Sunday afternoon football. Jennifer had a rib roast cooking in the oven. Arien was keeping to herself in her room making pictures pretty, or reading a book, or whatever the fuck else she got up to in there.

"Heh." *Stickin' pins in a voodoo doll of your ass, more than likely.*

He was halfway to the toolshed when Tanner called out to him from the house, "Hey, where you goin'?"

Without looking back, Kellan raised his hand in a wave. He needed to think, and he needed some time alone to do it. Away from the house, the football game he didn't give a shit about anyhow, and her.

Ever since the bonfire, he'd been mulling things over. Dwelling on what Arien said that night. How she could never be with him *and* his brother, as if the very thought was abhorrent to her. And wasn't that a load of horseshit? Yeah, she was all cozied up with Tanner, but Kellan saw her pretty eyes on him. The covetous glances. Too bad she didn't know, in his eyes, no other girl could ever hold a candle to her. And in his mind, it was her sweet lips he was tasting.

Still, Kellan couldn't allow himself to get too close just yet, but he was going to try to see things from her perspective. He'd let Tanner do all the sweet-talking. He was good at that flowery shit. And eventually, she'd have to come around. Because come hell or high water, he was going to keep her.

He wasn't going to leave winning her over to his brother. Kellan needed to make his own way into Arien's heart. He had to start somewhere, and with Christmas only a couple weeks away, there was no better time than right now.

The young Douglas fir was twice as tall as him. He tugged on a branch, the soft needles slipping through his fingers, pleased with his choice. "What do ya think, Tuesday? This one?"

Wagging her tail, she answered with a bark.

He chuckled, giving her head a pat. "Yeah, I reckon so."

Kellan cut down the tree. Securing it to the pull-behind, he only hoped Arien took the gesture for what it was. His humble peace offering.

Tanner and Dad helped him get the tree inside the house. Wearing the giddiest smile he'd probably ever seen, Jennifer came out of the kitchen, her hands clasped beneath her chin. "Oh, wow… Arien, honey, get down here."

He watched as she slowly descended the stairs, hair in a messy pile on top of her head, loose silken strands framing her gorgeous face. Dressed in a pair of black leggings that hugged her delicious curves and a cropped white UC sweatshirt, Kellan glimpsed the bare skin he was dying to get his hands on.

"It's huge," Arien squealed, seeing them wrestling the tree into the living room. "Are you sure it's gonna fit?"

Having heard that before a time or two, he couldn't help but snigger. *Don't you worry none, baby cakes. I'll fit just fine.*

"It'll be perfect right there next to the fireplace." Her mother pointed toward it with a gleeful nod, assuring her daughter.

"Okay, if you say so."

"I say so."

It took all three men to hoist the tree into its stand. Taking a step back to admire it, Dad pulled Jennifer close to his side. Kellan and his brother gathered Arien to stand between them, each wrapping an arm around her waist. It felt so right, and so good, to have his fingertips on her warm, soft skin. She was meant to be theirs, goddammit. This is where she belonged.

"Our first Christmas," Jennifer spoke on a sigh. "It's going to be the best one ever."

"Until next year." Rubbing her little baby bump, Matthew lowered his lips to her ear. "I love you."

"I love you, too." And she kissed him. "Shall we leave the kids to decorate the tree?"

"I think we should," he replied, nibbling on her lip. He turned to Kellan and winked. "Keep an eye on the roast, will you?"

The three of them stood there, watching their parents hurry up the stairs and disappear into their wing of the house.

"Jeez, well that was subtle," Arien scoffed.

"Yeah, well, Brooks men sure ain't known for it." Tanner chuckled, kissing her temple. "I love seeing them happy together. Be right back. I'm gonna go get the Christmas stuff, okay?"

"Yeah, okay."

Still holding onto her, Kellan squeezed his fingers into her side. She glared up at him. "You can let go of me now."

"What if I don't want to?" Pulling her in front of him, he held her close. "What if I like it?"

Arien turned her head away. "You don't."

"Oh, but I do."

"You hate me. I know it. Everyone else knows it, too." She pushed against his chest with her little fists, not that it got her anywhere. "Maybe Cassie believes all your bullshit, but you're wasting your breath on me."

Kellan tipped his head to the side with a smirk. "You're jealous."

"Don't flatter yourself."

"It's okay to admit it." Gripping her ass, he pressed her soft belly into his hardening dick. "And I don't hate you."

She squeaked, a little puff of air passing between her lips.

"But I don't trust you, either."

Kellan backed her up against the wall. His hands on either side of her head, he rubbed the hardness in his jeans into the thin fabric between her thighs. Arien pushed into him, and between the two of them they found the perfect friction. *That's my girl.* He groaned. Lips skimming her delicate neck, he captured the lobe of her ear with his teeth and picked up the pace.

God, he wanted to slide his hands up inside that fucking shirt and squeeze her tits, then rip it from her body. Kellan wanted her naked, to kiss her, to push his way inside her, but he didn't dare. The risk was too great. He could lose favor, and he'd taken this to the limits already. So instead of filling her up with his cum, he spilled inside his pants like a teenaged boy.

"See, I know you haven't been schooled in our ways, so you don't know any better. If you had been, you'd understand Brooks men love and worship their women above all else." Running his nose along her neck, he kissed the skin beneath her ear. "And we expect to receive it in return. Maybe one day, if you can look at me the same way your mom looks at my dad, then I'll trust you."

Tanner returned with a stack of boxes. "Everything okay?"

"Yeah, bro. You two start decking the halls without me." Kellan let a panting Arien go. "This jizz in my jeans is fuckin' sticky. Gotta take a shower."

He didn't intend on going back downstairs, but once Kellan was showered and dressed, he found himself there anyway. Standing off to the side, he watched her trim the tree with his brother. Saw how she smiled up at him. Their easy playfulness with each other. And dammit, he wanted that.

Arien held the topper in her hand. Tanner got down, gesturing for her to get on his shoulders. She did, and trying to keep her balance as he stood, she giggled. "I can't reach."

"Grab as high as you can and bend it toward you some."

You know what a ladder's for, bro?

Tanner wobbled, and laughing, Arien precariously swayed. "Stay still then."

Tipping the heavy tree forward, she tipped backward with it.

Chrissakes, he couldn't let her fall.

Rushing up behind them, Kellan pushed her upright before she toppled with the tree. "Whoa, easy there, girly."

And with both of them supporting her, Arien reached the highest branch. "I got it."

Yeah, baby, you got it, and we got you.

Nine

Just because it was Christmas didn't mean Tanner got to skip out on his chores. The animals still needed to be fed. Horses tended to. Stalls mucked.

He got out of bed extra early. Didn't matter he'd stayed up way too late last night watching Arien, Emily, and Grams bake cookies while he and Kellan got drunk on Bailey's mixed in Jennifer's hot cocoa. His stepmother excitedly insisted everyone had to open one gift to celebrate Christmas Eve. She got them all matching reindeer pajamas. He didn't usually wear them, but okay, he'd roll with it to make her happy.

It was well after midnight by the time he fell exhausted into his bed.

Still, Tanner was out the door by four. He had to be finished with chores, showered, and in his reindeer jammies before the sun came up at eight, if he wanted to be the one to wake Arien this morning. While he wouldn't be able to rouse her in the way he wished he could, he'd be there to see her lashes fluttering. Those pretty hazel-green eyes smiling up at him. Smell her alluring chypre fragrance. Feel the warmth of her silky-soft skin. That was all the motivation he needed.

It was dark outside, the house quiet, when he tiptoed across the hall to Arien's room at half past seven. Tanner peeked inside her door. Sunday slept in front of the fire that cast a warm and gentle glow upon the bed. He stood there for a moment, watching her sleep, wondering what she was dreaming of. Then carefully, so as not to wake her just yet, he slipped beneath the covers.

Jesus Christ, it was like she could sense he was there. Snuggling into him, her cute, little butt rubbed his front, waking up his reindeer-covered cock. He wrapped his arm around her middle, and burying his nose in her hair, breathed in the delightful scent of cocoa, mandarins, vanilla, and raspberries.

He kissed her crown. How the hell did Kellan do it? Tanner couldn't touch her without touching her the way his brother had. Not when her hot, pliant body was taunting his. Not when every molecule of his being screamed at him to take her.

Of course, he was being tested, and pure fucking torture that it was, this was only the beginning of it. The favor he and his brother had been granted could be taken away as easily it had been given. So, he would endure, just as every triad in Brookside had before him, and the same as those who would follow. Tanner would play by the rules, because a lifetime with Arien was more than worth it.

"Merry Christmas," he softly crooned, combing through her hair. "Wake up, pretty girl."

Unintelligibly mumbling, she rolled over, her face smooshed into his chest. "Not yet. Lemme sleep."

His fingertips skated up and down her spine. "But it's Christmas. Don't you wanna see what Santa left for you?"

Arien answered with a sleepy giggle, "I hate to break it to you, boo, but Santa isn't real."

Boo? Is that a city thing?

"How'd all those presents get under the tree then, *boo?*" he quipped, tickling her ribs. "C'mon now."

The dog jumped up on the bed. Tail wagging a mile a minute, Sunday joined the cause, licking her face.

"Okay," she shrieked, trying to catch her breath and laughing all at once. "Okay."

He and Arien were the first ones downstairs. The tree, laden with presents, twinkled beside the cold hearth. "I'll get a fire going. Why don't you make us some coffee?"

"Yeah, sure. Everyone's still asleep." She swatted his bottom. "I didn't have to get up so early."

"Kellan and Dad got up a long time ago."

"Well, where are they then?"

"I'd guess Kellan's still cleanin' up from chores, and my dad is wakin' up your mama." *The way I wish I could've woken you.* Tanner winked, swatting her back. "Coffee, girly, and make it strong. Don't think I got more than three hours of sleep."

He went left, toward the fireplace.

She went right, into the kitchen.

Hunkered down in front of the hearth, he'd just lit the kindling when Arien came tapping him on the shoulder. "Uh, it's not there."

"What's not there?"

"The coffee pot. It's gone."

Chuckling, he hitched his thumb behind him. "You walked right past it." Then under his breath, he added, "Merry Christmas."

Her squeal was loud enough to wake the dead.

He and Kellan had built her a hutch, for a coffee bar, that fit in the alcove between the living room and kitchen. Jennifer gave them advice on what to put in it. An espresso machine, milk frother, and one of those fancy-ass Nespresso machines. A variety of syrups—including the pumpkin spice one she loved so much.

Tanner might have been the one to come up with the idea, but it was his brother who ran wild with it. Kellan custom-fitted the drawers with pullouts to organize the pods of coffee and accessories. He even tucked a mini glass-front fridge between the two lower cabinets for water, creamers, and cans of soda.

Arien had his brother wrapped around her little finger and she didn't even know it. He'd never known Kellan to do stuff like picking out new coffee mugs or chopping down a Christmas tree. But he'd done it. For her.

A card was attached to the espresso machine with a big red bow. Tanner walked toward her as she read it. And then with a running leap, Arien was in his arms. *Oof.* Her legs encircling his waist, hands clasped around his neck, he held onto her bottom.

"I can't believe you and Kellan did all this for me." Bouncing on him *there*, she kissed his cheek over and over, repeating, "Thank you, thank you, thank you."

Fucking hell, you're killin' me here, girly.

He heard Kellan's amused chuckle from across the room. Arien must've heard it too. She slithered down his chest and made a mad dash for his brother. Flinging herself at him, she about knocked him on his ass.

She smacked a kiss to the corner of his mouth. "You *do* like me."

"Maybe a little bit." He smirked, lifting her up.

Giggling, her fingertips stroked his cheek. "You look ridiculous in reindeer."

"Oh, yeah?" Kellan squeezed her butt, his gaze slowly traveling down her pajama top. "I think they look damn fine."

Sandwiching Arien between them, Tanner wrapped his arms around her middle. He kissed on one side of her neck. His brother kissed the other.

And her breath hitched.

See, pretty girl? See how good we are together?

Did she feel it too? Fuck, if she didn't. She had to.

"I ain't jizzin' in my pants again." His breathing heavy, Kellan dropped his forehead to hers. "Make me some of that coffee?"

"Pumpkin spice?"

"Yeah, baby cakes." He chuckled deep and low. "You know how I like it."

With his gaze on Tanner, Kellan set her down. A lazy smirk creeping on his brother's face, he listened to Arien hum carols while she fiddled with her new gadgets. The season of love, peace, and harmony, Christmas is a time for miracles, ain't it? Could be they'd just gotten theirs.

"Here you go." Arien set down mugs in front of them. "Figured you both could use a Red Eye."

"What's that?" Kellan stared into his cup.

"Coffee, strong and black. Just the way you like it." She winked. "With a shot of espresso on top."

She flounced off into the kitchen.

Raising his brow, his brother looked over at him, then took a sip.

Truth be told, it was the best darn coffee Tanner ever tasted, and the most wonderful Christmas morning he ever remembered having. The five of them opened presents in their matching reindeer pajamas. He and Kellan refinished a cradle that Brooks babies had slept in for generations, filling it with tiny newborn things. Jennifer cried.

Arien popped cinnamon rolls and a breakfast casserole in the oven, wearing the cowboy hat and boots they got her. There was a custom saddle waiting for her and Daisy in the tack room, too. Then she set up her new tripod and took a gazillion family photos in front of the tree. Playing with the settings on her Nikon, swapping out lenses, she wouldn't let them get up and eat until she was satisfied with the images she captured.

Tanner was looking forward to next Christmas already. It would be even better than this one. At least he hoped so. Their new brother or sister would be here, and if he gave credence to his father's vision, which he did, they could be expecting a baby of their own by then.

"Get your coats." Kellan tipped his chin at him and Arien. "Meet me outside by the truck."

She scrambled for the door. His brother grabbed her wrist. "And keep the boots on."

He drove in the direction of the Tetons without a word. A three-seat sled and sixteen Alaskan huskies waited. The musher shook his head, chuckling at the comical sight of them, dressed in reindeer pajamas, coats, woolies, and cowboy boots.

Huddled together beneath thick fur blankets, Arien in between them, the dogs pulled their sled through the pristine snow in the forest. She shivered. Kellan passed her a flask. "This'll warm you up."

"What is it?"

"Fireball," he said, a shit-eating grin on his face. "I hear you like it."

"Tanner?"

He shrugged, rubbing a lock of her hair between his fingers. "You liked it well enough at the bonfire."

Taking a swig, she sputtered and gave it back.

"I wanna watch you dance again." Kellan reached across Arien beneath the blanket, taking her hand that was farther away from him. "Wearing nothin' but them boots…"

Her lips parted.

His arm crossing over his brother's, Tanner grabbed hold of her other hand. "He's just teasin' ya."

"Speak for your damn self, brother." Raising the flask to his lips, he tipped it back. "Can't deny she was hot. And just where'd you learn how to dance like that, baby cakes?"

"Miss Hattie's School of Dance." She snatched the flask from his fingers. "Thank you very much."

"Thank you, Miss Hattie." Nodding, Kellan sniggered.

"Asshole," she muttered with a grin, taking another swig.

Yeah, his brother sure loved getting a rise out of her. And Arien took the bait every damn time.

She wasn't shivering anymore. Tucking the flask in his pocket, Kellan let his head fall upon her shoulder. Snuggling closer, Tanner did the same. "Warm enough?"

"Uh-huh."

His hand slipped beneath all the layers, under her reindeer pajama top, to find his brother stroking her warm, velvet skin. Tanner laid his palm on her stomach. Arien dreamily sighed.

"How many more days 'til your birthday, little sister?"

"Twenty-six."

Nibbling on the lobe of her ear, Tanner whispered, "Baby, I don't think I can wait."

Ten

Arien kicked back on the sofa with her iPad, perusing YouTube for some kind of inspiration. Blueberry scones? Nope. Too ordinary. Prince Harry and Meghan Markle. Enough with that shit. Who the fuck cares?

"Meeting a pornstar?" Rubbing Sunday's head, she giggled. "Chrissakes, we live with two of 'em, don't we?" *Well, they think they are anyway, strutting around half naked, showing off their muscles all the damn time.*

Actually, in Kellan's case, it was his birthday suit and showing off way more than that. She chewed on her lip, distracted by the image in her head.

School project, Arien. Focus.

Flipping onto her stomach, she returned to her scrolling.

"Redemption from death row? Edging 101? Okay, YouTube. You're not helping me here."

Scroll.

Scroll.

Scroll.

"Ten things you should be buying at Aldi right now. Pass. We ain't got one." God, they were rubbing off on her. She was even starting to sound like them.

Swiss roll cake. "Maybe." Arien clicked on it.

Replaying it several times, she studied the video. Its aesthetic, the camera angles, how the vlogger spoke, and the presentation of the recipe. Arien's teacher wanted her to push herself out of her comfort zone. Still photography she was good at, but video? Not so much.

She was watching Mr. Preppy Chef roll his fluffy chocolate sponge cake with homemade whipped cream for about the tenth time, when she felt a hand rubbing her ass. The zing in her jeans unmistakable, his fingertips slowly trailed down the center seam. Fucker was teasing her. Too close, and not nearly close enough, she clamped her thighs together.

"Knock it off, Kellan."

His chuckle husky, he sat on the arm of the sofa. "Whatcha doin'?"

"Watching a video."

"I can see that." Arien didn't have to look at him to know he was rolling his eyes. "Of what?"

"Uhh…cake."

And he full on laughed. "Why?"

"Because I have this compulsion to create a decadent chocolate ganache." *And lick it off your skin.* Sitting up, she smacked his thigh. "Don't look at me like that."

"Like what?"

"Perplexed," she answered, wrinkling her nose at him. "I'm not really into chocolate. It's for school."

"You're watchin' some dude bake a cake." Letting his ass slide off the arm of the sofa, Kellan landed beside her. "For school? And yeah, you perplex me all right."

"Hey, pretty girl." Tanner came in and sat on the other side of her.

Acknowledging his presence, Arien began stroking his cheek and attempted to explain the assignment. "I'm just getting ideas for a visual arts project I have to do. Looking for a little inspiration, you know?"

Her gaze flicked from one brother to the other. Crickets.

"See, my teacher suggested a blog. Only catch is, in addition to photography she wants me to utilize videography, and that's not my strong suit. At all." Pursing her lips to the side, she sighed. "And blog about what? It has to be something creative, instructional or informative, and visually appealing."

"So, cake?" Kellan's brow lifted.

"Not necessarily just that, but yeah, food came to mind."

"That means she'll be cooking and we get to sample." Tanner reached behind her and nudged his brother. "I like it."

"I'd like Edging 101 even better…naked dancing." Squeezing her knee, he winked.

Glaring up at him, her nostrils flared. "Were you spying on me?"

"She said we're pornstars, bro." Confirming he indeed had been, Kellan smirked, flexing his muscles. "And the girl has no fucking clue. Yet."

Did he actually think she intended to find out? Beads of sweat erupting on her skin, heat flashed through her body. Sure, when Arien was alone in her room, she thought about it sometimes. And how could she not? She'd get all tingly, but she wasn't sure why.

Once, curiosity got the better of her and she googled threesomes. *Holy dirty, twisted shit.* That was a real eye-opener. All that fingering, fucking, and sucking. Double penetration, for chrissakes.

Her jaw dropped watching that one, but what did she know? The chick in the video seemed to like it.

She wasn't an idiot. Arien knew both Kellan and Tanner wanted her, and fucked up as it was, they were a package deal. She couldn't deny she had feelings she shouldn't be feeling for her step-brothers, and it had nothing to do with the fact they were related by marriage. Two months ago they were strangers. If anything, she liked that element of the forbidden when Tanner called her 'little sister'.

The thing was, Arien still thought this trinity thing and their stupid rules were fucking nuts. But yet, if she were being honest with herself, immersed in their strange-to-her culture as she was, it seemed less so every day.

"Asshole."

"Call me that again." Kellan wound her hair around his fist, pulling her head back. "Gets me hard."

"Asshole," she teased with a wicked giggle.

Tanner pushed on his brother's shoulder. "Cut the shit, you two."

Kellan combed his fingers through her hair. "Chill, we're just playin.'"

"Well I wanna know what our pretty girl here's gonna be makin' us." He put his feet up, laying his head on her lap. "I'm hungry."

Tanner tugged on the ends of her hair. Running his fingers through the strands that hung over her breasts, he brushed her nipples. Was it on accident or by design? Not that it made a dif-ference, because fuck if it didn't feel good.

Arien bit her lip. She might have even whimpered a little. Because he kept on doing it, over and over again.

Definitely on purpose.

Lifting the hair he'd been combing down her back, Kellan kissed her nape.

Tanner stopped, inhaled deep, and kissed the skin on her belly.

"Please..." Her fingers sank into his flesh.

He groaned, pulling on the ends hard. Then gently, purposefully, resumed his stroking, sweeping over her nipples with every pass. From the other side, Kellan hooked his arms through hers, gripping her shoulders. His teeth sank into her skin, and by pulling her back, he pushed out her chest, giving Tanner easier access and himself a better view.

Arien could see her nipples protruding against the fabric. So could he. And right then, she didn't fucking care.

"You'll see what an asshole I am," Kellan breathed in her ear, tugging on the tender lobe with his teeth. "Soon."

◭

Arien stood at the granite island, whipping frothy egg whites until they formed soft peaks. Gently, she folded in the honey, vanilla, and coconut flakes, before pouring the macaroon batter into a springform pan and popping it in the oven.

"That looks good, honey." Grams gave her a squeeze. "It's gonna turn out nice."

"I don't know what I was thinking, but the inspiration struck me like lightning and I just had to make this. Do you have any idea how hard it is to find fresh peaches around here in January?"

"Hm." She nodded. "Got 'em though, didn't you?"

"Yeah, they only had to special order them for me."

"Surrendering to your passion is a good thing. Listen to what speaks to you, then make it happen. And make it happen beautifully." Her blue eyes sparkling, Grams held onto her shoulders and drove the point home. "Absolute love. Passion. That's where you'll find joy. Settling for less will never feel right."

"We're not talking about peaches, are we?"

"Anything in life, dear." Smiling, she gave her arm a soft pat. "Now, let's get started on the panna cotta."

As Arien pulled the coconut macaroon base out of the oven, Tanner strolled into the kitchen. "Goddamn, something smells good. Hi, Grandma." He pecked her cheek, then peeked over Arien's shoulder. "Whatcha makin'?"

"Cake."

"For tomorrow?"

"No, I'm not baking my own birthday cake. That would be pathetic." She turned around. "It's a trial run for my blog project."

"You'll be trying out some coconut macaroon peach panna cotta cake for dessert tonight," Grams added with a nod.

"Isn't that what we had at that Italian place in Denver?" He grinned. "After the weddin'?"

"It is." Kellan pushed off the doorframe he'd apparently been leaning against. Arien hadn't even noticed he was there. "She wanted seconds, so I put a big, ole slab on her plate. Ate up every damn crumb too, didn't ya, baby cakes?" He winked at her.

Grams raised her perfectly arched brows. "Baby cakes?"

"Yeah." He chuckled. "Fits her."

"Uh-huh."

Walking over to her, Kellan half cocked his head. "What happened to the chocolate?"

"Told you, I'm not into chocolate."

"This one reminds you of home, don't it?" Tanner tucked some hair behind her ear. "You miss it."

"Arien *is* home," Kellan insisted.

"I just really loved the panna cotta. I do miss Denver, though," she admitted. "Can't get a green chili cheeseburger around here to save my life."

His features hardening, Kellan tucked his tongue into the corner of his lips. Glaring at the UC emblem blazoned across her chest, he snickered. "Right."

She watched him bolt out of the kitchen. "What the hell?"

Grams silently stood there, pressing her lips together.

Tanner shrugged. "Don't know how many times I gotta say it, Kel's a moody fucker."

He took his cranky ass upstairs right after supper. Didn't even stay for dessert.

Fuck him.

"Since it's your birthday eve, why don't you pick the movie, sweetie?" Her mom held out the remote.

"That's okay, Mom, you pick," Arien said, settling herself on the opposite side of the leather sectional next to Tanner. "There isn't anything special I want to watch."

"Oh, we can watch that *Harry & Meghan* documentary." Jennifer began scrolling through Netflix. "I haven't seen it yet."

"No, Mom. Please, anything but that." Vehemently shaking her head, she extended her hand. "I changed my mind. Give me the remote."

'*Thank you*,' Matthew mouthed.

Winking back at him, Arien clicked on the first movie she came to.

Pulling a blanket over the two of them, Tanner draped his arm across her shoulders. She grabbed the bowl of popcorn from the end table beside her, placing it on his lap so they could share it. "Extra butter."

"Just the way I like it."

"I know."

"What movie is this anyway?" he asked, shoveling popcorn in his mouth.

"*The Invitation*. Some horror flick. Mom and I both like them, so I figured that was a fair compromise since I vetoed the Harkles." Arien quietly giggled. "I grew up watching scary movies. We'd have mommy-daughter dates camping out in the living room with Michael, Jason, and Freddy, while most of my friends were watching Jasmine, Belle, and Ariel."

"Really?"

"Yeah, perk of having a young mom, I guess." Reaching into the bowl on his lap, she glanced over at Jennifer, cuddling with her husband, and smiled. "They're fun."

Licking butter from his fingers, Tanner set the popcorn back on the table. He put a pillow behind him and sat back against the arm, pulling her back to his chest. Then he adjusted the blanket, raising it almost to their chins, and wrapped both arms around her. "You good?"

Arien looked again across the sofa. Her mother and stepfather were too preoccupied with the movie, and each other, to pay them any mind. "Yeah, I'm good."

Underneath the blanket, his palm rested on her bare stomach. She pretended not to notice his fingertips lightly strumming her skin. Up and down, from the bottom of her bra to the waistband of her pants. Lazy circles around her belly button.

His cock grew hard beneath his sweats. It poked up against her ass. Arien pretended not to notice that either, but considering she was wiggling her way closer, Tanner was surely aware she knew.

His fingers delved into her sides, and raising his hips, he pressed himself into her. "I love how you're always wearin' these little cut-off shirts so I can feel your skin."

She turned her head toward her mother.

"They're asleep, pretty girl."

"They could wake up," she whispered. "My mom would *die*."

"Nah. Your mama loves me." With a kiss to her head, he nudged her. "C'mon, let's leave 'em here. We can finish the movie in my room."

Taking the bowl of popcorn with her, Arien followed him up the stairs.

In all fairness, he did turn the TV on.

Tanner fluffed a nest of pillows behind them and they snuggled together under the velvet comforter. His arm came around her, and pulling her closer, he kissed her hair. "Where were we?"

"Hmm, about fifty-nine minutes in," she answered, pressing the fast-forward button. "They were about to do it, I think."

"Do it?"

"Yeah, you know. Have hot vampire sex. See, our unsuspecting heroine doesn't know it yet, but she's an offering to that lord of the manor guy—who's really Dracula, by the way. Her family set her up to be his bride in exchange for prosperity."

"*Three. The magic number.*"

"You've seen this before?"

"*We are at our strongest when we are three.*"

The dialogue on the TV catching her off guard, she absently answered, "Whoa, uh, yeah."

"No need to watch it again then." Tanner put on a music channel and tossed the remote. "Now…" Scooping her into his arms, he rolled her on top of him. "…where were we?"

"Hmm, I dunno."

"Need a reminder?" Fingertips skated down her spine. Tanner grabbed her ass with both hands, pushing her into him. "Feel what you do to me, pretty girl."

She couldn't miss it. It felt like he was packing a Louisville Slugger in his pants. "But I didn't do anything."

"Baby, all you gotta do is breathe." Burying his face in her neck, Tanner inhaled. "And I'm dyin' from wantin' you so bad."

"Sorry," Arien said, almost as a question. She rubbed the stubble on his cheek.

"Don't be." Turning his head, he kissed her palm. "Happy birthday."

"Is it?" Glancing at the clock, she saw it was just after midnight. "Oh, look at that, it is." She looked at him. "Thank you."

Bringing her with him, he scooted back to sit against the headboard. Tanner held her on his lap, running his fingers down her hair. "You know what that means, right?"

"Uh-huh."

Green eyes burned into hers. "Can I kiss you?"

Please. I've been dying, too.

But Arien didn't have the air in her lungs to say it. Her heart beating faster, she could only nod.

The moonlight through his bedroom window felt sultry.

January turned warm. Stroking her cheek, Tanner leaned in, and for a moment, time froze. His lips brushed over hers. They were *so* soft. Arien hadn't expected that. Honest, tender, and sweet, his kiss was the destination in and of itself. She knew it would stay with her forever.

"As soon as I saw you, I knew..."

Blood pumping in her ears, Arien grabbed his face and pulled him closer. Lightly nibbling on her lip, he gently sucked it into his mouth. Rubbing his nose alongside hers. Sweet, buttery breath on her face. Fingertips lingering on her skin. His lips skated along her jaw.

"...I was gonna lose my heart."

And right then and there, she knew she'd lost hers, too.

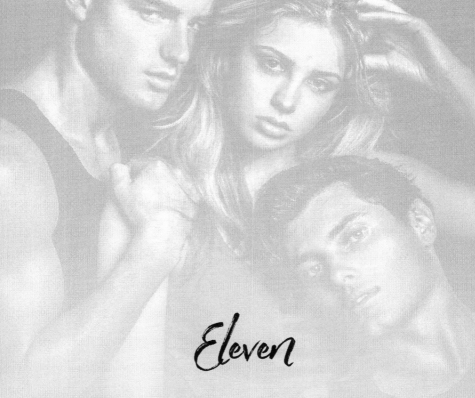

Eleven

Kellan tossed the little square box onto the bed. Wrapped in gold paper, he'd tied it with ribbon. What the hell was he thinking? He should've known better.

That girl put a spell on him or something. Enticing him with her delectable body. That beautiful face. The cute way she laughed. Christ, he could smell her everywhere. Arien almost had him forgetting she was going to leave them.

Sitting down on the edge of the mattress, Kellan expelled a breath. He picked up the box, twirling it between his fingers. He'd made the birthday gift himself. Three hearts hand-carved in beeswax, cast in sterling silver, to wear on her slender wrist. Should he even give it to her?

At midnight, he stole across the hall to her room, but it was empty.

He crept halfway down the stairs, and finding the house dark, went back up as quietly as he came.

In the stillness, he could discern muffled sounds on the other side of the door he shared with Tanner. A gentle groove tempered by a mere thickness of wood. And cracking it open, he found her kissing him.

Tanner's hands all over her.

Whispering sweet nothings in her ear.

Couldn't wait, could ya? She's mine first, dammit.

He took in the way she looked at him. Stars in her hazel-green eyes. Hanging on Tanner's every word. Fingers raking his scalp, Arien pulled on his brother's hair, his lips suckling a pink-tipped breast.

She loves him.

Looking away, Kellan closed the door.

He'd wait until morning.

The shower was running when he slipped inside her room. Quietly, Kellan shooed the dog out and turned the lock. Glancing around, he placed the little gold box on her dresser next to a photo she framed of the three of them. A book lay upon the night table, the laptop open on her bed.

He sat down. Inhaling her scent, his fingers rubbed the rumpled sheets where she'd slept. It aroused him, the desire he'd squashed down for so long crashing to the surface.

"Kellan? What are you doing in here?"

Steam billowing out behind her, naked beneath a towel, Arien stood in the open doorway. Beads of water dripped from the ends of her hair, gliding past creamy swells to disappear in the valley between her breasts.

Without answering, he stood and stalked toward her. With his hands on either side of her head, Kellan caged her against the wall. He trailed his lips over the pulse in her neck and breathed in deep. Filling his lungs with her, he held onto her breast, squeezing it through the towel.

"Kel," she squeaked, biting her lip.

He reached inside the towel for her nipple. Pinching it between his fingers and stroking it with his thumb, he nipped at her earlobe. "Don't let those flowery words and his sweet ways fool you, *little sister.*"

Arien whimpered.

"He and I are the same." His hand moved down her belly to the flesh he craved between her thighs. He cupped her pussy, a finger sliding up her slit. Warm and wet. All for him.

Breathing against her skin, Kellan heard the air catch in her throat. He pressed on her clit. "Maybe Tanner's what you want, but I'm what you need."

And he kissed her.

Her lips formed a bridge for all his pent-up feelings to flood into. Frustration. Desire. Anger. Lust.

But what of love?

It was there. The promise of it. All Arien had to do was stay and claim it.

I'm right here for the takin', baby cakes.

With his fingers clamped around her neck, their mouths mated, tongues touching in a wet, frenzied dance. Kellan rubbed her clit, feeling it swell beneath his thumb.

Her shaking thighs could barely hold her. He held her up so she wouldn't fall, loving the sound of her scream as she came.

"I think…" He smirked, licking the delicate sweetness from his fingers. "…what you really need, is us both."

Sitting in the window seat, Arien stared at nothing through the glass, absently tracing three silver hearts on her wrist. It felt like a lucid dream. There had to be something in the air or the water here, because this place was getting to her. Chrissakes, what she did was almost as slutty as that time Savannah Mason and two football players got caught by the principal with their pants down in the girls' bathroom.

It was during Arien's freshman year of high school, and to this day everyone still talked about it. Nothing happened to the quarterback and his buddy, of course, which was bullshit. But the poor girl was so slut-shamed she couldn't walk the halls after that. Her mom had to pull her out of school. How was that fair? Last she'd heard, Savannah left Denver to go to college in Chicago.

Even though she didn't have to worry about anything like that happening in Brookside, Arien couldn't convince herself that making out—okay, it was a little more than just making out—with her stepbrothers wouldn't come with some kind of repercussions. How could she resist their pull, though? Especially here, where she wasn't expected to. Her head told her she should, but her heart, and other parts of her anatomy, had an altogether different idea.

Like a moth to the fire, she was drawn to them. Gentle and sweet, Tanner was just so easy to be with. And Kellan? Hair bristled all over her body just thinking of that kiss. She'd never tasted anything quite like it.

Yeah, there was definitely something in the water here. Because Arien wanted to kiss them both again. And it was fucking with her head.

"Whatcha thinkin' about?"

Strong hands firmly kneaded her shoulders. Squeezing himself in behind her, Tanner wrapped her up in a giant hug, kissing the top of her head. Deep in her crazy thoughts, she hadn't noticed he'd come in.

"Nothing," she said, sinking against his chest. "Just zoned out, I guess."

"Don't believe ya." Tanner fingered the bracelet on her wrist. "It's okay, you know. I want you and Kellan to—"

"But it's not," adamantly, Arien disagreed. "It feels so messed up."

"It's fine. You're fine." His arms tightened around her.

She inhaled with a half-hearted shrug, blowing it out on a sigh. "I made out with both of my stepbrothers. That makes me a slut."

"Does not." Dipping his head, Tanner angled her face toward his. "Stop it. You're thinking like an outsider."

"I *am* an outsider."

"Not anymore, pretty girl." He turned Arien over, her chest on his, dragging his fingers through her hair. "You're a Brooksider now and we're gonna make you ours."

"I...I don't think...I don't know, Tanner."

Gorgeous green eyes gazed into hers, promising her everything, if only she'd willingly accept it. The corner of his mouth lifting ever so slightly, he took her face in his hands. Thumbs caressed her cheeks. Warm, soft lips gently swept over hers. Then with the fireflies dancing in her tummy, Tanner kissed her.

Breathless.

Weightless.

Limitless.

In the arms of her best friend, her stepbrother, the world outside the gate vanished, and every crazy, wild dream felt possible.

"*I* know." Tucking a strand of hair behind her ear, he kissed her forehead. "Me and Kel are headin' out in a while. Goin' to Jackson to have a few beers and watch the game. Why don't you come with us?"

"Thanks, but I can't. Got a study date with Emily and Grams."

Trigonometry is a bitch. Arien rubbed her temples. Cosecant, cosine, and cotangent functions were giving her a headache.

"A right triangle has three sides that can be uniquely identified by the hypotenuse using the Pythagorean theorem. What are the definitions of the trigonometric functions?"

Kiss my cute, little ass, Mr. Pythagoras.

Exchanging a glance with Emily, Arien dropped her shoulders.

What would she ever need this knowledge for anyway? Her brain hurt.

"Come on now, honey. You know this." Grams encouraged her with a wink. "Think of the mnemonic."

Sohcahtoa.

"Sine equals opposite over hypotenuse, cosine equals adjacent over hypotenuse, and tangent equals opposite over adjacent."

"Very good!" Clapping her hands together, she chuckled. "I think you two have had enough trig for one day, yes?"

"Who knew simple triangles could be so hard? Not to mention exhausting." Yawning, Emily gave Melinda Brooks a hug. "Thanks, Grams. See you at Uncle Matty's for dinner tomorrow?"

"Same as every Sunday, babydoll," she replied, hugging each of them goodbye.

Free of Pythagoras and his stupid theorem at last, they giggled all the way to the car.

Buckling in, Arien blew out a breath. With the sun setting, a shadow crept up the mountains, gradually ascending from its base to the snowcapped peaks. For a moment, it looked as if they were ablaze, glowing orange against a darkening sky, until the shadow engulfed them completely, extinguishing the fiery light. The marvelousness of the phenomenon never failed to mesmerize her.

"Pretty, ain't it?" Emily smiled at her. "I don't wanna go home, do you?"

"I'm so tired, Ems." Closing her eyes, she tipped her head back against the seat.

"The boys went to Jackson."

"How'd you know?"

"Jake and Billy went with 'em."

Her eyes flew open.

"*Who wants a fumbly-bumbly under the covers, if you get my meaning. I heard some of the boys get plenty of practice with the ski bunnies in Jackson.*"

They wouldn't.

Well, Tanner wouldn't.

Emily smirked. "Wanna go?"

Did she? "I dunno if I can stay awake through another stupid football game."

"But it's the playoffs." Emily waggled her eyebrows. "C'mon. They're either at Eleanor's or Pinky G's. We can surprise 'em."

Tanner *did* ask her to go, now didn't he? Biting her lip, she nodded. "Yeah, okay."

Kellan's red truck in the parking lot was hard to miss. Emily pulled into the spot beside his, and now that they were here, Arien was almost afraid to go in. What if he was practicing on some snow bunny? After kissing her, touching her the way he did, she'd die. *I'll kick him right in his Wranglers.* Perhaps she shouldn't feel that way, but she did.

The place was so packed, she and Emily barely made it through the door. The game played on TVs affixed to exposed-brick walls, not that anyone could possibly hear it over the music blaring from the speakers. Squished into the corner of the bar, Arien spotted their cowboys in a booth on the far wall.

Nervous tension draining from her shoulders, she released a breath. No bunnies in sight. Nursing on pints of beer, the boys were alone.

Pointing across the crowded bar, Emily waved. "There they are."

"Jesus, I feel like such a stalker."

"Don't be silly." She nudged her shoulder. "Look, they're happy to see us."

With that ever-present smirk on his face, Kellan locked eyes with her, raising his beer to his lips. After taking a long, slow swallow, he stood.

"How come Wyoming girls are just so damn pretty?"

Arien turned her head in the direction of the slurred voice. A group of guys wearing UC jerseys, a couple of them on barstools, the others standing, wedged together like sardines in a tin, were leering at her and Emily.

"Fuck's sake," Arien muttered under her breath.

Leaning into her ear, Emily giggled. "Are all the boys like that where you come from?"

"Sit right here and have a drink with me, baby." The dude squeezed the dick in his pants while patting his thigh.

Ewww.

"Does that usually work for you, Chad?"

"My name's not Chad."

Should be.

"C'mon, baby girl. I don't bite." He grinned. "Much."

A hand gripped her arm, yanking her away. "She ain't your baby." Kellan got right up in the dude's face. "She's mine. You so much as say another word to her, look at her, even breathe in her direction, and they'll be wipin' up your innards from the floor. Got that?"

"She really banging that cowboy?" Sneering, barstool dude looked at Emily.

Kellan grabbed his cousin by the hand. "Let's go."

Stumbling into him, she glanced back. "Well, you do know what they say, *Chad*. Save a horse, ride a—"

"Emily!"

Leading them away from the bar, Kellan busted out a belly laugh at the drunk, dejected voice behind them that said, "And the name's not Chad."

Arien slid into the booth next to Tanner, Kellan taking his seat beside her, while Emily took her place between Billy and Jake. Peanut shells were strewn about the table, along with a pitcher of beer, half-eaten nachos, and the remains of buffalo chicken wings. Reaching into the bucket, she grabbed a heaping handful of the salty nuts.

Tanner pulled her closer. "Hungry, darlin'?"

"I could eat something."

Kellan motioned for the server.

Jake smiled at her, his arm winding around Emily. "Had enough of trig, huh?"

"Had enough of Pythagoras." Rolling her eyes, Arien popped a peanut into her mouth.

"Ah, the triangle guy. Numbers are the building blocks of reality." He chuckled. "You know, he believed the meaning behind numbers was deeply significant, and considered the number three—the number of harmony, wisdom, and understanding—to be the perfect number."

"Is that right?" Cracking open another nut, she snorted.

"Truth." Jake winked. "It's also the number of time—past, present, future. Of the divine. And magic."

"Uh-huh, okay, is that where your, um…" Searching for the right word, Arien paused, twirling her hand in front of her. "… logic comes from?"

"Maybe." His smile grew. He tipped his head to the side. "Or maybe, it was just practical a hundred and eighty years ago."

The server came to take their order. Kellan spoke on her behalf. "Cheeseburger—well done. Do you have green chili?"

"I can ask."

"Do that."

Tanner squeezed her side. Jake ordered another pitcher of beer and a taco salad for Emily.

As the server left, Arien planted her elbows on the table. "You were saying?"

Glancing to Kellan, Tanner, and lastly to his brother, he nodded. "The wagon train encountered a mountain man on the trail going west. Our great-grandfather, Levi, fell in love with his daughter. People called her half breed, because her mother was Shoshone."

She gasped. "Assholes."

"Yeah, the world was different then. I like to believe people aren't as ignorant now. Anyhow, she thought no one would ever love her because of it, but Levi did. He wanted to marry her. The old mountain man gave him his blessing on one condition. He had to take her sister, too."

No fucking way.

Picking up Tanner's beer, Arien took a swallow.

"Marrying two sisters or two brothers was common among her mother's tribe, you see, as it is in India, Tibet, and other places in the world."

"So he married them both."

"He did." Emily combed her fingers through his long dark hair. "But that's just part of the story."

"Go on."

"The mountain man imparted many Shoshone beliefs and traditions to them. They believed in visions, dreams if you will, and he told them to settle by the lake on the three-headed mountain. If they heeded his words, the earth would bless them with endless favor and bounty. He'd seen it."

"And they believed him?"

"Nah, they thought he was off his rocker. Nippin' on too much whiskey." Sniggering, Jake wet his whistle with a swallow of beer. "Until they accidentally veered off the trail and came upon Brooks Mountain. It didn't take long for them to see what the mountain man told them was true. The earth blessed them with favor just as he said it would—even more than they ever dreamed of. Still does.

"So, yeah, maybe it's Pythagorean logic. The Shoshone." He smirked. "Or maybe just because Levi wanted my great-grandmother so badly. The pool of eligible mates was sparse here back then. There weren't a lot of people to start a family with in order to grow and prosper, so maybe the others did find it practical and went along with what the old man told them."

"Still ain't many people here." Tossing her chestnut waves, Emily snickered. "Less than half a million in the entire damn state. Betcha the prospects are dismal unless you're lucky enough to live in Brookside."

"But that's not what drives us, Arien. It's absolute love."

Rubbing Emily's back, Jake went on, "See, family is the most important part of our values. It's the trinity that binds us all together and sustains us."

"The old man must have been tripping on 'shrooms or something. A magic mountain? That's just crazy."

"Maybe he was." His dark eyes boring into hers, Jake implored, "But they shouldn't have survived. So many who set out on that trail west didn't. And look at what they left us. What they taught us. The community we have.

"You want to know what's crazy?" He ticked his chin toward Kellan. "Your man here can wrangle a hundred grand for a single bull. Tanner doesn't need to break horses, he talks to 'em. Every investment your stepfather makes for Brookside turns to gold. How can that be, huh?"

"I don't know."

"Because the old man was right, Arien."

The server came with the food. Smiling up at Kellan, she lifted the burger, smothered in mounds of green chili deliciousness, to her mouth. Tasting heaven, she moaned out loud, "Oh, God. Sooo fucking good."

"Careful now. You're gettin' me hard, baby cakes."

"Don't take much." Tanner rubbed her thigh. She'd swat him for that remark, if it didn't mean taking her hands off her burger.

With a cocky shrug of his shoulders, Kellan conceded to the fact, and they all laughed.

Devouring her orgasmic burger, the wild notions of Pythagoras and a crazy, old mountain man were all but forgotten. She'd been missing it, craving it, for months. And just like that, Arien knew what the next entry for her blog project would be. *Colorado green chili.* Why hadn't she thought of it before?

"How's your dad and Jennifer doing?" Billy asked.

Her ears pricked at the mention of her mother's name.

"Great." Arien could hear the grin in Tanner's voice. "Belly's growin'."

"I hope they're favored with a boy," Jake softly said. "The third son."

"What's wrong with having a girl?"

"Nothing." He gently smiled. "Girls are lovely. But three of anything brings good fortune with it. And so a boy, Matthew's third son, may negate his unfortunate luck…the deaths of his wives."

Fucking nonsense.

"Wow, you really are superstitious." Biting into her lip so she wouldn't laugh, her head bobbed from side to side. "My maybe baby brother is a lucky charm now?"

"In a manner of speaking." Reaching across the table, Jake took her hand. "Matthew has been given the most precious gifts of all. The love of your mother. A child. Still, he took great risk entering into a traditional marriage."

Not knowing how to take that, Arien snickered. "My mom's the third wife. Isn't that lucky too?"

Kellan and Tanner exchanged a wary glance.

"Maybe."

But his answer lacked conviction.

"At least, I hope so. For all our sakes."

Twelve

Arien and her stepfather were the only ones around to clean up the kitchen. Grams, Aunt Kim, and Emily had long since gone home. Kellan and Tanner were out, tending to their evening chores. Mom was taking an after-dinner nap, same as she usually did.

Rinsing off plates, Matthew stacked them in the dishwasher, while Arien took care of the leftovers. She was actually surprised they had any. Most often, her stepbrothers made sure they didn't.

Fuckers can eat. She giggled to herself.

"Want to let me in on the joke?" A wet plate in his hand, Matthew chuckled with her.

"There isn't one." Arien stuffed half a tray of lasagna into the oversized fridge and walked over to her stepfather. "Can I ask you a question?"

"Course, honey." He set the plate down. "You can come to me for anything, you know that."

"I know, but it's kind of personal."

"We're family, Arien." He pulled her in for a hug. "What is it?"

"Are you hoping the baby's a boy?" She felt silly asking, so she didn't look at him when she said it.

Matthew lifted her chin with his finger. "The only thing that matters to me is makin' sure Jennifer and this baby, he or she, are happy, healthy, and loved."

"Okay, good." She nodded.

"You know, you'll always be our girl." He stroked her cheek. "What's this really about, honey?"

"Jake told me having a third boy would be lucky, so…"

"You figured I was hoping for one?"

Mumbo jumbo. God, I'm stupid.

"Yeah."

"What else did Jake tell you?"

"Everything, I think." Turning away, Arien picked up the dish in the sink. "You really believe all that stuff?"

Standing right behind her, his hands kneaded her shoulders. "I do."

"Then considering what happened before, you must want the baby to be a boy."

"Christ, Arien." Gripping her arms, her stepfather turned her back around. "Yes, I can admit it. Just the thought of losing Jennifer, like I lost Heather and Amanda, scares the shit outta me. I can't go through that again. But your mama reassured me. She's not them, and she's seein' the doctor in Dubois instead of the midwife here, so there's nothin' to fear."

"Even though your marriage is traditional?"

"Heh," he blew out, giving a quick shake of his head. "Jake did tell you everything, didn't he?"

"John Jacoby mentioned it at Thanksgiving, too. Didn't make sense to me at the time."

"Don't you worry about it." His arms around her felt rather nice. "You, your mama…our family is all that matters, okay?"

"Okay."

"My beautiful Arien." Hugging her tight, Matthew kissed the top of her head. "I love you."

Growing up without a dad or a grandpa, she'd never heard those words from a man before. That had to be the reason tears sprang in her eyes. She hugged him back.

"And so do your brothers." *Maybe. Just a little.* "They're good to you, ain't they?"

Don't you dare cry, Arien.

"Uh-huh."

"You come to me if they're ever not, ya hear?"

She failed. Tears rolled down her face.

"Shhh…don't cry, darlin' girl." Wiping her eyes, he pressed his lips to her forehead. "We're always gonna take care of you."

This. It was the feeling she'd been missing all her life.

Getting up on her tiptoes to reach his cheek, Arien kissed him.

I love you too, Daddy.

Weary to the bone and Kellan couldn't sleep again. *Her fault, dammit.* He tossed. He turned. But it was no use. How was he supposed to sleep when she was right there across the hall?

If he could just hold her, tuck Arien's soft, warm body next to his, Kellan knew he'd be able to fall asleep. He didn't know if he could trust himself, though. Or her.

Chrissakes, it took everything in him to keep himself from plowing his dick inside her the last time he touched her. And fuck, he could feel it. She wanted him to.

I give up.

He whipped off the covers, hastily pulled on a pair of sweats, and took his ass across the hall.

"I could do this all night, pretty girl."

Fuck's sake.

They were so into each other, neither of them noticed him standing there. Arms folded in front of his chest, Kellan leaned back against the doorframe. Arien sat astride Tanner's lap, fingers in his hair, lips smacking, playing giddy-up on his dick. Well, kind of. It's not like they could do it for real—rules and all.

Kellan was a little miffed, quite honestly. Here she was, loving up on his brother, when he hadn't so much as gotten a kiss since her birthday. And hell, that was weeks ago.

He cleared his throat. Loudly.

Like two kids caught with their hands in the cookie jar, they froze.

"Don't stop on my account." Kellan pushed off the jamb. "I was enjoyin' the show."

Tanner looked over, his puppy-dog eyes silently begging him to play nice.

He got on the bed, kneeling behind her.

"I don't mind watchin' sometimes." Kellan trailed his fingers down her arms. Caressing his lips along her neck, he murmured in her ear, "Make him come, Arien."

"Kel."

That isn't what you want, brother?

"Suck his dick." He toyed with her panties. "Better yet, let's slip these off so I can watch you slide that wet pussy of yours back and forth on him."

"He's just fuckin' around with ya," Tanner soothed, his fingers coasting through her hair. "He don't really mean it."

"Guess that's a no then. Sorry, bro." Kellan snickered. "I'll just let y'all get back to it."

Giving his stepsister a thorough up-down, he backed away

from the bed. Then with a click of his tongue, he winked, and returned to his room across the hall.

Kellan slammed his door shut and he paced. That didn't go as he would've liked. Not. At. All. Maybe he'd left too much of the wooing to his brother. It had to be why Arien seemed to favor him, yeah? But being in tune with people, Tanner was better at that sort of thing. It had never been Kellan's strong suit.

One thing was for certain, he wasn't ever going to get any sleep now.

The door crashed open. Storming into his room, Arien got right up in his face. "Do you always have to be such an asshole?"

His mouth stamped over hers with a growl. Tanner coaxed. Not him. He took.

And Arien was his to take.

Holding her body to his in a vise-like grip, he kissed her hard and deep. Kellan wanted to bruise her tender lips, swollen from Tanner's kisses, and imprint her with his own. He pulled on her braid, steering her toward his bed, and laid her down on cream linen sheets.

Gasping, Arien got up onto her elbows. "What do you think you're doing?"

"Showin' you what an asshole I am." He pulled her panties down her thighs and flung them over his shoulder. "Gonna make *you* come."

She sucked in a breath, her pretty eyes widening.

His hand at her throat, he pushed her back down on the bed. "Tanner makes you come, don't he?"

Circling her clit with his thumb, she answered with a whimper.

He inhaled her, teeth grazing her skin. "Yeah, he eats this pretty pussy up, I bet."

Arien still didn't speak.

Kellan pushed her thighs apart and knelt between them. "Well, it's my turn, baby cakes."

"You take turns. Is that how it works?"

There she is.

"Nah. We love goin' two on one." He smirked, tracing her lips with his thumb. "Shall I call him in?"

"No," she protested, lifting her head up. "That's so…"

"So what? Dirty? Twisted?" He pushed his finger all the way inside her tight virgin hole. *Jesus.* "Look at that, baby, you're gushin' just thinking about it."

Clawing at the sheet, Arien spread her legs farther apart.

Kellan pulled his finger out slowly, only to slide it back in again. Arien reached for his wrist, holding him there inside her. Saliva dribbled from his mouth to her pussy, and with his thumb rubbing her swollen clit, he stroked her silky, wet walls.

Her hands went to her breasts. Squeezing them through her T-shirt, she lifted her hips, that sweetness he was dying to taste dripping down her thighs. She bit on her lip, trying to suppress her sweet, strangled cries.

He wanted to hear her scream.

He wanted Tanner to hear it too.

Give it up. C'mon, baby cakes.

His lips touched her clit. And that was all it took.

"Don't you get it yet? You can want both of us." Caressing her pussy, Kellan stretched out beside her. "You can love both of us. There's no need to choose. Me and Tanner can love you together, and there ain't nothin' wrong with that."

"Most people would disagree," Arien murmured into his chest, fingertips rubbing his cheek.

"Good thing we ain't most people then." His lips swept over hers. "Now, let me be an asshole and fuck that pussy with my tongue."

Taking her hand from his face, he kissed her palm and pressed it to his aching dick.

Pretty green eyes gazing into his, she wrapped him in her fingers.

All's fair in love and war, ain't it?

He'd fight dirty if he had to.

Arien was his to take.

⛰

Kellan and his father rode toward the house after checking on the bred heifers. They'd start dropping calves in a few weeks, so yesterday they brought them in to the cattle yard adjacent to the maternity barn.

Usually, he looked forward to spring and calving season. Hard work. Long days. Little sleep. He loved bringing cattle to market in the fall for the same reasons. But this year it only meant he'd have less time with Arien.

In a few short months, she'd be graduating. The baby would be coming soon after that, and then summer would fly by. *Summer always does.* That didn't leave him and Tanner a helluva lot of time to accomplish what they had to.

His brother came at him the second he and his dad rode up. "I need you to hurry and untack Gunner."

"What for?"

"I wanna turn him out with Airdrie." Tanner was grinning from ear to ear. "She's in heat."

"Late February's a little early, don't ya think?" Kellan asked, swinging off the saddle. "That'd have her foaling in December."

"A Christmas foal—how perfect is that?" His brother hooked an arm around his neck. "C'mon, I'll help ya."

Arien was fixing breakfast when they made it back to the house. Seeing her barefoot in a pair of yoga pants that hugged her ass and one of those cropped shirts that teased her soft skin made his dick hard. He walked right over to the stove, spun her around, and kissed her. Either she didn't notice her stepfather standing not three feet behind him, or she didn't care. Because she let him. So he went with it.

Kellan squeezed her ass, his lips lingering on hers. "Good mornin', baby cakes."

"Mornin."

Not wanting to miss out, Tanner cut in and took his turn. "Mornin', pretty girl."

"Someone's in a fine mood today." Arien giggled, and half turning to glance back at him, saw their father smirking there behind her. Covering her face with her hand, she gasped. "Oh, my God."

"Now, that's what I love to see. One big, happy family." Hugging her to his side, Matthew kissed her cheek. "It's a beautiful mornin'."

With a chuckle, Tanner pulled her hand away from her face. "What's the matter, little sister? Did ya think he'd be mad?"

"Not exactly, but Jesus..." Transferring bacon to a platter, she muttered, "...my mom would die."

"I keep tellin' ya, she won't."

"Don't you worry 'bout your mama. I'll take care of her." Rubbing her shoulders, Matthew glanced around the kitchen. "Where is she?"

"Still sleeping, I guess." Arien shrugged. "I haven't seen her yet this morning."

Tanner's brows shot up. "But it's already goin' on ten."

"She's tired is all." Dad didn't appear to be concerned. "Baby's takin' a lot out of her."

"Well, I'm near starvin' here." *For you.* Swiping a piece of bacon, Kellan kissed her. "Let's eat."

In his haste to get back to the horses, Tanner rushed through breakfast. Matthew went upstairs to check on his pregnant wife. At least that's what he told them. But Kellan knew better. Arien did too. It didn't surprise him Jennifer was so tired all the time. *All that fucking.*

He leaned over the back of her chair. Kissing her neck, his fingers brushed over her nipples. "Meet me at the back paddock in an hour."

"Why?"

"Somethin' I want you to see."

Just as he asked, he found her standing at the fence watching

Gunner sniff at the mare's raised tail. Running his hands down her arms, Kellan pressed in from behind her.

Arien angled her face toward his. "What's he doing?"

"Courtin' her," he breathed into her ear. "See how she's wettin' herself for him? Airdrie's showin' him some signs, but she's not quite ready yet."

Same as you, baby cakes.

"Look how patient he is. Gunner's a good stallion. She'll give in eventually, and when she does, he'll cover her."

"How do you know?"

"She wants to be bred."

Kissing her slender neck, Kellan slid his hand inside her jeans.

"You want that, too," he said, rubbing her pussy. "So wet for me. You're not quite there yet, either, but you will be soon."

Gunner covered the mare, and her breath caught in her throat. "Damn."

He couldn't take it anymore. Kellan tugged her jeans down to her knees and thrust two fingers up inside her. Arien let go of the fence. Head tipped back onto his shoulder, whimpering, while he sawed in and out of her pussy.

"Just imagine my cock inside you, little sister." He turned her around.

The look on her face told him everything he needed to know.

"Yeah, you love hearin' that. Gets you off, don't it? Just thinkin' of your brothers breedin' you."

"Yes. Fuck."

He rubbed her clit. He needed her to relax. For her pussy to open. She was just so tiny inside, and he wanted, he needed, to get another finger up in her.

"Yeah, take another one for me. That's my good girl," he praised her, three fingers wedged in to the second knuckle.

Moaning and whimpering, Kellan knew he was hurting her, as much as he could tell she liked that it did. *So perfect.*

"I know, baby, it hurts a little bit, but it feels so fucking good, don't it?"

"Fuck, Kel, please."

"Know what gets me off?" He pushed in to the hilt. "Hearin' you scream."

And fucking her fiercely with his fingers, he swallowed her cries.

"I know what you need, and you know I'll always take care of you, don't you?"

Because I fucking love you, dammit.

Mascara running down her face, she nodded.

"Stay."

Kellan stood beneath her bedroom window. Snow had fallen during the night. Pristine and pure and white, he shuffled through it with his boots. Back and forth. Over and over. He took a step back, and satisfied with his efforts, glanced up to where she still slept.

I ♡ U.

He turned away and smiled.

Thirteen

She missed them.

And it surprised her just how much.

Every morning when Arien woke up, Kellan and Tanner were already gone, and they didn't come home until long after she'd fallen asleep. Her stepfather too. Since calving season started, she almost never saw them at all, leaving her and her mother in the house on their own.

Just the two of them.

Same as it ever was.

Not that she didn't appreciate spending time alone with Mom. She did. Arien loved Jennifer like no other person in this world—traded Denver for Wyoming just for her, didn't she? Because after all the years of struggling on her own to make a good life for them, her mom deserved to share the rest of them with a man who loved her.

Thinking back, she couldn't remember her mother ever having a boyfriend until Matthew came along. If she dated at all, Arien wasn't aware of it. Jennifer worked a lot—she had to in order to pay the bills. That left Arien to take care of herself most of the time. She didn't realize what a toll that had taken, until she didn't have to anymore.

Arien had people—a real family who cared for her now. She had a dad who told her he loved her. God, hearing Matthew say that made her heart sing. She never thought she'd missed out on much, never understood why a girl's first love is her father, until she got one. And she loved him something fierce. Would do anything he asked of her. Same as she would for Mom.

She loved her brothers too. More than that, Arien was in love with them. Both of them. And she had no qualms admitting that to herself. Though neither of them had ever come out and said it, one morning she woke to see "I ♡ U" written in the snow outside her bedroom window. She didn't know who wrote it. Whether Kellan or Tanner, it didn't matter. She knew both brothers were in love with her, too.

And sweet fuck, did she want them. Arien thought she understood it now. Savannah Mason must've understood it, too. Why else would she have risked it all for a fleeting moment in the girls' bathroom?

"They believed in visions, dreams if you will..."

She had dreams of them often. Her brothers sharing a bed with her. Tanner sucking on her nipples. Kellan's face smothered in her pussy. Matthew kissing her tummy, round with his sons' first child.

Did she want that? Could she let go of the world outside the gate and live this crazy life? Arien was tempted. So very tempted. They'd woken up something dormant inside her. She wanted more than kisses. More than fingers in her cunt or a tongue on her clit.

More than a fat cock in her hand or salty semen in her mouth. What she craved, more than anything she'd ever longed for in her entire fucking life, was to feel Kellan and Tanner inside her.

And she'd never have that unless she married them. Both of them.

On this episode of Brother Husbands…put that on your blog.

Arien giggled to herself.

That's so fucked up.

Maybe. No, probably. Yeah, Arien had no misgivings with loving them both. It was the consequences of what would, undoubtedly, come with it. She'd have to live a lie outside the gate. Keep her loves—one of them at least—a secret from the world.

It would be so freeing to just let go. To live as she chose, love who she wanted, any way she might desire, without ignorant people condemning her for it.

Fuck the rest of the world, Arien. You can have a beautiful life with your brothers right here.

One big, happy family, right?

If only it were that simple.

"Earth to Arien." Fingers snapped in front of her face, interrupting her thoughts.

Startled, she glanced up. "Oh, hey, Mom."

"You must've been a world away. I've been calling you for a good five minutes now." She sat beside her on the sofa and brushed the hair from her eyes. "Is everything okay? What's got you so preoccupied, sweetie?"

"Just thinking."

"About?"

"Life," she said with a slow exhale.

Rubbing her belly, Jennifer smirked. "And by 'life' I'm guessing you mean your stepbrothers."

Arien choked on her own spit.

"I might be pregnant, but I'm not blind, daughter dearest. Think I haven't noticed how they look at you?" She chuckled. "We saw Tanner with his hands all over you under the blanket. Matt and me pretended to be asleep and had a chuckle watching you two sneak off upstairs."

"Mom, I…"

"Tanner's such a good, young man. I only have one question. Do you love him?"

Oh, boy. Here it goes.

"I do." She couldn't help but smile. "I love him so much I don't have words. He's my best friend."

"That's exactly how it should be, baby." Jennifer hugged her. "I never loved anyone until your stepdaddy. And he loves me well. It's the most incredible feeling in the world, isn't it?"

"Yeah."

"Have you and Tanner been having sex, Arien? Do we need to have the talk again?"

"No, Mom." Pursing her lips to the side, she eyeballed her mother's round belly. "He won't do that unless we get married."

Apparently, her mom wasn't aware of all their rules.

"Well, as I recall, kissing leads to touching, and touching leads to—"

"We haven't done it, Mom." Wringing her hands together, she sighed. "The thing is…"

"You want to?"

"Yes, but besides that, more important than that…" Nibbling on her lip, saline rushed to fill her eyes. "I'm in love with Kellan too."

She was quiet for a moment.

"Ohhh, I see." Jennifer glanced down at her stomach. "That's good, I suppose. If you're gonna stay here. Can't have one without the other, can you? Being it's their way and all."

"You're not mad? Shocked? Anything?"

"No, I'm not mad. I probably should've expected it." She rubbed the baby kicking away in her belly. "It's not the life I ever imagined for you, to be honest, or for this little one either. But most of us are lucky to find one true love in this lifetime, so if you've been so fortunate as to have found two? Then I'd say you're very blessed indeed."

"You ready yet, pretty girl?"

Arien turned from the mirror. Tanner swept into her room with no shirt on. Skintight Wranglers painted on his ass. She licked her lips. *Yummy.*

It had been a long and lonely month for her—Emily and most of the other girls, too. All the men pitched in during calving season. But it was over and done with for the most part, so they were going to the first bonfire party of the spring. And this time, she knew what to expect.

"Not quite." Arien crooked her finger. "C'mere."

"What?" Grinning, Tanner came closer.

"Kiss me, cowboy."

And he did.

Tender and sweet, Tanner had a way of kissing that snuck in and stole her breath when *he* wanted to take it. Soft-spoken, yet commanding, he burned at a constant simmer. But those expressive green eyes told her he was more than ready to dial it up a notch.

"You missed this, didn't you, little sister?" His lips brushing hers, he squeezed her breast. "I did too."

"So much." Arien cupped the bulge in his jeans. "You have no idea."

"You keep testing me, baby." He groaned. "I want inside you so bad."

"Fuck, I want you too." She kissed him again.

Tanner tugged on her lip with his teeth. "And Kellan?"

"Yes, and Kellan."

"That makes me so fucking happy." He squeezed her so tight, her feet came off the floor. "You're stayin', then. We'll have to plan a weddin' for the summer 'cause we take the cattle to market in the fall…"

"Wait a minute..." Tanner set her down. "...I start college in the fall. In Denver."

"You can take classes in Jackson. Or online."

"But I got a scholarship to UC." And she'd worked so hard to get it. "Do we really have to get married right away? Can't we wait? We'll still be together and I'll come home every break, I promise."

"We can wait." He softly kissed her lips, but there was no passion in it. "We can't be together, though. Not how we wanna be. Won't risk it. I love you way too much."

"Tanner..." *Jesus, he truly believes all that mumbo jumbo.* "...I love you. God, I love you so much, but I never imagined myself married at eighteen. I saw college, taking pictures, parties..."

And boys.

She already had the ones she wanted, though.

"I'm just gonna need a little more time, okay?"

"I can give you that. Anything you need." Rubbing a strand of her hair between his fingers, he nodded. "Finish getting dressed. I'll be waitin' downstairs."

They took the truck this time. Tanner was subdued, but Kellan was his usual smirky self. Arien sat between them in her flouncy short dress and the cowboy boots they got her for Christmas. She'd taken extra care to look nice for them.

"You wearin' panties under that dress, baby cakes?"

"Course, I am." She lifted the hem. "See?"

"Good girl." Kellan squeezed her thigh. "You look real pretty. Don't she, Tanner?"

"She does." He took hold of her hand, interlacing their fingers. "I tell her all the time."

A bonfire blazed in front of the big, old barn. Same as last time. And while the vibe was just as oddly sensual, everything seemed different. Maybe it was seeing Griffin locking lips with Cassie— and Shiloh. Maybe it was because Billy wasn't kissing on Emily. He couldn't, poor baby.

Birthdays. And Griffin and Emily recently had one. Cassie was in. Billy was out. Until he turned eighteen anyway. *Stupid damn rules.* It was going to be a helluva long year for him. He loved her cousin a lot, though. He'd get through it, just like Jake had. That's what he told her, anyway. But watching him look at his brother with Emily, so forlorn and with such longing, Arien wasn't so sure. She felt so badly for him.

"You okay, Billy?"

"Yeah, babes. This too shall pass, right? One year. That's all it is. Jake's been waitin' a helluva lot longer." He reached for her hand. "Can I say something?"

"Of course."

"If you love 'em, don't make 'em wait." Then he squeezed her hand tight. "A man who can't be with the woman he loves is missing a piece of his soul, Arien. I feel like I'm dyin'."

"Oh, Billy. I'm so sorry." She hugged him, paused, and pulled back. "Wait a minute…"

"Don't be angry with him, Arien. Tanner needed to talk it out with somebody and he couldn't do that with Kellan." He pulled her in for another hug. "He loves you. They both do."

I know.

They came back from the bar together. Tanner gave her a beer. Kellan slipped her a flask of Fireball and winked.

"You want to get me drunk?"

"Nah." He gazed downward. "Just hopin' I can get you to dance for me in them boots." He leaned into her ear. "Naked."

Arien gave him a good-natured elbow to the ribs. "How about we just go dance?"

"City girl like you? How many barn dances you know anyway, huh?"

"Asshole."

"You know it." His tongue tucked in his cheek, Kellan hooked his arm around her neck. Pulling her close, he lowered his voice. "Need me to prove it again?"

Please?

And with that, he kissed her.

Kellan didn't just kiss, he claimed. Fingers sinking into her flesh, he hauled her onto his lap. Full, soft lips sealed her mouth and he groaned. She smelled the whiskey on his breath. Tasted it on his tongue. Cinnamon heat setting her on fire.

Beneath her dress, he kneaded the globes of her ass, pushing her against the hardness in his jeans. *Fuck me, I want you.* Silk panties riding on rough denim, Arien gripped his nape, deepening their kiss. The room, the music, the people, everything faded away. There was only him.

"Goddamn, I need a cigarette." Shiloh's skinny-ass sister lit up a Marlboro and exhaled, blowing smoke up in the air. "Never kissed me like that."

"No offense, Cassie, but you were never mine."

"Neither were you. None taken."

"What'd I tell you about smokin', girl?" Wrinkling his nose, Griffin waved her smoke away from his face. "Now put that nasty thing out."

"Gonna make me?" Taking a drag, she smirked.

"I'll bend you over my lap and spank your ass 'til it bleeds."

"But, Griffy, you know how much I like it when you do that." Arching her penciled-on brow, Cassie's tongue peeked out to slowly wet her lips.

Griffy? Okayyy. Arien had to bury her face in Kellan's neck to contain her laughter.

Shiloh rolled her eyes. "Shut the fuck up, Cassie."

"And I won't be kissin' you, neither."

He kissed her sister instead.

She dropped the cigarette to the floor, stomping on it with her boot.

"It's thunderin' out there." Kellan smacked Arien's lips and helped her off his lap. "Let's have us that dance and go home."

"Yeah, c'mon, little sister." Tanner grabbed her left hand.

Kellan took the right.

Her stepbrothers. Her cowboys. Her loves.

She smiled, her gaze flicking between them. "Well, when you ask me like that, how can I say no?"

Lips at her ear, cinnamon fanned her face. "You can't."

"We won't let ya." Tanner pulled her to stand.

And they led her out to the floor.

Kellan drove them home, pulses of lightning illuminating the mountainous landscape. While not totally unheard of, thunderstorms in Brookside were unusual this time of year. Heck, it was snowing just last week. But these last few days of April had been unseasonably warm, heating up the atmosphere.

The dark skies opened, unleashing a torrential downpour, before they made it to the driveway.

Dashing through the rain with her stepbrothers right behind her, Arien was first up the stairs. Soaked to the bone, she made a beeline for the shower. She'd felt grubby before they left the dance, and now, peeling the dress from her skin, she felt worse.

This had to be a soap up, rinse off, get in, and get out kind of thing. She remembered reading about some guy getting struck by lightning in the shower once. It can travel through plumbing—who knew? Arien wasn't sure if that still held true, since pipes were mostly plastic nowadays, but better safe than sorry. She wasn't about to risk being electrocuted, and having them find her naked, wet, and dead.

It was the quickest darn shower she ever took.

But she took her time massaging body oil into her still-damp skin. Arien deeply inhaled the mandarin and berries infusing the air, fingertips skimming across her breasts and down her tummy, then exhaled on a sigh. *Now what?*

Get in bed and wait to see if one of them comes to her?

Be bold, tiptoe across the hall, and play "Eenie, Meeny, Miny, Moe" to pick a door?

"I can't," she said to herself, slipping into a pink cotton bralette and thong.

Thinking of them, her nipples stood out against the fabric. Arien liked the way they looked, how the top supported her breasts, making them appear plump and round. She turned from side to side in the mirror, inspecting her curves. *Hmm…not bad.* Her tushy still jiggled a little, but she'd toned up some since coming here. And anyway, Kellan seemed to like it—chrissakes, he was grabbing it all the damn time.

"All right." She giggled. "Time to go to bed."

Arien switched off the lamp on her bedside table.

Lightning flashed through the glass.

And she screamed.

Fourteen

Kellan came running through the door.

Tanner followed close behind him.

She couldn't move. Her heart pounding, choking on her breath, Arien held her hand to her chest, as if that would somehow tame its wild beat.

"Are you all right?" Taking hold of her arms, Kellan shook her from her frozen state. "What happened?"

She forced her gaze to his face, her voice whisper-thin. "Someone's out there."

He thrust her into his brother's arms, racing for the glass door. Cold wind and rain rushing in as he closed it behind him.

"Look at me, baby." Tanner lifted her chin. "Slow, deep breaths."

Keeping her close to his side, Tanner moved them toward the

window. It was hard to see, but Arien could make out Kellan running along the deck through the rain, then taking the stairs down at the end of the house.

"Did you see who it was?"

"No, he had a dark jacket on—with a hood. I couldn't see his face, but it was definitely a man."

The rush of adrenaline wearing off, she started to shake. Tanner sat her on his lap, running his fingers through her hair. "It's okay. You're safe."

"He was right there…" Arien tried to swallow, but her mouth was too dry. "…reaching for the doorknob."

"We won't let anything happen to you." He kissed her forehead. "I promise."

"Didn't see no one." Rainwater sluicing off his skin, Kellan locked the glass door. They never lock their doors here. There was no reason to. "You sure someone was there?"

"I didn't imagine it and I wasn't seeing things."

Sunday barked in agreement. *Good boy.*

Kellan nodded. "Don't leave her. I'll be right back."

She and Tanner were sitting on her bed with the dog when he returned thirty minutes later in a pair of dry sweats.

"What the hell took you so long?"

"Checked the house, bro. No one's hidin' in here, either. Made sure all the doors are locked—windows too." He took a seat on the other side of her. "Get down, Sunday. Go on now. Scoot."

"Who the fuck was that, Kellan?"

One of the ranch hands? A psycho serial killer?

"Dunno, but we're stayin' here with you tonight," he assured her, rubbing her nape. "Don't worry, okay?"

"Okay."

But she did.

Rain pattering against the window, Arien lay between them in the dark, her arm around Kellan's middle, Tanner's curled around hers. She was reminded of the last time they all slept together, squished on an old pullout couch back in Denver.

"*It's one night, Arien. Just make do.*"

Every night could be just like this. If only…

Kellan's hand covered hers. "Shhh."

"But I didn't say anything."

"Didn't have to." Bringing her hand up to his chest, he used it to rub his skin. "I can hear what you're thinkin'."

"Can you now?"

"Yup."

"Okay, what am I thinking?"

Kellan moved her hand back down his chest and over his rock-solid abs, to slide underneath his sweats. He curled her fingers around his rigid shaft and squeezed.

Tightening his hold behind her, Tanner kissed her nape.

"About time we show you…" he said, catching her lip between his teeth, "…just how good your brothers can make you feel.'"

Tanner pulled at her bralette, exposing the tips of her breasts. Kellan slowly swiped his thumbs across them, and drinking her in with his wicked gaze, rolled them between his fingers.

She hissed at the delicious zing between her thighs, sucking in air between her teeth. The three of them had never been together like this before, and Arien wasn't quite sure how to go about it. Reaching forward with her left hand, and behind her with her right, she took hold of each of them, rubbing their cocks through their sweats.

The brothers groaned at the contact, a sense of empowerment coming over her. This didn't feel sick, or twisted, or wrong like she thought it would. It was actually liberating.

Pulling her thong to the side, Kellan intensely worked her clit. All gruff and grit, there was nothing gentle about him. And Arien wouldn't want it any other way. Inserting his finger all the way inside, he fucked her, while Tanner held her open, pressing his fingers into her flesh, kneading her thigh.

Thick and hard and throbbing, she pulled him out of his pants. Craning her neck, Arien reached for him with her tongue. She swirled it around his head, tasting the salty precum, and sucked him into her mouth. Her breath catching, moaning on his dick, Kellan fingered her pussy.

"Fuck yeah, suck him. Look how good you take your brother's big cock."

His words sent a wave of tingles through her body. Fucked up or not, she loved this. Everything about it. Sucking Tanner. The musky flavor of him. How incredible it felt to have him playing with her nipples while his brother pounded into her with his finger.

It was so intense, Kellan rubbing her clit, fingering her at the same time. She lifted her hips and his cock slipped from her mouth.

Tanner pulled on her leg to bring her closer. The pad of his finger lightly touching her sensitive clit, swollen from his brother's vigorous rubbing, Arien whimpered. She squeezed his cock in her hand. He kissed her there, and soothing her with his laving tongue, that wave rushed through her once more. "Oh, fuck."

With one hand empty, she reached for Kellan and brought him to her greedy little mouth. He pushed his pants down his legs, kicking them off his feet, as she swallowed his massive dick. *Mmm.* Choking, her eyes watered, saliva dribbling down his length.

And the unrelenting wave kept coming.

"Mmm," Arien hummed on Kellan's dick, drowning in pleasure with every sweep of Tanner's tongue.

Removing her bralette altogether, Kellan plumped her breasts, pinching and pulling on her nipples.

Her mouth full of cock, she sighed. "Mmm."

"What a good little sister you are," he crooned, stroking her cheek.

She sucked him harder.

Tanner feasted on her pussy. Sucking on her clit. Licking up her lips. Spearing her hole with his tongue. His fingers and tongue wedged inside her, so overwhelmed with sensation, she gasped to get air into her lungs.

"Ohhh, that feels so good."

Her body in spasms, Kellan squeezed her throat.

"Oh, my goshhh," Arien screamed, the word drawn out with her breath. "Oh, fuck…" Unrecognizable sounds coming from her own mouth. "Oh, God."

Somehow, she found herself lying crossways, catching her breath, a brother on either side of her. Their long, thick cocks bobbing in front of them, they gently stroked her skin, caring for her as she came back from the most intense orgasm she'd ever had in her life.

Neither of them had come yet. Rubbing along the veins with her thumb, Arien took a brother in each hand.

"How many fingers you fuck yourself with, baby cakes?"

"Uhh…" *Why is he asking?* "…two, I guess."

"Gonna use four this time. Two for me and two for Tanner." Kellan held his hand on top of hers, stroking his cock. "One day you're gonna have both your brothers inside you at the same time."

Y'all are hung like horses.

"Don't worry, pretty girl." Leaning down, Tanner kissed her sweaty brow. "We'll work up to that."

"You like the thought of that, don't you?" Smirking, Kellan swept his tongue across his lip, and they placed their hands together, palm to palm, lining up their index and middle fingers. "Yeah, I know you do."

"Look at all that juice pourin' out of her, brother," Tanner said, like he was in awe at the sight of it.

Together, they pushed four fingers inside her.

Kellan leaned over and licked her clit.

Sweet Jesus.

"You have no idea how well-fucked you're gonna be," Kellan rasped, finger-fucking her with his brother. "Every mornin'. Every night. In your throat, your pussy, your ass. We're gonna fill up all these holes."

While Tanner kept his fingers inside her, Kellan withdrew. He went to work on her clit, fervently rubbing, holding onto her nipple the entire time. Then his brother added two fingers from his other hand to replace the ones he took out of her.

Filled with Tanner, silky, hot liquid seeped out of her with every thrust of his hands.

He pulled out, and reentering her with two fingers, Tanner slipped one into her ass.

Arien opened her lips to scream, but she couldn't make a sound.

"Relax, baby cakes. Let it happen."

Kellan didn't let up. Tanner didn't either. Her clit. Her nipple. Her pussy. Her ass. The sensations bombarded her.

I think I'm dying.

And she exploded. Literally.

Kellan tapped on her clit, and rubbing it some more, cum sprayed out of her. "See, baby, *this* is how it works. All of you was made for both of us, and you belong right here." He licked her from his fingers. "No one will ever come close to lovin' you like we do."

They lay back down, Tanner pulling up the covers. Kissing the back of her neck, he wrapped his arm around her tummy.

Wait…

Had it all been for her?

Neither of them had yet to take their own pleasure.

"Shhh…I can still hear you." Tucking her arm around his middle, Kellan kissed her. "Now go to sleep."

Fifteen

Tanner stepped from the stables into the midday sun. He gazed up at it for a moment, the rays washing over his face, and breathed in the scent of late spring, fresh pine, and hay. Nothing else like it. Considerably warmer than it had been this morning, he rolled up his sleeves, and headed in the direction of the house.

Arien was at school and his dad had taken Jennifer over to Dubois for a doctor's appointment, so there wouldn't be a home-cooked meal waiting for him, but he figured he could fix himself a sandwich or something. Toss a steak on the grill, maybe. He looked forward to the weekends when his pretty girl did most of the cooking. She thought they were all doing *her* a favor, sampling the culinary experiments for her blog. Not so. He understood now, why she always seemed to have a craving for those green chili cheeseburgers.

Course, the only thing Tanner craved was more of her. And he didn't mean her body, but hot damn, he wanted that too. Hell, a lifetime of her wouldn't be enough. It was so much more than just that, though. He was utterly, totally, and completely consumed by her, and he wanted her to be just as held by him. And Kellan.

Especially Kellan.

His brother worried him.

"Hold up, Tanner."

Speak of the devil.

Hopping the fence, Kellan caught up to him. "I'm starvin', man."

"We're on our own today," he said, hooking an arm around his brother. "Was just goin' to rustle up somethin.'"

"Jennifer ain't back yet?"

"Doubt it. I figure Dad'll make a day of it, ya know? Take her out to lunch and shit." Tanner stopped walking. "Hey, did you ever tell him what happened the other night?"

"No." Pursing his lips, Kellan exhaled. "I'm not so sure anyone was really out there. I think the storm might've spooked her."

"Arien was pretty convinced."

"I know, but…" He started walking. "…c'mon, there ain't nobody around here for miles and miles, and there ain't no one who's got the balls to come anywhere close to our girl."

Truth.

The townsfolk knew Arien had been claimed, whether she realized it or not.

"I s'pose you're right."

"No use worryin' Dad and Jennifer over nothin,'" Kellan assured him. "Besides, we took her mind off it real good, now didn't we?"

Damn right we did.

His dick twitched in his jeans thinking of it.

A small taste of how they'd love her together. *Fucking magical.* She responded to them so beautifully. He'd been right not to say anything to Kellan. Arien and his brother had grown closer lately. His brother finally seemed to be letting her in, and Tanner knew that didn't come easily to him. If Kellan learned she was still thinking about leaving, he'd close up again, and they could lose her.

Tanner was hellbent on keeping her here, and he'd resort to any means necessary to do it. So he'd be a fool to get Kellan all worked up over something that was never going to happen.

"You hear that?" His brother came to a sudden stop.

"What?"

"It's comin' from the breedin' shed." He pulled his arm in that direction. "You usin' it?"

"No."

Tanner preferred to do things as nature intended them to be. He turned his stallions out in open paddocks, where ready mares waited to be courted, covered, and bred, rather than force them on each other in an enclosed shed. It hadn't been used in a long time.

"Well now, would you look at that?"

He could see them through the dust-covered window. Jennifer, buck naked, all swollen tits and big pregnant belly, his father's hand up her cunt.

"Oh, shit."

Mother and daughter looking so much alike, Tanner couldn't help but imagine his Arien. Holding her, his fingers on her nipples—God, he loved sucking on them—while his brother worked a fist inside her. His dick more than twitching, he turned away.

"The old man should take it a little bit easier on her, don't ya think? She's near ready to pop."

"He won't hurt her. Dad knows what he's doin'." His brother smirked. "And Jennifer's lovin' every bit of it."

That she was, judging by the sounds of it.

"Must be where you get it from, Kel." Tanner snickered. "C'mon, we shouldn't be watchin'."

"Then they shouldn't be fuckin' where we can see 'em." Walking away from the shed, Kellan confessed to him, "I like watchin'.

Thinkin' 'bout breedin' our little sister." And he let out a groan. "Turns me on like nothin' else."

"Believe me, Kel, I get ya. I do."

He and his brother were of the same mind.

"She'll be so beautiful with our baby in her belly. I'm gonna fuck her hard—just like that. Milk her pretty titties."

"Damn."

"Go ahead. You can say it. I'm a sick fucker, ain't I?"

Maybe.

"If you are, so am I, brother." Yeah, he was consumed by her, all right. "I think about that all the time."

Gentler in his approach, tender and sweet, still Tanner's appetite was as demanding as Kellan's. His predilections no less deviant. Arien really had no idea what she was in for, but she would, and soon. They'd been preparing for this their entire lives. Sharing everything. Their bodies, their hearts, their souls. With her. Only her.

And in return, he wanted it all.

I think maybe we both are.

While young cattle grazed alongside their mothers, the whole town emerged to celebrate the arrival of warm weather. Every year, on the last weekend in May, for as long as Tanner could remember, they gathered in the square for a community cookout. There'd be dancing and drinking and fireworks, games for the kids. The start of summer was upon them, and with that came graduations, then a host of weddings until they went to market in fall.

Surely, his would be one of them.

The letter that came from Denver didn't mean nothing.

Tanner hadn't asked her about it. His brother hadn't either. Arien tucked it into her backpack when Jennifer gave it to her, and that was that.

Nothing had really changed. She wasn't acting any different. He imagined, if she'd given serious thought to leaving, she would be.

But no, Arien sat on a blanket with Kellan, Jake, and Emily, their parents, Grams, and Aunt Kim close by. Dad had Jennifer, her belly enormous, on a lawn chair. The baby was due any day now, and no matter what she did, his stepmother was uncomfortable, so she insisted she might as well be miserable eating some good barbecue.

"Got it, bro?"

Billy strategically balanced another plate of food on Tanner's arm, and he nodded. "Yeah."

Then carefully, they brought it over to the eager faces waiting for them.

Kissing his cheek, Arien made room for him beside her. It surprised him a little. She usually curbed the affectionate gestures in front of her mother. And respecting her feelings on the matter, they did the same. But Kellan was rubbing his fingers over the back of her hand and she was letting him. Jennifer might as well start getting used to it, he supposed.

Billy and Jake's parents came by, their father, a mirror image of his sons, albeit older, speaking with Matthew, before hugging his boys and his future daughter. Chuckling, Aunt Kim leaned into Arien's ear. "When I was thirteen, I thought he was the most beautiful man alive with that hair of his. Still do. I wanted to marry him."

"Why didn't you?"

"He was older. Much too old for me. And I didn't have a sister, nor he a brother, so…" Smiling, she shrugged. "William and Timothy were my absolute loves. Always will be. They gave me Emily and he favored her with his sons."

"Wait a minute…" Tanner watched her brows knit, looking on, as his aunt's old crush walked away with a blonde woman on one arm and a man on the other. "…I'm so confused."

"C'mon now, little sister." He pinched her butt. "Don't tell me everyone's straight as an arrow back in Denver."

"Old Gantry is bi, girly." Kellan sniggered. "His wife is straight. Her brother isn't. He loves them both and they're all blissfully happy."

"So they share him?" She wasn't really asking. "Well, that's convenient."

"The earth provides. Nature always finds a way," Tanner agreed.

"Aunt Kim never stood a chance, did she?"

"No, but I think maybe he was fond of her too," Kellan told her, waggling his brows.

Christ, if Victor Gantry had taken a liking to his aunt back then, and Tanner didn't think so, it sure wasn't that way. He was in his twenties already when she was a teenager.

"The day Aunt Kim got married, Gantry told Grams she was going to have one child, a daughter, and that child would be the wife of his sons. He saw it."

"Billy wasn't even thought of yet, mind you," his brother added. He clicked his tongue. "But here they are gettin' hitched…just like he said they would."

"Lucky guess is all. Wishful thinking," Arien said with a roll of her hazel-green eyes. "Dreams don't mean anything."

Sure about that?

"If you say so. We know different."

She giggled, popping a berry in his mouth.

"Your mama's tired. I'm gonna go ahead and take her home." Bending over, Dad kissed Arien on the cheek, then glancing to him and Kellan, he winked. "You boys stick close to your sister now, ya hear?"

As the sun dipped behind the mountains, the older folks dispersed and the little ones were taken home to be tucked into their beds, the rest of them taking the party to the field at the old barn. Spirits high, the music was loud and the liquor was flowing.

Griffin lit the fire, it burned tall, shooting sparks into a navy sky. "Five more days 'til we're free." Graduation was this Thursday. He kissed Shiloh. "And in two weeks, you're all mine."

His wait was almost over. *Lucky bastard.*

Pulling Arien with him, Kellan leaned back against the barn. Slipping her sips of Fireball, he kissed her.

Really want her dancin' in them boots, don't ya?

Tanner couldn't take it much longer. He needed to know what was in her head. And in her heart. He needed to bring about an end to all this damn waiting, too.

Griffin's lips locked on her sister, a put-out Cassie parked her ass beside them. "Hey, Kel. Arien."

"Hey, Cass."

Arien didn't speak.

Cassie had a shit-eating grin on her face. "You're comin' to the weddin', aren't ya?"

"What in the hell are you askin' me that for? Whole damn town's gonna be there."

Same as always. Everyone in Brookside turned out for every event. Funerals, graduations, weddings, and everything in between.

"I didn't mean *you*, silly. I know you're comin.'" The grin never leaving her face, Cassie smacked Kellan on the arm, turning toward Arien. "I was askin' your stepsister here."

"That's a stupid question. Course, she is."

With a devious-sounding laugh, she shrugged. "Well, I wasn't sure when she was headin' on back to Denver."

"Hello, I'm right here," Arien said, waving her hand in front of Cassie's face.

"Shiloh tells me you're real smart. Got yourself a grant *and* a scholarship." Tilting her head from side to side, she pushed out her lip with her tongue. "Congratulations, by the way."

"Change of plans, Cassie. Arien ain't goin' nowhere." Kellan possessively wrapped his arm around her shoulders. "She's stayin' right here."

"Ohhh, I see. Daddy called it, huh?" Lighting a cigarette, she blew the smoke in his brother's face. "Congratulations to you, then. And you too, Tanner."

And with a parting nod to Arien, she walked away.

Run along now. Off you go.

With Cassie out of earshot, he muttered, "I feel kinda sorry for Griffin. He's got himself a handful with that one."

"He can handle her." Kellan tossed back his beer.

"She's a bitch. Shiloh's the one I feel sorry for." Getting out from under Kellan's arm, Arien shifted her stance. "And why'd you say that?"

"Say what?"

"That I'm not going."

Kellan drained the bottle of beer and folded his arms across his chest. "'Cause you ain't."

Uh-oh.

She pressed her lips together. Tanner could almost see the steam coming out of her ears. Arien looked over at him. Her hazel-green eyes locked on his, Tanner shook his head.

Her gaze returned to Kellan. "I have until the end of June to accept my award package."

"That's what was in that letter you got?"

"Yeah." Her voice going soft, she stared down at her boots.

"And are you?" Gently lifting her chin with his finger, Tanner spoke just as softly.

"She ain't."

"I haven't decided yet," she admitted, chewing on her lip. "I'm so torn between…"

"You don't need to be goin' off to school." Kellan's fingers pressed into her arms. It almost sounded like he was pleading. "You can do that right here. This is where you belong, Arien. I love you."

"*We* love you."

"And I love you, but…" She looked up at the sky. "…this is just crazy. It isn't real."

He and Kellan exchanged a glance. After everything they'd shared with her, did she still not get it?

"Mumbo jumbo. Come on, you don't really believe all this superstitious nonsense, do you? It's bullshit."

Kellan's laugh was brisk. His pause was loaded. "Look around you, Arien. What do you see?"

Half turning, she gazed at the fire burning behind her, then slowly, her big eyes filling with tears, settled it back on them.

"There's your answer." He let go of her. "We take care of our own, and that includes you. Whether you believe our bullshit or not. Whether you accept our ways or not. *We* are your home. And you're ours."

Don't do it, Kel.

But he did.

He walked away, got into his truck, and drove off.

⸎

He never came back to the party.

He wasn't here when she and Tanner got home.

Jake had to give them a ride back to the house.

"Kellan just needs to cool off." His fingers sweeping through her hair, Tanner softly kissed her lips. "Don't worry, he'll be okay."

But will we be okay?

She nodded.

"G'night."

Arien plopped down on her bed. How had everything gotten so fucked up?

Because you went ahead and fucked yourself, that's how.

She hadn't meant to. Arien didn't plan on saying anything about the letter at all, unless she came to the decision she was going to go. It sat in her backpack, untouched. She hadn't been able to bring herself to pick up a pen and sign it.

But then she hadn't been able to commit herself to staying here, either.

And what gave Kellan the right to speak for her like she didn't have a mind of her own? He and Tanner believing in all that *'power of three'* mumbo jumbo. Dreams and visions and *'the earth provides'* bullshit. *Chrissakes.* It's a lie. A fantastic, wonderful, beautiful lie, but a lie just the same.

"Look around you, Arien. What do you see?"

It surrounded her, abounding everywhere she looked. Beauty, wealth, abundance, prosperity, community. But more than that, more than any other thing, she saw love.

Absolute love.

And that sure as hell didn't feel like a lie.

Tiptoeing across the hall, she sat on his unmade bed. Leather, musk, and wicked sin, he was everywhere. Yet the room felt so empty without him.

Pulling his pillow onto her lap, something fell from the linen case. Retrieving it, Arien held it in her fingers. A photo of herself taken last year for the high school yearbook. She flipped it over. Three hearts. And like yarn being wound, emotion gathered in her throat.

"This is where you belong, Arien."

She pulled the letter from her backpack, and scanning the contents one last time, she tossed it in the trash.

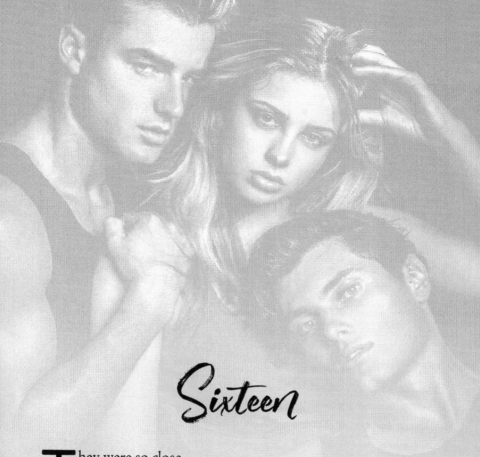

Sixteen

They were so close.

If Tanner moved even a fraction of an inch, he'd ruin her.

And Kellan would never forgive him.

"Fuckkk…please."

He kissed her, and sliding the underside of his dick over her clit, he hit the spot. Friction, wet and perfect. The delicate build, slow and deeply carnal. "You love me, pretty girl?"

Gasping for air, Arien stopped to lick her lips. "Ahh…you know I do…please."

The bundle of nerves beneath his head being particularly sensitive, Tanner remained patient, leaning into the sensations her body provided as opposed to fighting them. What was the point anyhow? Besides, the payoff was always worth it.

"Gonna stay with me, baby?"

Thighs shaking, her head thrashed against the pillow. A guttural sound erupted from deep within her throat.

It triggered him. His body seizing, mind numb, Tanner gave in. And growling, he came on her sweaty, hot skin.

Arien curled into him. Her head on his chest, he played with her hair and pressed a kiss to her crown. There had to be a way to fix this. Make everything good again. But he wasn't sure how.

Kellan had closed himself off again, shut her out, just as Tanner predicted he would.

He rubbed her back, feeling the goosebumps surface on her skin, and gently squeezed her bottom. "C'mon, you better get in the shower. Only takes you forever and a day."

"Does not."

"It does." Tickling her ribs, she giggled. "And you know it. Wouldn't wanna be late for your graduation, now would ya?"

"I'm never late."

"There's always a first time." He gave her ass a playful spank. "Go on now."

"Okay, okay. I'm going."

They were all in the living room waiting on Arien. Dressed in his best blue jeans and a white button-up, Kellan had his head tipped back on the sofa, staring up at the ceiling. Fidgeting in her seat, Jennifer went from rubbing her belly to pressing a hand at the small of her back.

"I got you, Mama." His dad took over. "You sure you feel up to goin'? Arien would understand if you didn't."

"I'm fine. Can't miss seeing my baby graduate. It only happens once." Choking up on her words, Tanner handed her a tissue. "Thank you, honey," she said, dabbing at her tired blue eyes.

"We could FaceTime you and—"

"Nope, I need to be there." Shaking her blonde waves, she held her hand to her chest. "I'm so proud of her. You know, that blog of hers is starting to take off."

"Yeah?" Like he didn't already know, Tanner grinned.

"Uh-huh." Jennifer nodded. "She got monetized. Her little school project has ten thousand subscribers on YouTube already."

"I didn't know that." Kellan's head shot up, glaring at him. "Why didn't I know that?"

Maybe 'cause you've hardly talked to her in five days, dickhead.

She came down the stairs in a pretty little dress and cowboy boots, carrying her cap in her hand, the gown draped over her arm.

Smirking at his brother, he winked. "That's our girl."

The ride into town was quiet. She sat in the middle of them in the back of the dually, yet neither Arien nor his brother spoke. They didn't look at each other, Kellan staring out the window while she looked straight ahead. But Tanner saw his hand reach for hers. He interlaced their fingers, and she let him.

Standing room only.

In true Brookside fashion, everyone turned out to see the latest class of graduates—all thirty of them—walk across the stage in their burgundy caps and gowns to receive their diplomas. This place wasn't just a town. Folks here weren't just neighbors. It was a true community, an extended family, that took as much pride in its future as it valued its history.

He and Kellan whooped and whistled as Arien's name was called. Jennifer, proud mama that she was, got all emotional, blubbering away through the entire thing. And for that matter, so did Aunt Kim. Matthew had an arm around his sister and his wife, consoling them.

They were still sniffling at the reception afterward.

Tanner and his brother stood back where most of the men were, next to the punch table, drinking the adult version out of clear plastic cups. They looked on while Arien took pictures with their cousin and her friends.

"How's my two favorite grandsons?"

"We're your only grandsons." Kellan smirked, slapping their grandfather on the back.

"So?" With a chuckle, he punched him in the arm. "Still my favorites."

"Hiya, Pops." Tanner passed him a cup of punch. "We're good. Everything's good."

"Glad to hear it, boy." He grinned, showing his teeth, and guzzled it down in one swallow. "So, when's the weddin'? I ain't heard no announcement yet."

"Uh." Tanner traded a look with his brother. John Jacoby wasn't a man to reckon with. He couldn't outright lie, so he'd just have to skirt around the truth. "Still workin' that out, Pops."

"Been holdin' off with the new baby comin' and all, but we're thinkin' September maybe," Kellan added for good measure. He had no trouble lying, evidently.

"Good, good," he said, glancing at their stepmother. "I gotta get me a slice of Maizie's cake. If I don't catch you before, I'll see you boys at the Archer weddin' next weekend. Pass on my congratulations to Arien, will ya?"

"You and Maizie's cake." Tanner sniggered. "We'll be sure to do that, Pops."

They waved as their grandfather moved along. Keeping his voice low, Kellan yanked on his arm as soon as the old man was out of earshot. "Has Arien been sayin' anything?"

"About what?"

"Denver." He tightened his fists. "I gotta know."

"Maybe you should try talkin' to her."

Kellan let out a mirthless laugh.

"Okay, maybe not." Tanner raked his fingers through his hair. "Don't know what Arien's fixin' to do, but if she decides to go and there's no stoppin' her, then I'll be goin' with her."

"You ain't serious."

"Sure am." Nodding, he turned away to ladle himself another cup of punch. "Not gonna lose her, Kel. I love her."

"You think I don't?" Head cocked, Kellan turned him back around.

"No, Kel. I know you do."

"You're not goin' anywhere and she ain't, neither." Seething, he slammed the plastic cup down on the table. "Bet your sweet ass on that."

They all sat together in the hospital waiting room. After complaining of her back hurting at Arien's graduation and all day today, Jennifer was in a room down the hall having the baby. His dad was with her. He and Kellan had visited with her early on. Attached to a bunch of hardware, she started hollering something awful, so they took their leave. Seemed to Tanner, the horses and cows had a much easier time birthing than humans did.

"Why's it taking so long?" Yawning, Arien laid her head on his shoulder.

He glanced at the clock on the beige-painted wall, running his fingers through her hair. They'd been here since suppertime. It was after three in the morning already. "Don't rightly know, pretty girl."

"Calves drop when they're good and ready. All there is to it." Hands clasped behind his head, Kellan didn't bother opening his eyes.

"Are you comparing our brother or sister to a baby cow?"

He sniggered. "Both of 'em come out the same way, 'cept mama cows don't yell so much."

"You're horrible." But Arien was giggling too.

At least they were talking a bit. He'd take it.

Another hour went by before their dad, looking worn out, his grin a mile wide, poked his head in the waiting room. "Who wants to come meet their new baby brother?"

"It's a boy?" Jumping out of her chair, Arien gasped like she couldn't quite believe it.

Matthew squeezed her shoulder, beaming with pride. "A big boy. Nine pounds."

"Is Mom okay?" Holding onto their hands, she followed their father down the hall.

"Your mama's just fine."

Looking a helluva lot better than the last time Tanner had seen her, Jennifer was sitting up in bed, a blanket-wrapped bundle in her arms. Cooing at the baby, she smiled. "Benjamin, your brothers and sister are here."

"His name's Benjamin?" Arien squeaked.

Huddled together, the three of them leaned over the bed to take a closer look. Dark hair. His eyes were closed, so he couldn't tell what color they were. Tanner reckoned he was a fine-looking boy. "He's got our dimple, Kel."

"Yeah, he does."

"He looks a lot like your daddy, don't he?"

Guess so. He just grinned.

"Awww, he's so cute." The baby curled his little fist around Arien's finger. "Can I hold him?"

"Course you can, sweetie." Matthew placed the baby in her arms.

Gazing down at him, she smiled. "Hello, Benjamin. You're our little lucky charm. Did you know that?"

The third son.

His father winked at her. "Born on the third day of June, at three thirty-three."

"That's a lot of threes," Kellan noted.

"You ain't kidding." And she kissed the top of their brother's head.

"Are you sure you can't come?" Arien stuck out her bottom lip, pulling the face she used to use on her mother as a child to get her way. It worked when she was eight, but it wasn't working now.

"I'm sure." Sitting cross-legged on the chaise end of the sectional, Jennifer nursed the baby, watching a godawful sci-fi movie on Netflix. "Benjamin's only a week old, sweetie. Can't take a brand-new baby to a wedding and expose him to all those germs."

What happened to all those antibodies in breastmilk she'd been going on about? But Arien didn't bother asking. "I'm told Brookside weddings are something else, and it's a lovely day. Do you good to get some fresh mountain air."

"There's going to be a dozen more of them before summer's over. I imagine I'll get to at least one." Rubbing the baby's back, she quirked a brow. "Maybe yours?"

"What on Earth ever gave you that idea?"

"Oh, I dunno. Except I did happen to see your award letter in the wastebasket." Her mom smirked. "So, I take it you're not going to UC."

"Doesn't mean there's going to be any wedding." Tucking her tongue in her cheek, Arien lifted her shoulder in a half shrug. "I decided to stick around for a while and help you out. You'll be needing it with the baby and all. I can take some classes online, maybe, and work on my blog full-time."

"Hmm…if you say so." The smirk never left her face. "Well, I'm going to enjoy having my little man here all to myself. And after I finish watching my movie, me and Benjamin are going to have ourselves a nice, long nap. God, I'm so tired."

"Okay, Mom." Arien kissed her cheek. "I love you."

"I love you too, sweetheart. Give my best to Shiloh and Griffin."

"I will." Watching him suckle, she touched the downy-soft curls on her brother's head.

Jennifer giggled. "Maybe you'll catch the bouquet."

Leaving the room, Arien burst out laughing and shook her head.

So, along with everyone else in Brookside, they went to the wedding without her.

The setting was beautiful. Pinterest-inspired Western chic with a Bohemian flair. As usual, Arien was seated between Tanner and Kellan, and Grams between him and her stepfather. Emily and her mom, flanked by Billy and Jake, were in the row directly in front of them, along with the rest of the Gantry family.

Taking her hand, Tanner leaned into her. "Our weddings aren't like what you're used to."

"What's so different about them?"

Besides the obvious.

"Well, for one, Griffin and Cassie are already married."

Arien wrinkled her nose.

"She's the elder sister." He chuckled. "They made it legal at the courthouse this mornin'. But the trinity ceremony is the real weddin.'"

Funny, the marriage certificate the world recognized was of little significance here. It was the part those on the outside would scorn them for, the triad union, that held meaning.

Turning her face to his, Tanner softly kissed her lips. "I need for you to always remember that."

Why?

Arien touched her fingers to his cheek. And not sure what to expect, with her Nikon ready on her lap, she waited for the ceremony to begin.

No bridesmaids. No maid of honor. No flower girl. Shiloh's three parents preceded her and Cassie down a lantern-lined aisle, where Griffin waited before an unlit fire, framed within a triangle of stone. Sheer tulle and lace. The brilliant rays of the setting sun turned gowns of champagne scandalously translucent, leaving no doubt as to what lie beneath them.

Turning to her, Emily sighed. "Miss Lilly creates the most beautiful dresses."

She couldn't make out what they were doing up there, or hear the words being said, but it was Shiloh's face Griffin had his gaze set on, his adoration for the younger sister apparent. At least it was to her. No one else appeared to notice. Cassie didn't seem to, either, or maybe she just didn't care. If she had, Arien might've actually felt a little bit of sympathy for her.

With the sacred fire now ablaze, festivities commenced. Revelry abounding in the growing darkness. The barn dances she'd been to thus far paled in comparison. Matthew stood from the table, extending his hand. "I need to get back to your mama and Benjamin. Don't like leavin' 'em. But I want a dance with my beautiful daughter before I do."

Why did hearing that make her want to cry?

She swayed in the shelter of her stepfather's arms, and with a kiss to the top of her head, he placed her hand in Kellan's.

They didn't move. Fingertips skating down her spine, he just held her tight in the middle of the dance floor. "I can't let you go."

Arien gazed into his eyes, melted chocolate flecked with green, and holding his face in her hands, she kissed him.

They were still dancing thirty minutes later, when Tanner tapped Kellan on the shoulder. "Grams just texted me, says we need to hurry home."

"She say why?"

Shaking his head, he showed them the message on his phone. "Nope."

The churning in her chest told her something was wrong. With her breath locked in her lungs, her brain wouldn't let her begin to process what that something could possibly be.

They weren't the first ones to get there.

Jake and Billy's father was exiting his truck as they pulled onto the drive.

Grams paced on the porch with the baby, tears marring her ageless face.

Arien tumbled out the door before Kellan could even park, tearing toward the house.

They didn't have to speak a word.

With just one look, she knew.

And she ran.

Seventeen

Kellan tore after her.

Screaming her name, he raced along the fence and through the field. He crossed the stream, following her into the pines. Hadn't he warned her never to come out here alone?

"Arien."

The wind carried his voice through the trees, a hushed, haunting stillness echoing in reply.

He kept going, twigs snapping beneath his feet, until he found her.

Staring up at the starry night sky, her knees drawn to her chest, she rocked.

Kellan got down on his haunches in front of her, but Arien didn't seem to see that he was there. "Baby."

"Tell me it isn't true." Still gazing upward, she didn't look at him.

I wish I could.

He gathered her in his arms, holding her against him. "I'm so sorry, baby, I can't. Your mama's gone."

Same as mine. Same as Tanner's.

It took a moment for the finality of his words to sink in. Then with her face crumpling, Arien scrunched her eyes closed, and cried for her mother.

At least she'd had one. He'd never known his. Kellan almost envied her grief. It's an inevitable part of loving someone. Because he couldn't grieve for the woman he never knew.

Sobs wracking her body, her tears soaked through to his skin.

This woman, he loved.

Wetness, unusual for him, trickled down his face.

Kellan stood, Arien in his arms, and he carried her home.

Pacing back and forth along the porch, Tanner spotted them. He sprinted across the yard. Embracing Arien from behind, he sandwiched her between them and kissed her tear-stained cheek.

Cars and trucks lined the long driveway. "Who's here?"

"Everyone, it seems like."

"Where's my mom?" Arien hiccupped against his chest. "I need to see her."

"You can't right now, baby." Tanner smoothed her hair. Their eyes meeting, his brother subtly shook his head. "Let's get you upstairs."

Kellan dressed her in one of his T-shirts and laid her on his bed.

Emily and Grams came into the room, Jake and his father behind them. He sat on the mattress next to Arien, combing the hair back from her eyes. "I'm going to give you something to help you get some sleep."

"But I don't want to sleep."

"He's a doctor, dear." Wringing her hands, Grams nodded. "You need to rest."

"I need my mom."

Gantry pulled a syringe from his pocket.

"Noooo…Kellan."

He kissed her brow. "Shh…I'm right here. We're going to take care of you, baby."

And, her eyelids fluttering closed, she fell asleep.

They all trailed Gantry down the stairs to Kim rocking Benjamin in the kitchen. "How is she?"

"Resting now." Grams took the baby from her.

Bending over the island, Kellan stared at the granite. "Where's Dad?"

"In the guest bedroom." Gantry clasped his shoulder. "I had to sedate him. He was…utterly distraught…inconsolable."

"What the fuck happened?"

"I came home with your father to see the baby." Her voice cracking, Grams rubbed her cheek against the newborn's silky hair. "He was crying his head off with the TV on, and Jennifer…" Looking toward the living room, she began sobbing. "…at first we thought she was just sleeping."

"Sheriff's been here. Coroner's comin'." Gantry lifted up the sheet.

Devoid of color, her face appeared waxen. A small trail of blood congealed at one nostril. But other than that, nothing looked amiss. His stepmother was as beautiful in death as she had been in life. Still, Kellan was relieved Arien hadn't seen her this way. He hated to think of that image haunting her dreams.

"I'm sorry, son," Gantry said, covering her. "I can't…she was healthy, as far as I know." Shaking his head, he exhaled. "We should know something after the autopsy."

"She was tired all the time." Absently, Tanner nodded. "But that's to be expected, I guess."

Grams carried Benjamin up to the nursery. And after the

coroner came and went, and everyone else had gone home, he and his brother returned to Arien.

A curse was upon them.

That's what his father always said. But then how else could he rationalize two dead wives? *Fucking Christ. Three.* Hell, he couldn't come up with a plausible explanation either. Kellan had to keep his wits about him. As much as he had to keep them all together. Because one thing was certain, something wasn't right here.

It took five days for Jennifer's body to be returned to them, and another two days to organize the funeral. In all that time, his father barely spoke. He'd go out to the barn or his office on autopilot, only to shut himself off upstairs at the end of the day. Grams and Aunt Kim took over the running of the house. Fending off well-meaning neighbors. Someone always seemed to be knocking at the door with a covered dish or donated breast-milk for the baby.

And Arien?

Kellan was worried about her. Tanner too. One minute she'd be sobbing and the next it was as if nothing registered at all. Only two things snapped her out of it. Her horse and Benjamin.

When Arien wasn't fussing over their brother, he'd be sure to find her with Daisy. Rubbing her down, braiding her mane, taking her out for a long ride. One afternoon, he even found her weaving crowns of wildflowers for the dang cows while the palomino grazed on the grass at her side. Kellan understood, though.

A horse can heal even the most broken soul.

While he and Tanner would mend her broken heart.

Looking out the window, Kellan tightened his tie. Emily, Jake, and Billy were here. Outside of his uncles, Grandpa Paul, and Grandpa Garrett, he didn't know much about grieving, and he was just a kid at the time. Grams and Aunt Kim were more than well-acquainted with it, though, and they assured him after today, the healing could begin.

Arien was already downstairs when he got there. With the baby to her shoulder, his father looking on, she patted his back, coaxing a burp from him. Kellan couldn't help but smile. She'd make a good mother one day.

And with the immediate family all here, they loaded into their vehicles and made their way to the cemetery.

Birth, life, and death are all part of an endless cycle. They considered the natural world to be sacred, and disregarded morbid practices that were commonplace elsewhere. Jennifer's unembalmed body lay inside a closed wooden casket of pine. For them, the purpose of a funeral was to honor her life, pay their respects, and return her to the earth.

The townsfolk were already assembled at the gravesite. Heads turning toward them, Kellan assisted Arien from the dually, and she froze.

"I can't do this." Hyperventilating, she grabbed onto his forearm with both hands. "Take me home."

"Baby." Stepping in front of her, his body shielded her from the onlookers.

Her blonde hair blowing in the mild June breeze, Tanner tucked it behind her ear. "We got you, pretty girl."

"No." Closing her eyes, she shook her head. "You don't understand. As long as I don't see my mom lying in a box, it isn't real."

"Arien, look at me." Kellan gently lifted her chin. "You don't have to look, but you need to say goodbye."

Tears erupting, she squeaked, "It's always been me and her. I don't even know how to exist now."

"You keep on doin' what you're doin', baby," he replied, kissing her forehead. "Your mama was so damn proud of you."

Swiping beneath her eyes, Arien nodded. "Look at us all... without a mother..." And the tears welled up again. "...I keep thinking how our baby brother will never know her."

"Yes, he will." And he pulled her against his chest. "He has you."

Arien laid the baby down in the cradle the boys had given her mother. Opening a book, she rocked him with her foot, determined to take in the beauty of an all-too-short summer. She lived for days like this. With the sun shining, not a single cloud in the bright azure sky, a soft July breeze fanning over her skin.

Five minutes in, after trying to read the same paragraph a dozen times, she gave up. Usually an escape for her, Arien found it difficult to focus these days. Her head kept spinning in a series of directions, trying to take her where she didn't want to go. Missing her mom just hurt so much. She tried not to think about it. Tanner and Kellan did their best to distract her. Didn't work, though.

Glancing down at her brother, she smiled at him. Dark curls like his daddy—and Tanner. Blue eyes like their mother. Arien wondered if they'd stay that way. She'd read a baby's eyes often change color. "I love you, lucky charm."

Even though he hadn't brought any, they were lucky to have him. What if whatever killed her mom had happened before he was born? Or before she met Matthew? She'd be all alone in Denver. *Waiting tables in a dumpy, ole diner, most likely.* Arien shuddered to think of it.

See? Her thoughts were all over the place.

They didn't know how or why Jennifer died.

Two days after the funeral, Doc Gantry—that's what Arien called him anyway—came by the house during supper, the autopsy report in his hand. The cause of death was undetermined, toxicology pending. They couldn't find anything wrong. Her heart just stopped beating.

"How's my girl?"

She looked up. Celadon eyes sparkled in the sun. "Oh,

Matthew." Arien started to get up. "I can have lunch ready in a jiffy. Where's the boys?"

"Sit." Nudging her back down, he took a seat beside her. "Boys are still workin'. Didn't come back to the house to eat. Came to see you."

"Oh?"

He slung his arm across her shoulders. "I'm worried about you. Want to make sure you're okay."

"I'll be okay…" She shrugged. "…one day. How about you?"

"Same," he said with a shake of his head. "I'm not quite there yet."

Arien rested her head on his shoulder. He stroked her hair. "You love them boys, don't ya?"

The thought of them made her smile. "Yeah, I do."

"There are no coincidences, Arien. No accidents. The three of you were born to be one."

"You think so?"

"I know so."

Lifting her head from his shoulder, she glanced up at him. "How?"

"I saw it." With a single nod, he lowered his gaze to the floor. "I know you think it's crazy. Most people would, but I can assure you it ain't. How do you think I know which investments to make? What to buy? When to sell?"

"You dream it?"

"And this town, everyone in it, is filthy fuckin' rich." He winked, an obvious smirk on his face. "The visions are a guide. You just gotta listen to 'em. So we listen and we believe. Our ways have served us well."

Not this mumbo jumbo again.

"You're saying you had a dream about Kellan, Tanner, and me?"

"Before you were even born." Matthew took her hand in both of his, and squeezing it, he held it on his lap. "It's common for a father to have visions of his children's future."

"The day Aunt Kim got married, Gantry told Grams she was going to have one child, a daughter, and that child would be the wife of his sons. He saw it."

"My first vision of you and your mother came the day after Heather's funeral. It was so strange, but so strong I couldn't ignore it. I knew your mama was the one the second I saw her, and when she showed me your picture..." Turning his face toward hers, her stepfather raised her hand to his lips and kissed it. "...I put that beautiful boy in her belly."

"You what?"

"Maybe I shouldn't have, but I'm so glad I did, or we wouldn't have Benjamin," he said, smiling down at his baby son. "I had to make her mine, and I had to make sure you came here with her, so the boys could make you theirs. But see, I kinda manipulated things and now I think we're all payin' for it."

You are fucking crazy.

"Do Tanner and Kellan know all this?"

He licked his lips, the brim of his hat bobbing back and forth. "They've been waitin' their entire lives for you."

Oh, God.

She clapped a hand over her mouth, bile rising in her throat.

"My boys won't beg, Arien, but I will. They love you. I love you," Matthew professed, his green eyes boring into hers. "Stay here with us. Help me make things right and put an end to all this wretchedness."

Stunned, Arien gave no response. She was trying to process everything he'd just said and nothing was making any sense to her.

"I'm doin' my part. Tellin' you everything." He flattened out a crumpled ball of paper, and standing, he placed it in her lap. Her award letter. "I want you to stay, but because you want to be here, not because you think you've got no other choice."

Then he walked away.

You're too late.

Not that it mattered. Arien had made her decision a while ago.

But she'd been duped, hadn't she? Set up.

Did Matthew ever love her mother? He genuinely seemed to. More importantly, Jennifer believed he did.

And for that matter, were Kellan and Tanner really in love with her? Arien thought they were, but now she wasn't as sure.

Madness. That's what this was. Sheer and utter madness.

Did one of them do something to her mom?

Stop it, Arien. They would never, and they were with you when she died.

Now she was losing her own damn mind.

Matthew must've said something to them. Both contrite, Tanner and Kellan kept to themselves and maintained a distance, giving her the time and space they thought she needed.

"Why are you fighting it?"

And apparently, they'd spoken to Jake. Or maybe Emily had. Didn't fucking matter.

"Fighting what?" Arien didn't bother to look at him, focusing instead on the dough she was kneading. Dutch-oven bread was up next on her blog.

Ignoring her bullshit, he came closer. "You love them. I know you do. So why are you fighting it?"

Jake had her all figured out, because isn't that exactly what she'd been doing for months now? Waging a war between her heart and her head?

Pushing the bowl away, tears rushed to fill her eyes. Her gaze met his. "I don't know."

"Arien." He wrapped his arms around her. "You love them and they love you. That's it. It simply exists. Forget everything else. The only thing that matters is what *you* feel. What's in your head can fuck you up, but your heart can't lie."

"I wish I could talk to my mom."

"What's stopping you?" Gently smiling, he inclined his head. "Go talk to her."

She hadn't been back here since the funeral.

And she didn't remember very much of that day.

Arien had sat through the service staring down at her shoes. Not once did she look in front of her. Even as they filed past the hand-carved casket, clinging to Tanner, she averted her gaze and whispered a silent goodbye.

She couldn't say who was there, the words that were said, or what they ate at the luncheon in the town hall after. It was all a blur.

The smell of burning sage. Intense and earthy. She remembered that.

Arien took the baby out of his car seat and walked toward the back of the cemetery on the outskirts of town. Water cascading over rock could be heard off in the distance. Birds. Wind rustling through pine.

She glanced at the gravestones as she passed. Surnames she recognized. The letters worn, barely discernible, many more than a century old.

"Levi Gantry, 1825–1906."

I know you.

The graves here told a story. Monuments serving as a reminder to Brookside's rich, historic past. Arien had a notion to photograph them. To preserve them somehow before the stone crumbled away. Maybe someday she would.

Too new, her mother's grave didn't have a stone yet. Next spring, once the ground had settled enough, her name would be here. Yet another chapter in their story.

"Hi, Mom." She sat down with Benjamin on the grass, placing the bouquet of wildflowers she'd picked beside her.

Now that she was here, she felt foolish talking out loud to the ground. Closing her eyes, Arien imagined her mother sitting across from her on the sofa at home, some low-budget horror flick on the TV.

"Me and Benjamin are okay. He's growin' like a weed. Wearing size three to six months already." She chuckled, kissing the baby's head. "We miss you, though. So much. It hurts so bad that some days I don't want to get out of bed. Probably wouldn't if it weren't for this little guy.

"Matthew misses you, too—something awful." Arien opened her eyes, tears escaping to roll down her cheeks. "And the boys. That's what I wanted to talk to you about. I don't know what to do…well, that's not exactly true. I know what I want to do. I guess, I just wish you could tell me I'm not crazy and you approve…gosh, this is stupid."

"I only have one question. Do you love him?"

She did love him. She loved both of them. They made sure of it, didn't they?

"Most of us are lucky to find one true love in this lifetime, so if you've been so fortunate as to have found two? Then I'd say you're very blessed indeed."

Sniffling, Arien swiped the tears away from her face and smiled. "I love you, Mom."

And a butterfly flitted past, landing on a stone to the right of her.

She gasped.

"Didn't mean to startle you, dear. Came by to visit my girls." Standing there, John Jacoby tipped his hat. "So sorry about your mama, Arien. I wanted to extend my condolences at the funeral, but you weren't up to talkin'. Told my boys to tell ya."

"Thank you." Clutching Benjamin tighter, she nodded.

"Hope they's takin' good care of you."

"They are."

He paused, his brow knitting in thought. "What are the odds, ya think? Three wives dead after birthin' his babies."

"Are you inferring something, Mr. Jacoby?" Shielding her eyes from the sun with her hand, she glared at the audacity of this man.

"You're gonna be my granddaughter, ain't ya?" His smirk reminding her of Kellan. "Call me Pops."

"Okay. Pops, then."

"Could be just a coinkydink, but it makes ya wonder, don't it?"

"No, it doesn't." Having heard enough of his ridiculous bull-shit, Arien got up from the grass. "I have to get home now. It's time for Benjamin's nap."

"Fine-looking boy." Stroking the baby's cheek, he grinned. "I'll be seein' ya, dear."

She hurried back to her car.

"There are no coincidences, Arien."

She punched the gas. "The hell there's not."

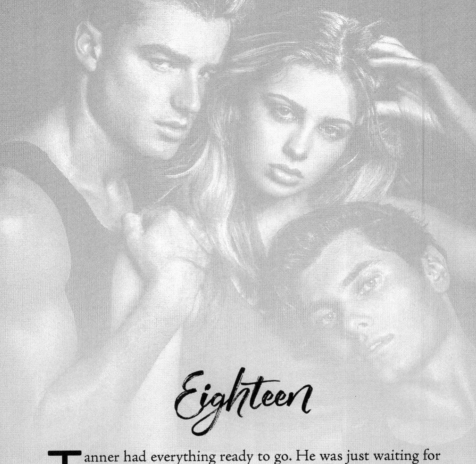

Eighteen

Tanner had everything ready to go. He was just waiting for his brother to get Arien down here. No doubt she was giving him a hard time about it too. Except for an afternoon ride with Daisy while the baby napped, she didn't leave the house often. Grams came by every day to help out with Benjamin and everything, but she insisted on doing it all herself. Kim seemed to think caring for their brother was her way of working through her grief, and to leave her to it, so they did for the most part.

But not today.

They'd drag her out of the house if they had to.

It seemed like he and his brother had been waiting for forever already.

He heard footsteps coming down the stairs, and grinned. *Got her.* Kellan could be quite convincing when necessary.

"I don't know what y'all are up to, but I've got things to do."

Her hand on her hip, head cocked, Arien tapped her bare foot on the wood floor. She was even prettier when she was all fired up.

Tanner chuckled. "Yeah, you do. With us."

"I have to start supper soon."

"No, you don't." He winked. "Already taken care of."

"The baby will be waking up and—"

"Benjie's not here. Dad and Grams went to Aunt Kim's for supper. You got any other excuses?" Before she could come up with any, Tanner turned to his brother. "Get her stuff?"

"Yup." Shit-eating grin on his face, Kellan held up a small canvas bag. "Right here."

Yeah, they'd planned ahead.

"Get your boots on, pretty girl." He smacked her on the ass. "We're takin' a little ride."

Under the late-afternoon sun, with the dogs chasing after them, they rode three abreast to the lake. It would be a bit chilly once it set, but it was warm right now. A dip in the water, then a starlight picnic. Just the three of them.

Tanner laid a thick flannel blanket out on the grass. Kellan unpacked the goodies from the saddlebags. Meatloaf pie, buttermilk fried chicken, orzo pasta salad, watermelon, raspberry crumb bars for dessert, and a jug of strawberry lemonade.

"Where'd you get all this?" Arien's eyes got bigger with every container Kellan set down on the blanket. "And don't tell me y'all made it yourselves."

"Hell, no." Grinning, his brother poured a fifth of vodka into the jug. "I can grill a mean steak, but Grams helped us out some. You're gonna love her meatloaf pie. It's been my favorite ever since I was a little kid."

"We do know how to cook, little sister." Tanner nodded,

elbowing his brother in the ribs. "Managed to feed ourselves some-how 'fore you got here."

"Could've fooled me."

Kellan pulled her down to the blanket and kissed her. "Well, you're a helluva lot better at it."

Glancing up from beneath her lashes, smiling sweetly, she took hold of their hands. "I know what you're trying to do. Thank you. This is really nice."

"So, you're done bein' mad at us?" Tanner asked her.

"I was never mad."

Nudging her shoulder, his brother smirked. "Yeah, you were."

"Maybe just a little." Leaning back on her elbows, Arien blew out a breath. "Not knowing the whole truth made me feel like I was lied to, you know?"

"Never once did I lie to you," Kellan insisted, threading his fingers into her hair.

"Me neither." Leaning on one arm by her side, Tanner turned her face toward his. "Yeah, we held back on some things. Things you weren't ready to know. I mean, you were already thinkin' we're all crazy."

Lowering her gaze, she giggled. "I still do."

"Oh, but I think you like our crazy, don't you, baby cakes?"

"Maybe," Arien teased, a grin on her face. Then she bowed her head. "I gotta know, though…"

"What's that?"

"Did you really fall in love with *me?*" Pressing a hand to her chest, Arien raised her chin. "Or a dream?"

"Both." And that was the truth. "You are the dream, pretty girl. Always have been."

"Loving someone isn't an accident, it's a choice. You don't fall. You choose it." Kellan took her by the arms, his face only inches from hers. "And *I* chose to open my heart and love you."

She nodded with a sniffle, tears sliding down her cheeks. "One more thing. Did Matthew know what was going to happen to my mom? Did he dream that, too?"

"Baby, no, I swear it." Holding her tight against him, his brother kissed her hair.

"If he did, and I don't think he did, he didn't tell us, pretty girl." His thumb tracing along her jaw, Tanner caught her tears. "And I don't believe our father would've taken the chance knowin' that."

"Or put himself through that again." Kellan made a fist, pounding it on his chest. "Dad's all tore up inside. He loved your mama."

"I know he did."

Tanner knew it too.

As surely as he and his brother loved her daughter.

So they took away her tears and took her to the lake for a swim. Not for long, though. Up here, the water never got very warm, and with the sun setting, the temperature on the mountain was quickly dropping.

Tanner wrapped a shivering Arien in a blanket. "Maybe we should go back or start a fire. It's cold."

"Nope." Kellan passed her a flask of Fireball. "Can't or we'll miss it."

"Miss what?"

His arm around her, he pointed up at the sky. "See that hazy band of light there?"

"Yeah, what about it?"

"That's the Milky Way," he said, and falling back onto his elbows, Kellan took her with him. "The edge of the galaxy in our little corner of the universe. A bunch of stars we can't see individually with the naked eye. Gas. Dust. That's why it looks like that."

"It's beautiful."

"They say there's maybe two trillion other galaxies out there. We're just a tiny speck in one of 'em. Ain't that some crazy shit?" Kellan slowly turned to look at her.

"It's surreal if you think about it."

"Too fantastic to be true and yet it is."

Fiddling with the bracelet on her wrist, Arien snickered. "Is that supposed to be an analogy?"

"Maybe." Exchanging a glance with him, his brother winked.

Tanner took her hand. He kissed her palm. "I love you, pretty girl."

"*We* love you." Kellan took and kissed the other. "And more love is just that. More."

"I love you too," she said, palming their cheeks. "Both of you."

Puffing out his chest, his brother grinned. "Then bein' it's the middle of August, and you ain't hightailed it back to Denver yet, I'm thinkin' you're plannin' on stayin'."

"Plans change. Dreams do too." Arien's head bobbed side to side. "So, I thought I might."

Tanner grinned too. "In that case, we've got somethin' we've been wantin' to ask ya."

They said it together, "Will you be our wife?"

"I must be crazy too." Biting on her lip, Arien inclined her head. "Because I will, yes."

Kellan slipped the oval-cut diamond on her finger while Tanner kissed her. Then his brother kissed her. And they kissed her together, tasting the cinnamon on her lips. Couldn't stop. It was sweeter now, because she was really, finally theirs.

Lying on the blanket, Arien held their hands on her chest, the three of them staring at the night sky. "Did you see that?" Letting go, she pointed straight up. "Looks like it's raining fire."

Shooting stars.

"The Perseids." Turning his head to look at her, Tanner smiled. "Didn't I tell you it was better than the Fourth of July?"

He'd told her, but Arien had to see it for herself. Same as how they loved her. He and Kellan could tell her over and over and over, but she had to feel the truth of it to see how good and perfect and beautiful it was all on her own.

And he was so fucking thankful that at last, she did.

"Two weeks?" Arien threw her hands in the air. "No way we're going to be able to pull that off."

It had been decided that the first day of September, the day after Kellan's twenty-third birthday, was *the* day. After knowing the months—heck, probably years—of planning Shiloh put into her wedding, and seeing it with her own two eyes, the idea of putting together such a monumental event, in such a short amount of time, seemed nothing short of impossible.

Sniggering, an undaunted Emily, Grams, and Aunt Kim watched her panic set in from across the table. "You doubtin' our abilities?" Rubbing her hands together, the latter woman assured her, "Don't you worry 'bout a thing. We got this, girly."

"We've done this a time or two, dear." Grams reached over and patted her hair. "Already got Maizie on the cakes."

"You told her, right? Nothing fancy."

"Naked cake." With a bouncy toss of her curls, Grams chuckled. "She knows."

Damn cake was the least of her worries, though. Arien turned to her cousin. "Hope you're up for shopping. We're gonna have to go to Jackson and pray we can find a halfway decent dress on the rack."

"Don't be turnin' into no bridezilla on me now."

"I'm not. I promise." Running her hand through her hair, she blew out her cheeks. "I'm just freaking out, because what in the hell am I doing?"

"Relax." Emily came over to her and placed her hands on her shoulders. "We're not goin' to Jackson and you're not gonna get no tried-on-a-gazillion-times sample gown from the rack. I'm takin' you somewhere better."

She took her into town.

Miss Lilly had an oddly elegant shop on Main Street. Stained glass obscured the view through the windows. Emily pushed the door open, a small brass bell announcing their arrival, and taken aback by what she saw, Arien's jaw dropped.

Victorian-flocked wallpaper. Sofas covered in purple velvet. It looked like a brothel from the 1800s.

"Probably because it was, Miss Brogan," a sultry voice came from the open loft overhead. "Show her around, Emily. I'll be down in a minute."

What the hell kind of creepy *Twilight Zone* shit was this?

Arien shook it off. Emily didn't seem fazed at all. The woman must've just guessed what she'd been thinking, right?

Bolts of luxurious fabrics were neatly stored in cubbies built into the far wall. Sketchbooks of designs and photos of long-ago brides sat on antique tables. A small collection of dresses on display. All of them sensuous and beautiful.

Her fingers running along the sleeve of a dreamy dress in pale-lavender organza, she turned to Emily. "This would be so pretty on you."

"It's gorgeous."

"You're my maid of honor." And she squealed, "Try it on."

Tilting her head, Emily bit her lip. "We don't do that for our weddings, though."

"Don't care." Arien pulled the hanger off the rack and handed her the dress. "I'm doing it for mine. Try it on, and if you don't like that one, then choose another."

"But…"

"Do as she says, Emily." Insanely alluring in a black mid-length gown, Miss Lilly appeared at the top of the stairs. "We can allow her that much."

She slowly descended, her long, black hair swishing with every step. Exotically beautiful with almond-shaped eyes of lush forest green, framed in a thicket of black lashes. Arien wondered if she was related to Billy and Jake in some way.

"My congratulations to you, Miss Brogan." Taking both of her hands, the woman swooped in. She smelled as exotic as she looked. "Those Brooks boys have been favored indeed."

"Thank you, and call me Arien."

"Lovely name." Giving her hands a brief squeeze, she let them go. "Do you have a vision?"

Oh, God.

She chuckled. "For your gown, dear."

"No," she admitted with a shrug.

"Just leave it to me then."

Emily came out in the lavender dress. The silk organza beautifully draping her nubile curves, she was positively stunning. Inspecting her, Miss Lilly tipped her head from one side to the other. "Turn around."

Her cousin did.

"It suits you." She nodded, pinching the sheer off-shoulder sleeves. "I'll take it in a bit and add some lining to the bodice."

Emily made a face.

"Not to worry, dear." Miss Lilly pinched her cheek. "Just enough to cover those pretty tits of yours. I'll leave you enough to entice my nephews with. Besides, it's Arien's day."

Ha! I knew it!

The corners of her lips ticking up, a wicked smile rose on Emily's face. "Your turn."

They stood her on a raised platform in front of a mirror. "Take all your clothes off. I need to get your measurements."

Arien stripped down to her bra and panties.

Miss Lilly glanced up from her notepad. "I said all of them. That means nude."

Emily nodded.

She unhooked her bra, tossing it on top of her clothes, and slipped off her panties. Arien wasn't ashamed of her body, but it took everything in her to keep from covering herself. Besides her mom, only Kellan and Tanner had ever seen her naked.

"Stand up straight." The dressmaker got right to work. Measuring her from every conceivable angle, she'd stop and scribble on the paper. "Perfectly proportioned. Not too skinny, like some people we know, eh?"

Thanks, I guess?

Emily snorted.

Lilly stood before her. Weighing her breasts in her hands, her thumbs traced around the areolas. The flesh puckering, her nipples beaded. Arien held her breath, an all-too-familiar tingle between her thighs. "Breathe, my lovely one. That's it. Now close your eyes."

She looked to Emily.

"It's okay, Arien. Just go with it."

The woman toyed with her nipples. Arien could feel them swell. "Beautiful. That's perfect. They will be pleased." Then abruptly, she stopped, and began to sketch. "You can get dressed now. I'll see you next week for your fitting."

At a loss for words, she didn't speak until Emily started the car. "What the fuck was that?"

"What do you mean?"

"She. Touched. Me."

"Ohhh that." Giggling, Emily pulled out onto the street. "Wasn't nothin' sexual about it."

The hell it wasn't.

"Not like you're thinkin' anyway." Taking her hand, Emily squeezed it. "You know how Shiloh's gown was cut real low, showin' all that cleavage and her graceful shoulders? All Cassie had to offer was her bony backside—she ain't got no titties." Emily snickered. "You do, though. See, Miss Lilly's creation is made especially for you, to showcase your beautiful body in the best way possible. It's our custom."

Arien glanced down at her nipples poking against her shirt. "My ta-tas?"

"My cousins are going to be so proud." She smirked.

"That's sexist."

"And that skinny bitch is gonna have to eat crow."

What the fuck have I gotten myself into here?

"Why?"

"Because you won."

Nineteen

Opening the door to her bedroom, Kellan found her at the vanity, putting on her makeup. Reminded of the first time he ever saw her, he stood there for a moment, just watching her. This beautiful vision of a girl, who became his stepsister then, would become his wife today.

He glanced at his watch.

Couple more hours, baby cakes.

They'd make it legal at the courthouse in Jackson this morning. A piece of paper didn't hold any more meaning to them than that, but he knew it meant something to Arien. Besides, he'd never admit it to anyone, not even her, but the fact that it was his name forever linked with hers in the county records made Kellan feel some kind of way. Like he had more of a claim to her. He didn't. Except for this one afternoon when she belonged only to him.

He tiptoed in, coming up behind her. His hands on her shoulders, he leaned over, slipping them inside her robe to squeeze her breasts. "Happy weddin' day." Kellan kissed her neck, murmuring in her ear, "I love you."

"I love you too." She giggled. "Isn't it bad luck to see me before the wedding?"

"Nah." He nibbled on her earlobe. "Besides, they'll whisk you away from us before you know it to put you in Miss Lilly's dress. We don't get to see you after that."

'Til you're ours.

But right now, you're just mine.

Kellan lifted her from the chair, and pulling the clip from her hair, he kissed her. With nothing beneath the silk she wore, his fingers swept over every square inch of skin, pressing her soft body into his hardness. Fuck, he could hardly wait to be inside her. And he'd never have to lie awake alone again.

"It's time to go, wifey." He squeezed the cheek of her ass. "Get dressed."

"I'm not your wife yet. Don't jinx us."

He smirked. "Soon enough."

Sitting in the front seat of the dually with his father, Arien fidgeted all the way to Jackson. Maybe it was because Grams insisted on keeping the baby home with her. Made her anxious to leave him.

Chewing on her lip, she slid out of the truck. He and Tanner were there to catch her. She looked real pretty in a short lace dress and her boots.

Kissing her cheek, Matthew put a small bouquet of flowers in her hand. "I love ya, Arien. So beautiful," he rasped, his voice all choky. No doubt she reminded him of her mama.

Nudging him, his brother tipped his chin at the flowers. "Why didn't we think of that?"

"I dunno. 'Cause we weren't, I guess."

"Never you mind, it's for her daddy to do," he said over his shoulder, presenting her with his arm. "C'mon, daughter."

Looking at him, Tanner shrugged, and they followed the pair inside.

Kellan took off his hat as he stepped through the door. There wasn't much to it. He and Arien filled out some paperwork, and holding her hand, they waited for their names to be called. She gnawed on her lip. He squeezed her knee. "You're okay, baby cakes. Breathe."

Glancing up at him with those big green eyes, she nodded, swiping on some gloss.

"Brooks and Brogan?"

"Kellan Brooks, do you take this woman…"

He gazed down at her. The flowers she clutched were shaking. "I do."

"Arien Brogan, do you take this man…"

She looked into his eyes, but he saw her reaching behind her to grab his brother's hand. "I do."

No, dammit. This was *his* time. He was going to share her with Tanner for the rest of their lives. All Kellan wanted was this one fucking moment.

Tanner let her hand go.

Kellan slid the slender diamond band on her finger.

"I now pronounce you husband and wife. Congratulations, you may kiss your bride."

Mine. Only mine.

He memorized how beautiful she looked right then. He never wanted to forget. Then he kissed his wife.

They took her away from them all too soon.

Each taking a turn, he and Tanner kissed her goodbye at the door of the room she'd never sleep in again, and watched her disappear down the stairs. Embracing them, their grandmother chuckled. "Don't look so sad, it isn't forever. You'll see her again in an hour."

Then she, too, was gone.

Tanner followed Kellan into his room, taking a seat beside him on the bed. "I s'pose we should get ready too."

"Yeah. Just gotta change my clothes. That'll take all of two minutes."

"Same." He chuckled. "You nervous?"

"Nah." Kellan slid his brother a look. "Okay, maybe a little. Makin' small talk with all them people. You know I hate that."

"I know."

"You nervous?"

"Kinda." Tanner laid back on the mattress, clasping his hands behind his head. "More so for Arien, I think. She don't know and… her mama ain't here…it's got to be weighing heavy on her heart."

"I know. Dad's too."

"Yeah." Quiet for a moment, Tanner swallowed. Kellan watched the muscle slide up and down his throat. "Gonna miss this room?"

It didn't sound like a question.

"Why would I? We're gettin' a bigger and better one at the end of the hall."

A whole darn suite.

"Just seems strange when we come back these ones'll be empty."

"Not for long, Tanner." He smiled, hooking an arm around his brother. "Our children'll be sleepin' here someday."

"Imagine that."

He could.

"C'mon." Kellan pulled him up. "Let's get hitched."

As the grooms, it was their duty to welcome each guest as they arrived. God, how he usually hated that frivolous shit, but for some reason it hadn't been as loathsome as Kellan thought it was going to be. With most of the townsfolk here, he, Tanner, and their father stood off to the side, anticipating the start of the ceremony.

Grams and Aunt Kim, holding three-month-old Benjamin, joined them. His baby brother smiled at him with his big blue eyes and his heart melted. He was doing that all the time now.

His aunt put the baby in his arms and he kissed his pudgy cheek. "How's my little butterball?"

"That's a horrible nickname. Benjie ain't no turkey, Kel." Chuckling, Tanner rubbed the dark curls on his head.

Matthew took the baby from him. "You're Daddy's big boy, ain't ya?" Holding his son to his chest, he rocked and swayed.

In a cloud of lilac, Emily appeared, skip-dancing across the grass toward them. Grabbing her by the hand, Kellan twirled her around. "Ain't you a sight. Tryin' to put poor Billy six feet under?"

"Just you wait." Giggling, she kissed his cheek. "Your bride looks so beautiful. Happy weddin' day." Turning to Tanner, she wound her arms around his middle. "Love you, Cuzzy. Y'all might want to get movin', 'cause she's ready."

Kellan, Tanner, and Matthew waited for Arien at the perimeter of the stone triangle. The assembly gasped, whispering amongst themselves, when it was his cousin in her pale-purple dress who preceded her. It should have been Jennifer.

He saw her then. And the air left his lungs. Surrounded by a halo of dazzling light, Arien looked so beautiful with the setting sun shining down upon her. Ivory and champagne, the flowy, voluminous layers of her sheer skirts shimmered. And the bodice...*Oh, Miss Lilly, you've outdone yourself—she's perfect*...was exquisite. A plunging, deep V-neckline of next-to-nothing tulle, embellished with embroidered appliqués of vine and feather lace.

How had they been so favored?

Kellan glanced to his father. Matthew squeezed his hand, as surely as he was Tanner's on the other side of him.

She began walking toward them, alone. And his heart ached.

Forbidden to come any closer to the stones, Emily kissed her cheek, and keeping Arien's flowers for her, took a seat with Grams, her mother, and Benjamin in the front row. With no one to offer her to them, Dad stepped forward, and taking her hands in his, he tied a ribbon around her wrist and whispered in her ear.

Kellan couldn't hear what he said, but whatever it was made her cry.

Then her hands joined theirs. He on her right. Tanner on the left.

The trinity ceremony, while sacred and symbolic to them, was actually very simple. No judge. No priest or officiant. It was the intent in their own hearts that married he and Tanner to her and she to them. Not a prayer recited by some stranger in a cassock or decreed by a stamp on a meaningless piece of paper. The three of them would forge their own covenant in blood and seal it with fire.

Together, the three of them stepped inside the triangle of stones and extended their joined hands.

Matthew tipped his chin and Kellan opened his left palm, the blade slicing quick and deep into his skin. Before Arien could utter a sound, her bleeding flesh was bound together with his. She cried out with the second cut. Tanner didn't so much as flinch.

"*Omne trium perfectum.*" Everything that comes in threes is perfect.

Bound to his brother and his wife, Kellan led them to the woodpile in the center of the stones. His father unwound the bloodied bindings, tossing them on top. As an old Shoshone poem was read aloud from the sidelines, Tanner stacked a second diamond band, slightly different from the one he'd given her, on Arien's finger. She gave a ring to each of them. Then the fire was lit and it was done.

Flames shooting up into the darkening sky behind them, he and his brother kissed their wife.

"That's it?" Her smile was radiant. "We're married?"

"Forever and ever, baby cakes."

"You've got yourself two husbands now, pretty girl."

Looping her arms through theirs, she giggled. "Gosh, I'm a greedy one, aren't I?"

▲

With this being one of the last weddings of the season, the party would go on well into the wee hours of the morning. Not for them, though. Now that everyone had eaten, the cake had been cut, and they were on their way to being pleasantly soused, Kellan and Tanner could make a getaway plan to take Arien to a private party for three upstairs.

A glass of champagne in her hand, she tipped her head back, laughing along with Emily, Billy, and Jake, while his brother was out on the dance floor with Grams. Imagining her nipples beading beneath the appliqués that barely concealed them, Kellan leaned over the back of her chair and said in her ear, "Drink up, baby. Not waitin' no more."

"Ahem." With Benjamin in his arms, Matthew stood beside him. "If you don't mind, your butterball here would like a dance with his sister before I tuck him in his crib for the night."

And that was the end of that. Arien was out of that chair, lickety-split, cooing with a baby on the dance floor. Hell, it seemed like all three of them were being pulled in different directions all night long. It was a wonder they'd gotten to eat any of their dinner, for chrissakes.

"Hey, Kel." Cassie approached him, rubbing the side of her neck. "Happy weddin' day."

"Thank you."

"How's it feel?"

"Couldn't imagine bein' any happier." Glancing down at her, he grinned. "Yet I know I will be tomorrow."

"Heh." Lighting up a cigarette, she exhaled a plume of smoke.

"How's married life treatin' ya?"

"I remember feelin' like you do right now." She paused, taking a long drag. "Ain't gonna last, though. Trust me."

"You drunk, Cassie? What the fuck you talkin' about?"

"You went to the courthouse this mornin' and felt special, didn't ya? Like you finally mattered. But it's Tanner she really loves, just like Griffin and my bitch of a little sister."

Cassie was drunk, but nonetheless his Spidey senses tingled, her words hitting him like a ton of bricks. She was wrong, though.

Lowering his voice, Kellan balled his fists. "Arien loves us both, Cassie. And surely, Griffin loves you."

"No, he don't. Not that I care all that much." She gave him a dismissive wave of her hand. "He only tolerates me to be with her."

"Don't believe it."

"Can't tell me it hasn't been obvious to you all along." Stubbing out her cigarette, Cassie shrugged. "I dunno. Maybe it'll be different for y'all. It's easier for brothers to share, I think. I can't stand to be in the same room with 'em. 'Specially now."

"Why?"

"He only wants her. Barely touches me." And she turned into him. Her arms around his middle, Cassie began blubbering on his new shirt. "Shiloh's gonna have a baby, Kel."

Sweet Jesus, someone come take her.

"Gantry says I'm too skinny. The asshole." She sniffled. "If I don't put on some weight I'll never have one of my own. Haven't had a period in more than a year."

Quit the damn cigarettes then, girly. And while you're at it, stop shoving your fingers down your throat. But he didn't dare say it.

"You'll never know what that feels like."

"I'm sorry." Rubbing her back, he could feel every bone in her spine.

Cassie looked over to the dance floor. Oblivious to everyone else around them, Tanner held Arien in his arms, and lost in a lovers' embrace, they kissed. Like they were the only two people in the world.

"I heard she only stayed for the baby. And him." Running her finger up and down his chest, she glanced up. "But then, maybe I heard wrong."

"You did." Putting some distance between them, Kellan took a step back.

"Well, if she ever leaves you out in the cold, you know where to come find me."

Fucking cunt.

He watched them together on the dance floor. And all these images starting playing in his head. From crying on his brother in the U-Haul to the two of them trimming the tree.

Tanner kissed her before you.

For fuck's sake, she reached for him, speaking her vows to you.

Kellan turned away and strolled over to Grams. "Tell 'em I'll be upstairs in fifteen minutes."

Maybe it was true.

Arien might love his brother, but Tanner sure wouldn't be the one to fuck her first.

Spying from the sitting room, he could see her.

In an ivory silk robe, she chewed on a fingernail, pacing at the foot of the oversized bed. Arien didn't know her old room would be gone when his grandmother escorted her up the stairs. He and Tanner remade the suite just for her. Meant for it to be a surprise. Besides, did she really think they'd keep separate rooms and take turns visiting her across the hall?

You made your bed, baby cakes. Now you're gonna lie in it. With me. And my brother. Every. Fucking. Night.

He was trying to ignore the churning in his gut, trying to convince himself what Cassie said she heard wasn't true. But the longer Kellan waited, the angrier he got.

Tanner opened the door and softly closed it behind him. He saw the relief wash over her face. The unmistakable joy as she jumped into his arms and kissed him.

Setting her down, his brother tenderly combed his fingers through her blonde waves. "I want you, pretty girl."

"I want you too." Sliding her hand inside his boxers, Arien kissed him again.

"Slow down, baby. We have to wait for Kellan."

He smirked. *Yeah, you do.*

"Where is he?"

"He's coming." Tanner kissed her forehead. "We should be ready for him."

"Huh?"

Pushing the silk off her shoulders, it landed in a puddle on the floor. Standing there naked, her back was to him. Kellan couldn't see her face as his brother led her to the bed. He peeled off his boxers and drew back the covers. Then, with his cock jutting outward, Tanner sat back against the headboard.

"C'mere, pretty girl."

She hesitated.

"Are you scared?"

"Not exactly." Arien got up on the bed, and pulling her between his thighs, Tanner held her back to his chest. "Shiloh told me it's gonna hurt."

"Maybe a little bit." Kissing on her neck, he rubbed her nipples. "But then with how much we've been finger-fuckin' you, it might not."

"That thing between your legs is a helluva lot bigger than your fingers."

And my thing is bigger than his, baby cakes.

"Relax, pretty girl," Tanner soothed, massaging her shoulders. "Kellan'll get you nice and wet. Make you feel good. He ain't gonna hurt you."

"What are you gonna do?"

"Hold you."

I think that's my cue.

"You love me, pretty girl?"

"More than the moon and the sun in the sky."

Arien didn't notice him at first.

Kellan stood at the foot of the bed, fisting his dick. She glanced up and he smirked, smearing precum around the head with his thumb.

"Kel." She nervously smiled at him.

He climbed onto the mattress without a word and spread her thighs wide.

"What are you doing?"

"Shhh, it's okay, baby." Tanner rubbed his lips across her face. "As the eldest, your virginity is his to take, but I'm right here."

Happy weddin' day, wifey.

Strumming through her pussy with his fingers, he found her wet enough to take him. "Hold her ankles, brother."

Fuck, yeah. Nice and open.

He needn't bother with the preliminaries. Kellan notched the head of his dick to her hole, and with everything he'd been holding back, drove all the way inside her. He covered her mouth with his and growled, sealing off her scream.

Sweet fucking Christ.

Tight, wet heat strangled his dick. She felt so good, he thought he might be dying.

Arien was in his blood now. His hips in the cradle of her thighs, he gripped her shoulders and fucked her. Hard. Fast.

Teeth nipping her skin. Licking the salt from her pulse as she cried.

Why don't you love me like him?

He didn't even try to prolong it. Tanner could finish her. Kellan let himself come. And when he pulled out his cock, he pushed the seed that escaped back inside her.

Then he backed away from the bed.

"Kellan?"

Glancing at the bucket of champagne, he snickered. This wasn't how he'd planned it. He was anything except tender in bed, but he wanted to love her right, make it special. Didn't matter now.

She didn't have to love him.

He'd take care of her. Put his babies in her belly.

And he'd love her anyhow.

Twenty

I t felt like a piece of raw liver dragging across her cheek.

Smelled like it too.

"Ewww." Arien woke to a furry face and sloppy puppy-dog kisses. "Dammit, Sunday, what did you eat this morning? Stinky breath."

Wrinkling her nose, she gave the dog a scratch between his ears. The pillow to her right was empty. She brushed her fingers across the smooth cotton case. Cold. Its occupant long since gone, if it had ever been slept on at all. The light coming in through the windows told her it was near mid-morning already. Arien sat up, and twisting the diamond bands around her finger, took a glance around the room. She was alone.

"Guess the honeymoon's over, huh?" His tail wagging, Sunday

dropped his head onto her lap. "Why aren't you out there with them? They leave you to keep me company?"

Maybe she shouldn't have expected today to be different from any other, but she had. Then again, Arien thought she'd feel like a different person now that she was their wife, but except for the rings that weighed heavy on her finger, an unfamiliar room, and a raw ache between her legs, everything was the same.

She lifted the sheet, almost afraid of what she'd find, and inspected her naked body. No bruises. No blood. Nothing to see down there at all. After being so thoroughly deflowered, it surprised her. Because what the hell was that last night?

Tanner holding her legs open while Kellan plowed into her without so much as kissing her first. Like she was just a receptacle for his dick. The whole thing was some seriously weird, fucked-up, *Handmaid's Tale*-like shit.

He didn't kiss her after, either. The fucker stumbled into the other room and never came back. Maybe he was drunk and passed out. Arien couldn't think of any other reasonable explanation.

Being her bladder was about to burst, she got out of bed. Immediately upon rising, thin, milky liquid ran down her thighs. The remains of what her husbands had left inside her. It felt like pee. "Gross."

Clenching her thighs together so it wouldn't drip onto the floor, Arien hobbled into the en suite and relieved herself. *Jesus.* She hadn't paid much attention to it when she came in here last night, but this bathroom was glorious. Triple vanity—of course. An enormous walk-in shower, and a big soaker tub.

The entire suite of rooms was pretty darn impressive, actually. After her shower, she stripped the sheets off the bed and went on a self-guided tour. Floor-to-ceiling windows with a stunning view of the horses grazing in the paddock, the stream, and the ridgeline beyond. Stone fireplace. Walk-in closets connected to the bathroom on either side. A lounge area with a TV that took up just about an entire wall. Pulling the throw down off the back, Arien sat on the goose-down stuffed sofa, and held it to her nose.

It smelled like Kellan.

Tanner was the first one through the door. She'd just gotten their lunch ready, and running to him, Arien clasped her hands around his neck to bring his lips to hers. Dirty and sweaty, she didn't care. His hands dropping to her ass, she slung her legs around his waist, kissing him with a voracious hunger that came out of nowhere.

"Damn, girl." He kissed her crown as her toes touched the floor.

She whirled around, just as hungry for Kellan. Before she could throw herself at him, his arm came around her waist and he pecked her cheek. "Lemme go wash up."

"But I missed you," Arien called out after him. "I woke up all alone and—"

"Ranch can't run itself."

The fuck?

Tears sprang to her eyes. Dashing them away, she turned back to Tanner. He shrugged. "I think he's hung over. Been a moody fucker all mornin'." Taking her in his arms, he kissed her forehead. "Sorry you woke up 'fore we got back. Figured you'd sleep 'til noon after yesterday."

"I didn't."

"Well, we're home now, pretty girl. Griff and the boys got it from here." He grinned, toying with a lock of her hair. "Dad took Grams to Jackson for the day, so we've got the house all to ourselves."

"Oh, yeah?"

And he waggled his brows. "Yeah."

After a meal that Kellan barely spoke a word through, they went upstairs. Tanner went straight for the shower. His brother sat down in a wide wingback chair by the window, like a king taking his throne.

Grabbing her by the hand, he jerked her toward him. "Ride me."

"What?"

He smirked, and pushing his jeans down his legs, Kellan started fisting his cock. "Take those off. And ride me, just like I taught ya."

His molten-chocolate eyes never leaving hers, Arien bit her lip, and sliding her shorts down her thighs, she did as he said.

"I'm gonna watch you get yourself off." He pulled her down onto his knee. "Now slide that pussy back and forth on me."

Kellan dug his fingers into her ass. Pulling her forward and pushing her back, he maneuvered her on his leg. With her pussy splayed open on his skin, her clit pressed up against the bone. Arien grabbed onto his shoulders for leverage. Fuck, it felt so good. Her head tipping back, she took over the movement on her own. And he let go.

She watched him watching her as he stroked his cock. Arien had half a mind to bend over and taste the precum that oozed from his tip. She started to, and snickering, Kellan nudged her away.

"That's it. Look at your pussy drippin' juice all over me," he huskily murmured, biting into her nipple. "You need my dick… need a fucking so bad, don't you?"

She did, but couldn't answer.

With a twist of her nipples, Kellan demanded one. "Don't you?"

"Please, Kel."

He tapped on her bottom with his fingers. "I'm taking that ass before you give it to Tanner." Kellan moved her up onto his belly. Sliding her pussy on his hard abs, Arien burrowed her face in his neck as he worked his finger into her. "Want to fuck it 'til you bleed."

She whimpered.

"You think I'm sick?"

"No," Arien squeaked. She shook her head, fingernails denting the skin of his broad shoulders.

"Why do I love hurtin' you?"

She stilled, and raising her head, Arien looked into dark, pain-filled eyes. "You do?"

"Yeah, I do."

With no other warning than that, Kellan impaled her and she screamed.

"*That's* what I was lookin' for."

The sound of her own heart beating whirred in her ears, the whole of her flesh pulsing thick, and heavy, and slow. What was happening to her? Surely, he'd split her in two and she was dying.

He moved then. Lifting his hips from the chair, he groaned, driving into her over and over and over.

All she could do was hold on for the ride.

At least it didn't hurt so much anymore, the throbbing fullness in her backside beginning to feel oddly pleasant.

Kellan worked himself into a sweat fucking her. Then yanking her head back by her hair, his teeth at her neck, he let out a growl. He pulled her forward, his lips claiming hers, and breathless, he kissed her. "I could never, ever hurt you as much as lovin' you hurts me."

What the...?

Tanner came out of the shower, a towel low around his hips.

Kellan eased her off his lap, and he stood, pulling up his jeans. He glanced at her, his lips parting as if he wanted to say something, then perhaps thinking better of it, closed them again. And he left.

▲

It was already getting dark when Matthew and the baby returned home from their trip to Jackson with Grams. Arien and her boys were watching a movie, nibbling on chips and roast beef sandwiches. Well, Kellan and Tanner were watching. She'd just been pretending to.

Something was going on with him, and it sure as hell wasn't a hangover. Even Tanner seemed to notice. She hadn't seen him in a funk like this in a long time...well, not since their brother was born.

Poor little guy was tuckered out.

Her stepfather was loaded down with bags in one arm and a sleeping baby in the other. Arien got up from the sofa to help him. "Here, I'll take Benjamin and put him to bed."

"It's okay, darlin', I got it," he said, letting the bags drop to the floor.

"No, I can—"

"Dad said he's got it. Sit down, Arien." Kellan tugged her back beside him and he patted her knee. "We're watchin' a movie here."

As soon as Matthew went up the stairs, Kellan turned his head her way. "You are not that baby's mama. Let the man be a father to his son. If you want a baby to take care of so bad, me and Tanner'll give you one."

"Asshole."

He snickered. "Yeah, but I'm your asshole now, ain't I?"

"Kellan…" Tanner started. Arien didn't stick around to hear what he had to say. She rose from the sofa, and turning on her heel, ran fast up the stairs.

Kellan made it so obvious—the something going on with him, was her.

The smell of fresh paint lingered. Curled up in a chair, she wracked her brain. They'd only been married a day, for fuck's sake. What could she have done to upset him?

She had put on Miss Lilly's diaphanous gown that she got felt up for *"to get the placement of the appliqués just right"*—didn't she? She walked down that aisle alone, everyone's eyes on her, shaking in her new white boots, without a clue what was coming.

It was like that movie on her birthday, *The Invitation*, except she was the offering.

"We are at our strongest when we are three."

Fuck their *unum onem inem*, or whatever it was, mumbo jumbo.

Got her hands sliced open for his ass. She rubbed her palms. That shit hurt.

Everything had been fine, though. In fact, it was magical and wonderful until…she got up to dance with Matthew and…

He was talking to Cassie.

God, maybe he didn't love her. Maybe he really wanted to be with Cassie, he just couldn't because of their stupid fucking rules. Kellan was tethered to Arien for life now, in every possible way. *Does he resent me for it?*

Her face in a throw pillow, she didn't even realize she was sobbing until she heard him walk into the room. Sniffling, she lifted her head. "Why?"

He just stood there.

"Why did you make me love you if you didn't really want me?"

"Is that what you think? 'Cause you got it all twisted, baby cakes." Raking his fingers back through his hair, Kellan let out a harsh breath. "I can't do this."

And he stormed out.

▲

In spring, when the snow melts and the grass begins to grow, the cows move up on the mountains for grazing. Then in the fall, they're taken back down to winter in the valley, where they're provided shelter and supplemented with hay. Wild animals will naturally do this all on their own, but the domestic stock on the ranch had to be rounded up and herded to go where they needed to be.

This time of year, with summer near its end, the cattle were dispersed over many square miles of mountain and forest. Often tucked away in remote woodland clearings, it could take days, sometimes weeks, of hard riding through trackless wilderness to find them all.

It takes a dozen men on horseback to move three thousand head of cattle.

Over the coming weeks, they'd be rounding up close to ten times that number.

Kellan hated to leave her. He would have hated it any time,

but especially now. Married only three days when he left, Arien was back home with Tanner and his dad while he was stuck out here chasing after cows.

Maybe it was for the best. Probably was. He wasn't in a good frame of mind to be around folks. Particularly his wife.

But then he remembered the look on her beautiful face. Her tear-stained cheeks. She was crying, as plaintively as when her mama died, and that was fucking with his head. It wasn't like Arien to turn on the waterworks as some girls were known to do. Kellan hurt her heart and he knew it. Even worse, he meant to.

What if he was wrong and Cassie was full of shit? Then Arien should never forgive him, because dammit, he wouldn't.

And if he was right, perhaps he only had himself to blame. He should've tried harder. Opened up to her sooner. He didn't possess flowery words like his brother. Kellan was who he was. Made no apologies for it, either. He showed her he loved her in other ways. At least he thought he did.

So yeah, it was best he was here, away from her, where he could clear his head and think. Figure out his shit.

"One more night." Wiping sweat off his brow, Griffin pulled up alongside him. "Can't wait to be back home in my bed."

Shut the hell up.

"You whinin' already, Archer?"

This was just the first roundup of many. They'd go home for a couple days, then ride out again. And again. And again. The process would be repeated until the count was right and all the animals had been found.

"Can't tell me you ain't dyin' to get back to your wife, too."

"Don't you worry 'bout me none." He lashed out, "Take care of *your* own damn wife."

"What the fuck's up your ass?" Griffin side-eyed him, then smirked. "And Shiloh ain't got no complaints. We're havin' a baby come spring. Just found out."

"I heard." *Congrats and all that shit.* "And what about Cassie?"

"Not sure what to do about her."

Now that wasn't the answer he was expecting. Brow raised, Kellan swiveled his neck, eyeballing the lead rider at his side. "The fuck, man. She's your wife. Don't you love her?"

"Course, I do, but she don't make it easy."

"What do you mean?" He never found it difficult to get into her jeans, but Kellan had a feeling that wasn't what he was talking about here.

"Cassie ain't a lovey-dovey kinda girl, you know? She can be downright coldhearted."

He wouldn't call her affectionate, no. But she wasn't coldhearted. Not in all his years of knowing her. Cassie had feelings. It just wasn't easy for her to show them.

Kinda like you, asshole.

"Shiloh and her ain't never been close the way most sisters are. I don't think they even like each other all that much. Some days, I worry they might kill each other. Everything's a competition between them two, and I'm in the middle. You have any idea how hard that is?"

His brows cinched together briefly before he shook his head. "Can't say that I do."

"Well, you're lucky. You and Tanner's always been thick as thieves, so Arien'll never have to put up with that bullshit."

Ouch.

Kellan and his brother were as close as brothers could be. Loved each other deeply. Always had. Always would. Yet, Griffin's words hit home.

"Ever since we found out about the baby, Cass won't even let me come near her. Guess that's my punishment for gettin' her little sister pregnant first."

"Does it matter?"

"Does to her, I reckon."

For a while, they rode without talking. The only sounds were the clops of horse hooves, cows snorting and grunting. Kellan turned to his friend. "I don't know shit, but before it gets worse, you need to talk to Cassie. Alone. Just the two of you."

His chuckle sardonic, Griffin huffed out a breath. "She won't."

"Then make her."

That night, Kellan lay awake in his bedroll, staring up at the stars. His miserable state was of his own making. Arien might not forgive him. But if he wanted any chance at all, he was going to have to take his own advice.

Looking none too pleased with him, Tanner was waiting to take the horses when they returned the following morning. "You're a real asshole, Kel."

Fair enough, he deserved it, but right now his only thought was to get to his wife. "Think I don't know that? Goin' to talk to her and don't come lookin' for us."

"Yeah, okay." He grabbed the horse's reins. "What the hell can you possibly say?"

"Gonna start with I'm sorry, 'cause I am. After that, I don't rightly know."

Nodding, Tanner clasped his shoulder. "Good luck to ya, brother."

"Where are you taking me?"

"You'll see."

Arien was in his truck. Backpack at her feet.

Kellan found her in the kitchen taking pictures of blueberry muffins. He walked right up to her, covered in dust, the stench of a three-day-ride all over him, and took the Nikon out of her hand. "I love you."

Then he kissed her.

And she let him.

He only told her to pack her camera, and to bring along some of them muffins, then he went upstairs to shower.

Her eyebrow arched, she peered over at him. Reaching for her hand, Kellan smirked and kissed it, before holding it on his thigh.

He turned into the Tetons.

"Oh, wow."

Arien took the camera out of her bag and let the bag drop to the ground. Kellan sat beneath a tree, just watching her do the thing she loved most. She peeked back at him. Sunbeams catching in her hair. Joy lighting up her face. This is all he ever wanted her to be. Happy.

He tipped his chin at the wide, pristine lake in front of them. "It's called Jenny Lake."

Tears filled her pretty green eyes at the mention of her mama's name.

"Photographers come from all over to take pictures here." Kellan pulled her to sit down beside him. "I guess 'cause of the mirror-like reflection of the Tetons on the water. The visitor center we passed was a photography studio back in the 1920s."

"Really?"

"Yeah. We can go see it, if you want."

She smiled up at him. "I'd like that."

"Thought you might." He put his arm around her, holding her to his side. "Next time, we can hike and explore a little. Hidden Falls and Inspiration Point's just a few miles from here. You can take lots of pretty pictures from there."

"Okay." Her head fell to his shoulder.

Dragging his fingers through the silky strands, Kellan kissed her hair. "I'm sorry."

"What happened?"

Slowly, he blew out a breath, because God, wasn't he a doofus? "I got it in my head you only stayed 'cause of Benjamin and Tanner. Not for me."

"Jesus, Kellan. Why would you ever think that?"

Chewing on the inside of his cheek, he shrugged noncommittally. "You don't love me the same as him, but that's okay—"

"Shut. Up." Straddling his lap, Arien flicked the hat off his head. "Just shut up. I'll have you know, I made the decision to stay *before* Benjie was even born. Tossed my award letter in the trash."

"But Dad gave it back to you."

"He did." Smirking, she palmed his cheek. "The deadline to accept had already come and gone, but your dad called UC and told them about Mom. They granted an extension and gave me the option to register for online classes. I took them up on the offer."

"We can pay your tuition, Arien. You don't need their money."

"I know, but see, *I* earned it."

His fingers gliding over her arms, he nodded.

"I have a vision of my own. My YouTube channel keeps growing and I started a website. I want to put a studio in the house and I'm thinking about putting all the recipes from my blog into a book."

I'll build you one.

Plans for her studio running through his head, Kellan grinned. He'd do anything to keep that smile on her face. "Gonna give that preppy chef dude a run for his money, huh?"

"Maybe." She giggled.

"I'm really proud of you, you know that?" His lips skimmed hers. "But I have one request, baby cakes."

"What's that?"

"Chocolate." He winked. "I'm into it."

Her fingers clasped behind his neck, Arien tossed her head back and laughed. Gazing into her pretty greens, Kellan loosened her braid, combing it apart with his fingers. Hands buried in the sunlit strands, he brought her lips to his, and he kissed her.

Even better. She kissed him back.

"You know, when I got here and found out about 'your ways'..." Arien threw her fingers up in air quotes. "...I thought you were all drinking the Kool-Aid."

"I remember." He grunted out a chuckle.

"Mumbo-jumbo talk. Sacred trinities. Triad unions." With a shake of her head, she snorted. "C'mon, that's crazy, right? How can anyone be in love with two people at the same time? Marry them. Course, I didn't know much about how loving someone works back then."

"And now you do?"

"I do," she answered. "It's not the most common thing, obviously—at least it isn't out there—but I know now, you absolutely can be in love with two people. Because I am." Arien took his face in her hands. "You scare the hell out of me and calm my soul at the same time. And maybe that's what love is—a total contradiction that somehow balances out."

Overcome, he tried to swallow. The muscle played in his throat.

"So, you're right, Kellan. I don't love you both the same. I can't. But then you and Tanner are two different people, aren't you? Each of you makes me feel special and loved in your own individual way."

And that's the way you love us back, ain't it?

He thought he got it now.

"You told me once, I needed you both. And I do. I love you, both of you, in equal measure."

"You are real smart." Bringing her face to his, Kellan sipped more kisses from her lips. "And I'm an asshole."

"Yeah, but you're my asshole."

Damn right, I am.

"I still think y'all are crazy, but I couldn't imagine my life without both of you in it."

He squeezed her tight. "Don't even try."

Twenty-One

Fall was almost worse than calving season in the spring.
She'd missed her cowboys.

But now that the cattle had been rounded up, sorted, and sent off to market, she had them back. And they were making her forget about all the nights she lay here alone in their big bed with only the dog to keep her company.

Arien closed her eyes. Warm lips kissed every part of her body. Her tummy. Earlobe. Inner arm. Wrist. Rough hands touched every inch of her skin. Two hard cocks, one on each side, the tips weeping, prodded into her thighs. She wanted them both inside her.

"Open up your pussy for me, pretty girl."

He didn't have to ask her twice. Drawing up her legs, she reached for her lips and spread herself wide. Tanner dove in with his tongue. He slurped on her pussy, then sucking on her clit, he exchanged his tongue for his fingers.

Watching, Kellan lay alongside her and stroked her hair. "Such a good listener, you are. Doin' what your big brother tells you to."

Wicked.

She opened herself even wider. Tanner slid another finger up inside her.

"We're gonna breed you, little sister." Kellan licked up her neck, dragging his teeth down the skin. "Fill you up with our cum."

That's all he had to say.

With an orgasm from his brother careening through her body, he kissed her.

"I love you, baby." Kellan breathed, smacking his lips to hers once more. "We love you. Now I wanna see you take Tanner's big, fat dick in your sweet, little pussy. Then when you're ready, I wanna see you take more."

Oh, fuck.

Tanner slid under her. Facing Arien away from him, his hands on her hips, he guided her down onto his thick cock.

"Look at that." Kellan got between their legs, placing her feet up on his brother's thighs. "So fucking beautiful."

Hands squeezed her breasts from below. Tanner pinched her nipples. He fucked her while his brother watched, jerking himself in front of her.

He reached out, his thumb rubbing over her clit. Up and down. Up and down. Then he leaned over and kissed her there.

Kellan licked and suckled at her clit, his brother inside her. Limbs shaking, Arien fell back against Tanner's chest.

"Want us both, wife?"

"Oh, God." She could barely speak. "Yes."

And four of his fingers, along with Tanner's cock, were wedged inside her gushing pussy.

"Fuckkkk."

"C'mon, baby cakes, I wanna see this sweetness dripping off my wrist."

"God," Arien repeated the word again and again, her voice climbing an octave with each delicious stroke.

Just when she thought she was going to explode, Kellan pulled his hand away. Licking her wetness from his fingers, he tipped his chin at his brother and lay down beside her.

Gently, Tanner positioned her, straddling her trembling legs over Kellan's middle. Rubbing her shoulders, he leaned over from behind, kissing the skin beneath her ear. "You got this, pretty girl. I love you."

His palms rubbing her nipples, Kellan proclaimed the same, then kissing her, he pushed himself inside. Fingers squeezing the breath from her throat, he fucked her, saying the words, "I love you," over and over.

Tanner gripped her bottom, his wet tip poking at her cheek, his thumb circling the hole. That's not the entrance he took, though. He went lower, stuffing his dick inside with Kellan's.

Sweet fuck.

So full. If felt so strange, yet so incredibly wonderful, filled up with the two men she loved.

Kellan put her arm behind her back. Tanner held it, and gripping her hip with the other, he and his brother found their rhythm.

It was glorious.

Savannah Mason, wherever you are, I hope you're living your best life.

Because fuck that world outside the gate. No one should have to hide in the girls' bathroom or walk down the hall in shame. Loving them both was right and beautiful and perfect.

A heart can't lie.

This would never feel wrong.

Arien was where she'd always ache to be.

Between the cowboys who loved her.

Arien sat Benjamin in his swing. Waving his little fists, he grinned a gummy smile, swaying back and forth, while she and Grams unpacked the groceries for Thanksgiving dinner. Just shy of six months old, they needed to keep him occupied somehow to complete the task. And if they were really lucky, he might fall asleep in it and nap.

The island, and every square inch of counter space, was taken up by bags and boxes that needed sorting. "All this for one meal."

"Looks like we brought the whole store home." Grams chuckled, pulling her shoulder-length curls through a hair tie. A few strands escaped it, framing her flawless face.

"You ain't kidding." Arien blew out a breath, delving through a bag of produce. "I don't remember there being so much last year."

"Well, you did add some things to the menu, dear."

"I did, didn't I?" Shaking her head, she flicked her gaze over to Grams. "Why'd I do that?"

"You tell me." Smirking, she sorted through the bag of foodstuffs. "Just a year ago I was teaching you how to bake a pie, and look at you now."

"Ice water. The trick to a perfect crust."

"That's right." Grams subtly nodded, a smile coming onto her face.

"Seems like only yesterday, and like forever ago."

"Time is funny that way." Her smile turning wistful, she tucked a lock of butter-blonde hair behind her ear. "Just yesterday Tanner was born, then I blinked, and he's turning twenty-three."

"Day after tomorrow." At least his birthday cake didn't have to compete with pumpkin pie this year. Arien got everything she needed to make him his favorite—white chocolate with pistachios.

"I swear, the older you get, the faster time flies." Turning around, Grams leaned back against the black granite counter and sighed. "We seem to mark its passage by the milestones of those who come after us. One of these days you'll understand my meaning."

"I think maybe I already do." Unbidden tears filling her eyes, Arien's gaze went to the baby, fast asleep in his swing. "Benjamin's this reminder of how long my mom's been gone. *Almost six months already*. I hate that in my mind, his birth will always be tied to her passing."

"As it must be for Matthew, too. I remember how he would get sad when the boys' birthdays came around. Same goes for John Jacoby, I imagine." Grams drew her in for a hug. "I'm not saying you're ever going to forget, because you won't, but life has a way of giving us our joy back. You're always going to miss her, Arien, but as time passes it won't hurt as much, and one day you'll see Benjamin as a reminder she's still here with you."

Maybe.

She wanted to believe that, see it that way. But right now the wound was too new, the pain too fresh, to imagine when that day might come. She had dreams of her mom that were so vivid and real, she'd wake up forgetting she was gone. Arien would go down to the kitchen, expecting to see her sitting there with her coffee, and upon finding it empty, she'd remember.

Grams began emptying another bag. Kellan's body wash. Her shampoo…

Oh, shit.

Shit, shit, shit.

…a pregnancy test.

"I think this is yours, dear." Like she was passing her a tube of toothpaste, Grams handed her the box.

She'd meant to slip it into her purse. "Yeah, thanks."

"How late are you?"

Arien chewed on her cuticle. "Ten days."

Grams embraced her once more. Holding Arien's head on

her shoulder, she smoothed the hair down her back. "See, what did I tell you? Life has a way."

Two pink lines.

Not that she was surprised. Her period came every month like clockwork. She'd never been late before. Not once.

Arien brushed her teeth, misted her face with thermal spring water before slathering it with moisturizer, and exhaled. She knew Kellan and Tanner would be thrilled about the baby, and she was too, but she wasn't sure how to tell them. Because it should be a special moment, right? Should she casually blurt it out? *Can I have the popcorn? Oh, by the way, I'm pregnant.* Leave the stick on the table and let them make the discovery themselves? *Ewww, but I peed on it.*

"What's takin' you so long in there?" Kellan asked from the other side of the door. "C'mon, baby cakes, the movie's all queued up."

"Keep your britches on." They were going to watch *National Lampoon's Christmas Vacation.* It was Tanner's favorite holiday movie. "I'll be out in a minute."

"We got snacks." He poked his head through the door and winked. "And just so you know, these britches are comin' off."

She didn't doubt it for a second.

Kicked back on the sofa, munching on Chex Mix, her husbands waited for her, the opening credits of the movie frozen on the big TV screen. Taking her place between them, they settled in closer, cuddling up to her on either side. Tanner reached for the remote.

"Wait. I want to take a selfie of us first." Arien held up her phone. Lining up the shot, they scrunched in even closer. "I'm pregnant."

And she tapped the shutter button.

Kellan smirked. "We know."

"But *I* didn't even know until five minutes ago." *Not for certain anyway.*

"That box of tampons under the sink's been sittin' there unopened since October." Tanner proudly grinned. "We've just been waitin' for you to tell us, pretty *mama*." And he kissed her. "I'm so happy. Love you."

"Me too, baby cakes," Kellan softly murmured in her ear, kissing along her neck on the other side. "You happy?"

"Course, I am." Worrying her lip, Arien's gaze flicked from one brother to the other. "Just don't want either of you to go all Cassie on me."

"What do you mean?" Sitting back against the sofa, Kellan's head cocked.

"Shiloh told me she's not handling it well at all—her being pregnant." Lowering her head, Arien shrugged. "And only one of you can be the father—"

"Stop right there." Flecks of green in melted chocolate seemed to vanish.

Tanner turned her face toward his. "Any child that comes from you ain't his or mine. It's ours. And that's all there is to that."

"He's a Brooks." Squeezing her knee, Kellan nodded.

His brother socked him in the arm. "*She's* a Brooks."

"Oh, boy," she muttered, glancing up at the ceiling.

"*Girl.*"

Shaking her head, Arien laughed. Because if the gender of their baby was the only thing those two were going to compete over, then God, how lucky was she? *Pretty darn lucky.* There'd been a few bumps in the road at first, and surely more would come, but all in all, forging ahead with her cowboys, life was damn near close to perfect.

With her husbands' hands rubbing her tummy, Arien reached for the remote and smiled.

Say hello to your daddies, lovebug. You don't know it yet, but you're the luckiest one of all.

Matthew tucked the baby in beside her and kissed her on the cheek. Without the glow of moonlight coming in through the windows, the bedroom was cloaked in darkness. Cradling Benjamin's head in his large hand, he looked down at his son and whispered, "Daddy'll be home 'fore you know it. Be a good boy for your sister, 'kay?"

Carefully removing his hand from beneath his son's head, he kissed him, then swept his fingers through Arien's hair. "You feelin' okay, sweetheart?"

"Yeah, I'm good." She reached up and palmed her stepfather's cheek.

Except for needing a little nap now and then, she was fine. Morning sickness didn't plague her like it had her mom. She hadn't tossed her cookies once, or even felt the least bit queasy.

"Thanks for bein' here for me. And him." Squeezing her shoulder, he kissed her again. "I'll be back in time for supper tomorrow. Anything you want me to bring back for you?"

He was flying out to Denver. Brookside business.

"No, thanks." Arien smiled. "Got everything I want right here."

"The boys got an early start. Should be comin' in 'fore too long. Go back to sleep now. Love you."

"I love you, too."

Then he was gone.

With the baby nestled beside her in the middle of the big bed, Arien closed her eyes. She couldn't have been asleep that long. It seemed as though only five minutes passed, when they opened again.

Breaking the silent stillness in the cavernous house, she could hear the echo of footsteps creeping downstairs. Her body prickling, Arien froze for the briefest moment, before she was able to take a breath.

The boys are home.

Something still felt off. The clatter ascending the stairs unfamiliar, she ventured out from beneath the covers and tiptoed down the hall. Arien stopped just before she came to the landing, stepping back into the recess of a doorway. Flushing cold, clammy sweat erupted on her skin. As determined as she was not to make a sound, she was certain the pounding in her chest could be heard throughout the house.

He didn't see her.

But she saw him.

Dressed in black, his face hidden under a hood, the man turned right at the top of the staircase. Heading straight for the wing where Matthew and Benjamin's rooms were, he seemed to know where he was going. He opened the baby's door and stepped inside.

Arien didn't waste another precious second.

Adrenalin pulsing through her, she ran back down the hall and locked her bedroom door. That alone wouldn't be enough to keep someone out if they wanted in. She didn't even bother dressing. Wrapping him in blanket, Arien scooped her brother from the bed, swiped the keys to Tanner's truck off the dresser, and slipped out through the glass door to the deck.

She didn't feel the snow beneath her bare feet.

She didn't think. Only one word repeated in her head.

Run.

Twenty-Two

Tanner stood at the expanse of glass, surveying the wintry night sky. Obscured by a veil-like layer of clouds, moonlight passed through crystals of ice, forming a halo around the shrouded orb. Yeah, something was coming. He could feel it.

His wife, none the worse for wear, bustled about the kitchen with the womenfolk, chattering amongst themselves. Couldn't tell by looking at her she'd come through such a harrowing ordeal not forty-eight hours ago. Strength, and an unshakable spirit, wrapped in a soft outer layer, is what she was. He saw it in her from the start, and it's what he loved about her the most.

A frosty burst of air swept into the room, the front door opening behind him. He didn't bother turning around. It had to be Gantry. Everyone else was here.

"Tanner." Kellan appeared at his side. "C'mon, brother. We're gonna talk private while Arien's occupied. No use upsettin' her none."

A meeting of the minds. Their families, connected since way back, had always been close. They took a seat, joining their father, Victor, and his sons, in front of the fire. The elder Gantry rested his elbows on his knees, fingers steepled beneath his chin. After an audible exchange of air, he spoke, "Someone was here all right. Left behind some footprints in the snow. Followed 'em to the stream and they disappeared."

"Course, they did." His brow knitting in thought, Matthew cocked his head. "He waded through icy water all the way back to town?"

"Looks like it."

Judging by the twist of his lips, Kellan didn't seem to agree. "That's an awful long way. Fucker would freeze to death first."

"Good," Tanner exclaimed, slapping his thigh. "Hope he did."

"More'n likely he was only in the stream long enough to keep us off his trail. Must've had a sled or a horse stashed in the woods somewhere."

"Good thinkin', Jake."

Clasping his hands behind his head, Kellan sat back with a smirk. "Well, if he went into the water, then he came out of it somewhere, too."

Billy tapped his brother's shoulder. "We can take the horses out in the morning. Ride the stream. See if the trail picks back up."

"Yeah, we should." Jake nodded.

A bunch of cowboys playin' detective. Sure, why not?

"The storm." Tanner snapped his fingers. "Tell 'em, Kel."

"Tell 'em what?"

"The night of the storm, remember?"

"Damn." His eyes widened. "It wasn't her imagination."

"Don't think so."

Matthew leaned in. "What you talkin' 'bout, son?"

It was Kellan who answered, "Back in the spring, we heard Arien scream and went runnin' to her room. Said she saw someone."

"He wore a hood. She couldn't see his face," Tanner added.

"Sonofabitch. And you didn't think to tell me?"

"I went out and looked around. Didn't see no one." Shaking his head, Kellan twisted the wedding band on his finger. "It was rainin' somethin' fierce that night. Thunder and lightnin'. Figured the storm just spooked her."

We figured wrong, brother.

"Hasn't he taken enough from me? He wants my boy now?" Gritting his teeth, Matthew plowed his fingers through his hair. "And my girl?"

Huh?

"He?" Kellan looked as confused as he was.

"Your grandfather." Dad's fist slammed down on the coffee table. "John Jacoby."

What in the ever-loving hell? Christ, if that wasn't the most preposterous thing Tanner had ever heard. "Pops wouldn't hurt anyone, 'specially a baby."

"No?" Matthew gripped the arm of the sofa. "I know different."

"Matt." Victor pulled on Matthew's shoulder.

"What? It's no secret the bastard blames me for what happened to Heather and Amanda. Weak heart, my ass. I suspected somethin' then. Couldn't prove it, though." Lip curling, he let out a harsh breath. "Still can't. But after Jennifer…now I'm certain."

Jesus Christ, are you sayin'…?

"No, Dad."

"I'm sorry, Tanner." Reaching over Kellan, he squeezed his knee. "I know you love him, but I believe it to be true. Wouldn't be sayin' so if I didn't."

"But the autopsy had nothin', so how?" Kellan wondered out loud, rubbing the two-day growth of scruff on his face.

"Dunno."

"And why?" Tanner didn't believe it. What could possibly

motivate a man to end the lives of three women and leave their newborns without a mother? Two of them his own daughters. It was inconceivable. And unless he missed the plot, isn't that what his father was alleging here?

"Not sure of that either." He looked away, staring off at nothing. "To hurt me, I reckon."

"I'm inclined to agree with you." With a subtle shake of his head, Victor Gantry sighed. "Three seemingly healthy women dead shortly after birthin' your babies. That's not just an unfortunate coincidence."

"Damn right it ain't." His fist shook in the air. "It's a curse. And that curse has a name. John Jacoby."

"But Dad, Pops was at Griff's wedding when...you know... when it happened." *See? You're wrong.*

"You sure about that, son?"

Did he see him that night? He must've, but Tanner couldn't swear to it. "Pretty sure."

"Should be easy enough to check, Matt." Victor squeezed his shoulder. "We'll talk to Archer. See if anyone else was missing from the weddin' while we're at it."

"I saw him." Arien sat down next to him on the arm of the sofa. How long had she been standing there? Tanner brought her hand to his lips and kissed it. "At the cemetery. He didn't come right out and say it, but what he inferred was quite clear."

"You never mentioned it." His features softening, Matthew gazed at her.

"Didn't believe him. Wrote it off as the ramblings of a grieving man."

"My beautiful Arien." Matthew went over to her, and in a tender embrace, smoothed the hair down her back. "Daddy's so sorry, baby."

"There are no coincidences. You told me that, remember?" She pulled away and reached for his hand. "C'mon, food's ready."

Tanner watched his brother shovel mashed potatoes in his

mouth like their dad hadn't just announced he suspected their grandfather of being a murderer. While everything looked really good, and he was sure it was, Tanner wasn't hungry. He had way too much on his mind.

The mothers he only knew through stories and photographs. Jennifer. The more he thought about it, the more he had to agree, death didn't befall them by accident. There were too many similarities to chalk it up to happenstance.

Three wives.

Three deaths.

Three sons.

Dad had to be swallowed up by his own guilt and grief to think John had anything to do with it. Pops might be eccentric, but he was no killer. Though it was becoming apparent, someone in Brookside was.

When I find out who you are, motherfucker, I'm gonna end you with my own two hands.

Tanner glanced to his wife, bouncing Benjamin on her lap as she ate her dinner. Bile rose to his throat just thinking of what could have happened to them if she hadn't gotten out of the house. How had Matthew survived it, not once, but three times? Might as well just put him in the ground with her. Arien was everything in the world to him, and he couldn't imagine a life without her in it.

Victor Gantry and Aunt Kim were sleuthing across the table between forkfuls of Arien's braised short ribs. With the go-ahead from Jake, Emily was on her phone messaging Shiloh to ascertain if John Jacoby had an alibi. All of them bound and determined to find evidence to convict the man. As if.

This ain't no episode of CSI.

"You okay?" Arien's fingers trailed up and down his arm. "You've barely touched your supper."

"Yeah, pretty girl." Breathing in chypre from her hair, Tanner kissed her temple. "I'll eat later. Gotta go check on Airdrie. Promise I won't be too long."

He couldn't sit here, listening to the nonsense for another minute.

The mare was due to foal soon. She'd been pacing some this afternoon and her teats were waxing up.

Airdrie came over to him the moment he approached her stall. She lowered her head in greeting, and Tanner rubbed her muzzle. "How you feelin', Mama?"

The horse whinnied softly, looking for more rubs.

"Not tonight, huh?" He patted her, giving her a handful of oats.

Airdrie's ears pointed forward, a signal to him they were no longer alone.

"I know that was difficult to hear, Tanner, but we're all in this together, okay?" Jake's hands pressed down on his shoulders. "Grams, Kim, Emily, my dad, and yours. All of us. Whether it turns out to be Jacoby or not, we're gonna figure it out. But until we do, you need to keep Arien and Benjamin close."

"Day and night, one of us will always be with 'em."

Turning around, Tanner gave Jake's arm a squeeze. That was a given. He and Kellan had already talked about it. Their wife and baby brother were not going to be left alone, in the house, or anywhere else for that matter.

"Good, and you know we'll help carry the load here."

That he did. "Appreciate it."

Later, after everyone had gone home and he'd managed to eat some dinner, Tanner stretched out on the sofa with his brother. His mind was still reeling, and surely Kellan's was too. They sat in contemplative silence, not even the TV on, while Dad took Benjamin upstairs to bed.

Carrying a plate of cookies she'd baked for Christmas, Arien set it on the table and got herself comfy in between them. He loved how she did that. Never choosing to sit beside one over the other, she always kept them both close to her. The three of them together. The way they were supposed to be.

"Baked these just this morning. Chocolate cheesecake." She winked, feeding each of them a cookie. "Whatcha think?"

This girl. God, how he loved her. Only she would think to bake cookies in the middle of all this crazy shit.

"Mmm-mmm." His mouth full of cookie, Kellan kissed her. "You know how much I love me some chocolate."

Tanner glanced up at his father trudging back down the stairs. And it seemed that, all of a sudden, he looked a hundred years old. Shoulders hunched. Eyes red and glassy. Like the weight of the past twenty-three years had finally caught up to him. Maybe it had.

"I'm going to keep you and Benjamin safe, Arien. I promise." Getting on his knees in front of her, Matthew reached up to tenderly touch her hair. "So beautiful, just like your mama."

"You must miss her so much." She palmed his cheek.

He nodded. Tears ran down his face. Tanner looked at his brother. Never in his life had he seen his father, the manliest of men, weep. Wrapping his arms around Arien's middle, Matthew kissed her belly.

Arien peered over at Tanner, and then Kellan, a question on her face.

He and his brother traded a look, and nodded.

She held their dad's face in her hands, and wiping away the tears, she gently whispered, "I'll always take care of you, Daddy."

Then softly, she kissed his lips.

Twenty-Three

A rien tucked the frame in a box on a nest of gold tissue paper. Pleased with herself, she carefully wrapped it, tied it with ribbon, and placed it under the tree. "Last one and done."

A thumb in his mouth, his butt in the air, Benjamin slept on a blanket beside her. Grams prattled from the kitchen, prepping the prime rib for tomorrow's dinner, to her son who wasn't answering. Matthew was passed out, snoring as *White Christmas* played on the TV.

She raised her gaze to the windows, the landscape outside blanketed in fresh, powdery snow. *Dreams come true here, Bing.*

Kellan came in through the side door. Barely shaking off his boots, he walked into the living room. "Tanner sent me to get ya. Go put your coat on. Hurry up now."

"Why?"

"It's time."

So as not to disturb her, they watched from a perch in the far corner of the large foaling stall. Tanner had his kit at the ready, in case she needed assistance, but Airdrie was doing fine all on her own. She'd lie down on the deep bed of fresh, clean straw, only to get up again. Up and down. Up and down. Arien was getting anxious for her. But once the mare's water broke, she stretched out on her side and stayed there, making herself as comfortable as she could.

A foot appeared first, then another, followed by a nose. Airdrie pushed her baby out, Tanner easing himself into the stall. He ruptured the membrane covering the foal and quietly backed away, rejoining Arien and Kellan on their perch. Looking over at them, he grinned. "It's a fine filly."

"Well, there you go. You got yourself a girl." Kellan smirked.

"Gunner got himself a girl." He elbowed his brother in the ribs, then kissing Arien's cheek, he rubbed her tummy. "But we're gonna have one too."

"Sorry, bro. I keep tellin' ya, it's a boy." Kissing her other cheek, he murmured against her skin, "I saw it."

"Well, hate to disappoint ya, but I saw a girl."

She giggled. "What are you going to name her?"

"Noëlle."

"Perfect."

Tanner kissed her. "Merry Christmas."

Arien looked on in awe as Airdrie licked her foal clean. She recalled that afternoon at the paddock fence with Kellan, when they'd witnessed the creation of this beautiful creature, and now here she was to see the miracle of its birth. How magical was that?

"C'mon, it's late, and he's going to be here all night. Let's get you to bed."

Noëlle made her first attempt to stand up on her wobbly legs. In his element, Arien and Kellan left Tanner to tend to Airdrie and her baby.

"Wake up, pretty girl," Tanner crooned, dragging his fingers through her hair. "Merry Christmas."

"Shhh, it's early yet."

Arien didn't have to crack an eye open to know it was still pitch dark. Was he just coming home? Had he slept at all?

"I know." His head dipped to her breast, sucking a nipple into his mouth. "But it's gonna take a *long* while to wake you the way you like me to, the way I only dreamed of last year. Nothin' I love doin' more than lovin' on my beautiful wife."

God, this man.

"Even whispering to the horses?"

"Even that." Slipping his tongue inside her mouth, he kissed her. "But after this baby comes outta you, I'm gonna fuck you ridin' on Tux's back."

She felt that. Right where he wanted her to.

"Love these pretty titties." Her nipples in his fingers, Tanner rubbed his scratchy cheek against the pillowy flesh.

She smiled in the dark. Holding him to her, her fingers threaded in his damp hair. "Oh, yeah?"

"Yeah." Rolling Arien onto her side, he pulled her in close. "Love every little bit of you."

His lips touched hers. Kissing her, Tanner's hand swept down her bare skin, and over her hip, parting her thighs. She opened. Freely. Willingly. Gladly. Wanting him. She'd always want him.

"Love how your clit swells when I touch you," he murmured. His fingertips skimmed the nub of flesh. "Love suckin' on it. The way you taste..." With a groan, Tanner pushed two fingers inside her. "Love seein' your pussy stretch open for my brother, skin all shiny and tight. And then somehow, you make room for me too." Stroking her walls, he worked her into a frenzied state of desire. "Damn, girl, I don't wanna hurt you, and I know it's gotta, but I love fuckin' you that way."

"You can't hurt me, baby." She pulled on his hair. "Don't you know there's nothing I love more than having both of you together inside me?"

"Yeah?"

"That's us, my sweet cowboy, and I love us. I love how we fuck."

And she did. Every precious, twisted second of it. But then given the chance, what woman wouldn't? Two men to love and adore her. Two men to worship her body in ways one man alone never could.

Gnawing on her neck, Tanner stuffed another finger inside. He knew what she needed, and she knew what he wanted.

"Go on, baby. Give it to me. Please, I want your hand in my pussy, all the way to the wrist."

"Goddamn, we're sick fucks, ain't we?" He kissed her, reaching for a bottle on the nightstand. "You sure?"

Arien pulled her legs back. "Maybe we are, but I love that about us, too."

"Relax, my pretty girl." Generously bathing her pussy in lube, it coated his hand and fingers. "Breathe."

She gave him complete control of her body, the ultimate submission. Tanner worked his hand into her gently and slow. With that sultry celadon gaze trained on her, three fingers became four. It was in this moment, before his hand became a fist, when eyes spoke without words and her body had a language all its own. At her most vulnerable, Arien could just let go, and succumb to the intrusive, heavenly burn.

"Is this okay?" Those magic words that made her even hotter.

"Keep going. Please." Exhaling, she nodded. "Are you all the way in?"

"Almost, baby. So tight." Fervently rubbing her clit, he kissed her. Warm fluid spurting from her body, he slipped all the way inside, limbs shaking, muscles and flesh quivering in response.

"Does this hurt?"

Yes, it hurts, and it's wondrous. Please.

"Please, do it harder."

Nothing else existed. Completely connected to her body, mind, and emotions. To her sense of trust and love for this man. The combination was utterly euphoric. So aroused, the feeling, and their connection to each other, was spiritual.

"Open your eyes, little sister. Look at me."

Arien didn't realize she'd closed them. "Fuck, I love when you say that."

"I know," he said with a smirk, and kissed her. "You love me, baby?"

Such a feeble word, when the feelings she had for him and his brother were all-consuming, but there wasn't one that meant more.

"So much."

"I love you."

And she orgasmed, the force of it stealing her ability to emit sound, her muscles contracting and fixing on his wonderfully stimulating hand inside her.

"How's it feel?"

Bliss. Indescribable bliss.

Maybe she was slightly masochistic. But then her cowboys were a little bit sadistic, so together they were perfect. It might seem straight-up pornish but they'd taught her to love that feeling of fullness. She craved them and they knew it.

"Oh, God…" Arien held onto his tatted wrist, keeping him there inside her. "…don't stop."

She'd always crave them.

"I won't."

Not ever.

He was trying to be in the moment.

It was Christmas, for fuck's sake, the first one he'd celebrate with Arien as his wife, and the first ever for his baby brother. Not that Benjamin would remember it or anything, but still.

Checking his phone every five minutes, Kellan's mind was on

other things. So far they'd come up with nothing. No tracks going into the woods. Griffin recalled seeing Pops sitting with a slice of Maizie's cake at his wedding. Shiloh confirmed he'd signed the guestbook. Much to Tanner's relief, and his too, truth be told.

But Jake called him yesterday. Victor thought he might be on to something. So while they all sat on the floor in their matching plaid pajamas—hey, at least she'd foregone the reindeer—opening presents, Kellan anxiously waited for word.

Benjamin sat on his father's lap, big blue eyes transfixed on shiny red wrapping paper, trying to get his little fist in his mouth. Arien laid her head on his shoulder, camera in her hands, smiling as she watched Tanner rip it off for him. *Next year, baby cakes.* They'd be here in front of the tree with a child of their own.

He went to get up to start picking up the mess. She stopped him. "Sit. There's one more."

Arien crawled through discarded ribbon and tattered wrappings to the tree. Glancing over to his brother, he shrugged. Poor guy had to be beat, up all night seeing to Airdrie and her foal. They'd passed each other in the dark. He was leaving and Tanner was just getting home.

"This one's for both of you." She put a gold box on the floor between them.

"Don't just sit there starin' at it," Matthew prompted them. "Open it."

Kellan untied the ribbon. Tanner tore away the paper. They removed the lid.

"What's this?" Lifting the frame from a nest of gold tissue, Kellan's eyes sought hers.

Biting her lip, she smiled. "An ultrasound picture."

"I coulda told ya that, Kel." His brother sniggered, then paused. "Baby A and Baby B?"

"Twins." And she grinned. "So maybe you're both right."

Holyyy shit.

They were. He already knew it.

Kellan reached for her, and pulling Arien onto his lap, Tanner's arms around them both, he kissed her. "Two?"

She nodded.

"We shoulda been there with you." Pressing her against him, his brother kissed her hair.

"Sorry, I just went in for bloodwork," she said with a smack to Tanner's lips. "I didn't know Doc was gonna do that. Swore him to secrecy. You can come with me next time."

"I thought you were gonna go to the clinic in Jackson."

"Changed my mind." Getting off his lap, Arien nestled in between them. "I want to have the babies here at home if I can, that way you and Kellan can both stay with me."

Something warm and wet snaked its way down his face. Hooking his arm around her neck, Kellan swiped at it.

"Three little ones runnin' around the house." Matthew chuckled, wiping drool from Benjamin's chin.

Omne trium perfectum.

"Everything that comes in threes is perfect, right, Dad?"

He nodded, and gazing down at his infant son, the muscle played in his throat. "And once again, we've been favored."

You ain't kiddin'.

It wasn't until many hours later, long after their dinner of prime rib had been eaten, that Kellan stopped glancing at his phone.

Jake appeared at the door. "Can you meet us over in town in an hour?"

He glanced behind him. Tanner slept, a piece of eggnog cake still in his hand. "Yeah."

"Good." He tipped his chin, squeezing his shoulder. "I'll let him know."

"What'd he find out?"

"Didn't say."

Didn't or wouldn't?

"I'm on my way to Emily's. Takin' her home. Just be at his office at ten."

"Yeah, okay." Kellan waved to his cousin sitting outside in Jake's truck. "I'll be there."

And rubbing at the back of his neck, he quietly closed the door.

Twenty-Four

t was going on three in the morning when he slipped into bed beside her. Kellan held her from behind, fingers tracing circles over the flesh where new life grew. He put all his other feelings aside. They were the ones who mattered the most to him. His brother, their babies, and his wife.

Arien rolled over, sleepy hazel eyes gazing up at him. "Where've you been?"

"Helpin' Jake out. That's all." Sweeping the hair back from her face, Kellan held his lips to her forehead. He didn't want to tell her yet. And anyway, she was safe. "Go on back to sleep."

"You're keeping something from me, aren't you?"

He nodded. "I can't talk about it right now, okay?"

"Okay."

"I just need to hold you."

Arien kissed his chest, her arms squeezing around his middle.

Closing his eyes, Kellan tickled his fingers along her spine.

Tomorrow.

He'd tell them all about it tomorrow. How Victor studied every photo taken at that wedding. How he combed through his mother's medical records searching for some kind of clue.

And he'd found one.

"Amanda was taking insulin during her last trimester to control her blood sugar…gestational diabetes."

Even after seeing the proof with his own two eyes, Kellan found it hard to believe.

"It's not entirely uncommon with pregnancy. Some women are unable to make enough insulin on their own to meet the demands of their changing bodies," Victor had explained in terms he could understand.

Amanda was nineteen when Kellan was born, and otherwise healthy. The condition would have resolved itself, and her blood sugar would have normalized, in the weeks following delivery.

Heather, her older sister and Tanner's mother, didn't have it. Neither did Jennifer.

"Look at the dates on the vials, son."

It wasn't a weak heart or diabetes that killed them. But an intentional overdose of human insulin did. Its onset rapid, the effects would have been felt in as little as two minutes. Confusion, fatigue, clammy skin, before losing consciousness, though they were likely injected while asleep. Eventually the heart just stops. The substance degrades, leaving the body just as quickly, not that anyone would have even thought to look for it post-mortem.

Three empty vials. Two more than twenty years old. One of them new. Each once contained a thousand units in ten small milliliters. Death can occur with as little as twenty, but in that quantity, it's certain.

I'm so fucking sorry, baby.

With the sound of Arien breathing against his throat, her heart beating against his skin, Kellan gave in to a fitful slumber.

⛰

They left Arien at home with Emily and Benjamin. She'd endured enough pain and there was no reason for her to witness this. Grams and Aunt Kim stayed behind to keep her busy, helping her style the YouTube set in the new studio he and Tanner put in for her in a spare room behind the kitchen.

New Year's Day. The Sunday after Christmas. Seven subdued faces gathered in the parlor of Victor's house. Not yet noon, his wife, who had to be in her forties but sure didn't look it, brought in a bottle of Macallan on a tray of rocks glasses. The voluptuous blonde had always reminded Kellan of a mature Pamela Anderson. She set down the tray, kissed her husband's cheek, and taking her brother by the hand, quietly left the room.

Jake metered out the whiskey in generous doses. The single malt warming his throat, with its notes of peppery clove as he swallowed, Kellan exhaled, and steeling himself for what was to come, poured himself another.

From his left, a hand clamped down on his shoulder. Archer. "Easy, bro. We got your back," his lead rider assured him.

Matthew paced.

Tanner, numb and in disbelief beside him, slowly sipped, rotating the glass in his fingers.

So it had to be him.

Kellan would be the one to confront his grandfather.

He still couldn't fathom it, how a man could murder his own flesh and blood. Pops never really cared about him or Tanner, did he? He couldn't have loved them. If he had, he wouldn't have left them without a mother.

Long, black hair pulled back in a queue, Victor stood before him. "Are you ready, son?"

"Yeah." Downing his shot, Kellan nodded.

It was a short walk through town from the Gantry home to his grandfather's place that sat alongside the stream. With the holiday, and the January wind bitter, there weren't many folks wandering about the square. And even though the sun was shining, it held no apricity for him.

Kellan stepped up on the porch, walking past the childhood ghosts of the countless times he and his brother had played here, and knocked at his grandfather's door. Licking his lips, he held the cold air in his lungs until the old man answered it.

"Well, well, happy New Year, my boy." His grandfather smiled at first, until he observed the others behind him. "What do we have here?"

"Hey, Pops." Kellan smirked, attempting to be his usual self. Acting job of his life. For now, he had to turn everything else off. He'd think about it all later. "We gotta talk to you. It's important."

Side-eyeing Matthew, he curtly nodded. "Can do. C'mon in, the heat's gettin' out."

None of them taking a seat, they assembled in the living room.

"Maizie, make some coffee, will ya? We got company."

"That isn't necessary, John." Victor stepped forward. "We won't be long."

"What's this all about?" His cold blue gaze settled on Kellan. "I'm guessin' you ain't here to ask about my trip."

Hope you had a real good time in Vegas, 'cause you won't be playin' poker again anytime soon.

"No, Pops." He lowered himself to sit on the arm of the sofa. "I'm sure you heard a man broke in at the ranch some weeks ago."

"Yeah, I recall Maizie mentioned it." He leaned back against a bookcase, and crossing his feet in front of him, lit a cigar. "Think the girl musta imagined it, though."

That so?

Pursing his lips with a nod, Kellan shrugged. "Well then, my *wife* must've imagined it twice."

"C'mon, boy. Use your damn noggin." Seemingly annoyed,

Jacoby waved a hand through the smoke. "This is Brookside we're livin' in, not Denver."

"We found a set of footprints leading to the stream," Victor added, casually moving toward the center of the room.

"So?"

"We were hopin' maybe you seen something, Pops. That's all."

Tanner was the one hoping. He'd idolized their grandfather his entire life. To know what John Jacoby had done, what he'd tried to do, had hit him the hardest of them all.

"Nope, ain't seen nothin' or no one." He set his cigar down in the ashtray. Crossing his arms over his chest, he tipped his chin. "Maybe it was your daddy here. Ever think of that?"

"Christ, that's absurd," Matthew objected.

"It ain't." Jacoby half turned in the man's direction, a twisted grin contorting his face. "Wouldn't put it past you to sneak back into your own damn house. Get your dick into the girl. Everyone knows you're weak for a young blonde with a tight cunt."

"Shut the fuck up." Moving fast, Kellan stood toe to toe with his grandfather.

"Well, he is, boy. You should know," he said with a wink. Then looking up at the ceiling, he chuckled. "Course, there was a rumor…" His gaze went to Victor and he smirked. "…ah, never mind."

"Enough with this bullshit." Kellan went to the bookshelf, retrieving the plastic bag containing the empty vials and syringes from its hiding place inside a box of photos. They'd discovered it while searching his house the other night. He tossed the bag onto the coffee table. "Why'd you do it?"

"Do what?" The smirk never left his face.

"Murder my mother."

"I did no such thing." His head slowly moved from side to side. "I could never hurt my sweet, darling girl. Your daddy's the one to blame."

"You lying bastard." If looks could kill, his grandfather would be dead, Matthew's expression murderous.

"Not lyin'. It's all his fault. See, he was partial to my Amanda. Always showerin' affection on her. Can't say I blame him for that. She was so easy to love." Thinking of his daughter, John tilted his head to one side, his wistful smile almost eerie. And then it was gone. "He didn't do right by her sister, though. Coulda tried harder."

"What are you sayin', man?" Holding onto Matthew's wrist, Victor took another step closer.

"He didn't love my Heather."

"I *did* love her."

"Had a funny way of showin' it." With a roll of his eyes, he picked up the cigar. "Givin' her younger sister a baby before her."

The fuck?

"What? Are you hearin' yourself, Pops?" Habit. Kellan hadn't meant to call him that. He no longer deserved the endearment.

Jacoby shrugged. "It didn't sit right with her, I reckon. Your daddy and everyone fussin' over Amanda. Leavin' her out."

"Heather wasn't left out of nothin'."

Tanner came to stand at Kellan's side. "What about me?"

"Didn't matter, boy." Their grandfather reached out to grasp his brother's shoulder, but Tanner backed away from his touch. "In her mind, your brother and her sister would always come first."

You fucking piece of shit. How dare you lay that on him?

Kellan shook his head in disgust, curling his arm around his brother.

"Amanda was still warm when she told me what she done." Not a hint of emotion. He could've been talking about the weather, or the projected value of cattle. "She gave me the vials and syringes. Told me she was sorry, begged me to never tell a soul, and I didn't. Not Maizie, or even my brother. I'm thinkin' she musta been from his seed, never could trust him. And I couldn't trust Heather no more, either. She left me no choice. Couldn't trust her not to hurt your brother or you."

"*You* killed my mother?"

"To protect you, boy."

Jesus. Fuck.

Hadn't they been trying to tell him that? Tanner had to come to the realization of it on his own, he supposed. They'd been wrong about one thing, though. Never would've thought it was Heather who killed her sister. This was so fucked up. Like that wouldn't weigh heavy on Tanner's heart.

"And Jennifer? Was that to protect me, too?"

"Nah." Cigar in his fingers, his hand flopped over, ash dropping to the floor. "That was to keep you here. Couldn't have you chasin' after some stupid chit all the way to Denver."

Tanner's green eyes widened. "You're mad."

"Knew with her mama gone, she'd never leave that baby behind. Did ya a favor." Grinning, he drew smoke into his lungs and exhaled. "Besides, your daddy was too happy fuckin' her, and he don't deserve the favor of a third son after what he done to my girls."

"I can't hear any more of this." Scrubbing his face, Tanner turned away.

"Get him out of here." Victor nodded to his sons. "I'll go talk to Maizie."

"You can't do this, boy!" Jacoby shouted in protest as Jake and Billy restrained him. "I'm your blood."

How the fuck dare you?

Kellan pointed to Dad. "*That* man is my blood. Tanner. Benjamin. Arien is in my blood and she's carryin' mine." Looking upon the man he once called his kin, Kellan balled his fists. "I'm a Brooks. You ain't shit to me no more."

"It's over, son." Matthew watched as they led Jacoby out the door. "Let the council deal with him now."

A curse had indeed been upon them.

And it had a name.

A name he would never speak of again.

Twenty-Five

Gazing at snow softly falling on the mountains, Arien rubbed her fingers over her tummy. Three months along now, it was no longer flat, but she didn't have a bump yet, either. More of a thickening, she supposed.

She chuckled to herself, remembering the day she got out of that U-Haul a little over a year ago. If anyone had told her then, this was the place she'd think of as home, she would have told them they were fucking crazy.

Actually, I did say that. A lot.

Funny, how she never thought of Denver anymore. Not like that. It was just a place. She had fond memories of it, but her heart wasn't there. This land had seeped into her skin, as much as her cowboys had stolen her heart and branded their names upon her soul. Everything and everyone she loved was here.

Turning from the window, Arien kicked back on the sofa with her iPad and began to write.

My blog turns one today, and I honestly can't believe it's been a whole year since I wrote that very first post. You can bet we'll be having some coconut macaroon panna cotta cake here at the ranch tonight to celebrate. Like all new beginnings, it brought a lot of excitement, and hope, and thrill, and a sense of adventure. Along the way, I've learned so many things, and I realized that I know nothing still.

When I started this little school project of mine, I thought I had a pretty good idea what I was getting myself into. I didn't. But then nothing could have prepared me for what was to come. This blog, the website, and YouTube channel are a labor of love, a constant source of inspiration and creative energy, that fuels my passion and feeds my soul. The food styling and photography, cooking and recipe creation, storytelling and editing—I am grateful for every single moment of it.

There's so much I still need to learn, and so much I still want to share with you. My blog is not a niche blog, but whatever you find here, you can be sure it's something really special, and unique, if not a little unconventional.

I couldn't reach my hundredth post by my blogiversary like I was planning to, and I didn't share as many photographs of this beautiful place I'm lucky enough to call home as I wanted, but I hope to rectify that. Between getting married, having twins on the way, and Sunday always at my feet—well, let me just say, ranch life can be pretty crazy sometimes…

Warm breath fanned her face. Soft lips skimmed her cheek. "Mornin', pretty girl."

"Hey, cowboy." Arien smiled up at Tanner leaning down over the sofa from behind her.

He kissed her lips, hopping over the back of the couch like the paddock fence to sit beside her. "Whatcha doin'?"

"My anniversary post." Snuggling into him, she laid her head on his shoulder. "Thought I'd work on it while I was waiting for you and Kellan. Where is he?"

"He's comin'."

"We don't wanna be late." Arien brushed her fingers along his jaw. "I'm never late."

"Well, you were once."

She lifted her head. "When? Name one time…"

"Back in November." Tanner bent over and kissed her tummy. "How's my babies?"

"Think you're cute, huh?"

"Well, you seem to think I am." Taking her face in his hands, he joined his mouth to hers and slipped his tongue inside.

Then a pair of strong hands settled on her shoulders, while lips caressed her nape. "She thinks I'm cuter, don't ya, baby cakes?"

"You're both pretty darn cute, I guess." Arien shrugged with a smirk.

"So, what do you wanna do after we see Victor, wifey? Anything special?"

He was doing another scan. Kellan and Tanner would get to see the babies today.

"Being we've got the house to ourselves." Her smile sultry, she palmed his cheek. "I thought we'd just grab a quick lunch and come home."

"Oh, yeah?" Kellan raised his brow, the pupils in his chocolate eyes dilating.

"Yeah."

"I love that plan." Tanner smacked a kiss to her lips.

"I love you."

"We love you too, baby cakes."

I know.

Her husbands raced up the stairs to get cleaned up.

And Arien picked up where she'd left off.

…And crazy can be a good thing. A wonderful, amazing, beautiful thing. I sure wouldn't trade it. If I've learned anything at all this

past year, it's that dreams, like plans, can change—my grams told me that, and she was right. So now I can pat myself on the back, because I know I did just fine.

Better than fine.

She'd never have to chase after that feeling again.

Kellan and Tanner were her heart, and with them, she was home.

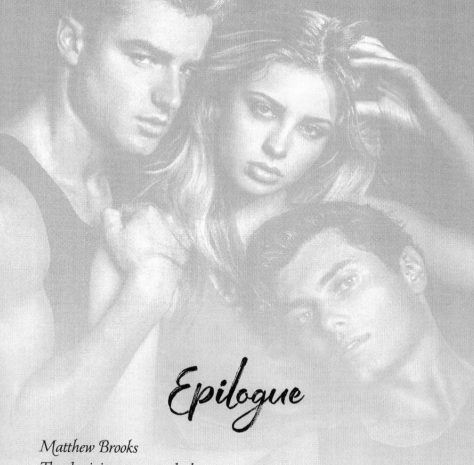

Epilogue

Matthew Brooks
Thanksgiving, ten months later...

He was a lucky man. Favored. Blessed. Call it whatever, and having buried three wives most folks wouldn't think so, but he was a lucky man indeed.

Generations before him had lived in this house, and many more would follow. From his seat on the overstuffed chair, Matthew looked around at all the people gathered here. His family. His legacy.

Benjamin played at his feet. Stacking building blocks of wood, his youngest stopped to glance up at him, gifting his daddy with the brightest smile. Except for Jennifer's big blue eyes, the boy was his spit. God, how he missed her.

Across the room, Tanner was cooing at four-month-old Harper. With her dark curls and light-green eyes, his granddaughter reminded Matthew of his son at that age, except she was a helluva lot prettier than him. Cayden napped on Kellan's chest, his golden hair, the color of freshly laid straw, sticking up like a porcupine. It was as soft as down, though. His blue eyes had already turned kind of hazel, more brown than any other color.

Three beautiful babies. See? Blessed.

And he had a feeling there were more babies coming.

Emily was a Gantry now, their families further entwined. They hadn't made an announcement yet, but knowing Billy and Jake, and how newlyweds are, he was expecting one before too long. She and his mother laughed with Arien and Shiloh in the kitchen, while his sister, carrying trays of food out, grinned from ear to ear. Familiar with that kind of smile on a woman, Matthew couldn't help but wonder who put it there.

Kim came over, and sitting on the arm of his chair, she kissed him on the cheek. "Hey, Matty."

"Whatcha so happy about?"

"It's Thanksgiving." She ruffled his hair. "Can't I be happy?"

"Not like that."

"Like what?"

His gaze flicked briefly to Victor Gantry. "Never mind." It wasn't for him to ask. Folks find their joy where they can, he supposed.

"Everything okay, big brother?"

"Look around you, little sister." Wrapping an arm about her waist, Matthew leaned into her. "We have so much to be thankful for. Everything's just fine."

His family was happy and healthy.

The ranch was thriving.

And the sonofabitch was dead.

Rot in hell, you worthless piece of horseshit.

Not that he believed in a heaven or a hell, but even if he did, hell was too good of a place for the bastard.

Good thing the law of the land don't apply in Brookside.

They deal with murderers their own way.

Everything that comes in threes is perfect.

And even after his wives, Matthew still believed it.

All he had to do was take a look at the big, beautiful, crazy, happy family they gave him. He had his three sons, his beautiful Arien, his grand-babies...

Just like he always saw it.

Yeah, he'd been favored, and he was grateful.

He was a lucky man.

Epilogue

John Jacoby

He'd known this day would inevitably come.

He didn't fear death.

His only regret was leaving Maizie a widow, not that she would miss him very much. But then she always did love his brother better. Still, she'd be alone now. He hoped his ungrateful grandsons checked in on her from time to time.

Those boys were all she had left.

They marched him to the top of the three-headed mountain, water tumbling from the rock. Looking down into the craggy gorge, he refused to say its name.

He turned around, and spreading his arms wide, he stepped off the edge.

Look, baby, I'm flying.

And when he plummeted into the icy water, she was there to catch him.

The End

Acknowledgments

I've literally just typed 'The End' to Arien, Kellan & Tanner's story. And I already miss them. But I have this strange feeling we could be heading back to the ranch one of these days. While their story may be over—for now anyway—I think some of the other folks in Brookside want theirs to be told. I reckon, we'll see.

The Pinterest board and the playlist for *The Third Son* on Spotify and YouTube are open. By the time you read this, I will be well into writing *Son of a Preacher Man*, Book 6 (Omg, can you believe it?) in the *Red Door* series—yes, Kodiak is coming next!!! I've included the sneak peek after these acknowledgments. Beyond that, I have another twisty standalone, *Whiteout*, coming in 2024, as well as Matt's story, *Rhythm Man*. But I'm getting ahead of myself, so…

I could never do this on my own, and I have so many people to thank for going on this crazy ride with me. More than that, I couldn't imagine (and I don't want to) taking it with anyone else. Family isn't always blood, some we choose for ourselves, and I'm so grateful these amazing humans are part of mine.

My loves—**Michael** and **Raj, Charlie, Christian, Josie Lynn** and **Josh, Zach** and **Sam, Jaide, Julian, Olivia**, and baby **Jocelyn**. I love you more than words. Thank you for putting up with your mama's crazy.

My beautiful editor extraordinaire, **Michelle Morgan**. Gosh, I'm so darn lucky she loves me. And I love her. After seven books together, we've got this synergy that could never be replicated. Thanks to her I have never feared the dreaded red pen. And editing is still my favorite part of the writing process. xoxo

Linda Russell and her wonderful team at **Foreword PR**. My Linda…I can't say enough. My evil twin who licks all the covers first!!! She loves cowboys—who knew? And cracking whips. She does that a lot. And I love you for it!!! xoxo

My cover queen of hearts, the beautiful and insanely talented **Michelle Lancaster**. She sent me 539 images from the shoot for this cover—can you imagine that? Like, how in the hell was I supposed to choose just *one* when they were all so perfect? She nails it each and every time—**Lochie Carey, Anthony Patamisi**, and **India Woollard** depict Kellan, Tanner & Arien to a T!!! Aren't they gorgeous? I can't thank you all enough—much love to you!!! xoxo

Lori Jackson is the magic maker. I say that every time, but she outdid herself with this one. This cover is flawless, and I couldn't give her a lot to go on, because how do you explain this story? But somehow she got me and…*voilà*!!! Absolute perfection. I love you, Lori!!! xoxo

Ashlee O'Brien—Where do I even start? We began our journey together. I was getting ready to release my debut, and she had just launched Ashes and Vellichor. She made the trailers for *Serenity* and it's been her and me ever since. Not only did she make all the pretties and alpha read every page of this "cowboy cult triad" (I love that—her words!), she's my family, my *'book daughter'* (her momma lets me borrow her), who's been with me every step of the way. I *love* my model covers, and I will always have them, but I wanted to give readers the choice of an alternate cover, and I wanted that cover to represent the story on the pages inside just as much as the models do. Ashlee is the only one who could do that, and she exceeded any expectation I could've ever had. She's stuck with me. I'm keeping her. And, girly, you already know I love you the mostest!!! xoxo

Stacey Blake of Champagne Book Design makes the pages so darn pretty—she's so talented! Unfortunately, I have to write this before she formats, so I've yet to see this one. But I already know it's perfect, because she's the best!!! I love you, Stacey!!! xoxo

My beta team—**Charbee Balderson, Jennifer Bishop, Heather Hahn, Kim Lannan, Devon Lomas, Marjorie Lord, Lee Ann Mathis, Anastasia Meimeteas, Melinda Parker, Sabrena Simpson, Rebecca Vazquez**, and **Staci Way**, together with my **ARC team**—as always, thank you isn't nearly enough, but thank you. Here's to Fireball, Kit Kat bars, and lots of laughs, because no one has more fun than us. I love and appreciate you all so much!!! xoxo

Bloggers, Bookstagrammers, and **Booktokkers**—It would be remiss of me not to recognize your continued support of my often twisty stories. I wish I could name each and every one of you here, but I see you. I'm beyond grateful every time one of you likes a post or shares a graphic. All the beautiful edits, reels and TikToks. You're so amazing!!! I appreciate every single thing you do, big or small, to support me and share my books with readers. There isn't one indie author who would be anywhere without you, your love of books, and your dedication to us—so a gazillion times, thank you!!!

The beautiful **Redlings** in my Facebook group, *Behind the Red Door*. You know how much I love you all!!! If you're not there, you should join us—most wonderful group of humans I know.

And as always, my lovely **readers**. For those of you who are new to me—welcome to my madness, and thank you for reading this book. I hope you loved kickin' your boots off in Brookside for a while. There's a place called the Red Door you should probably visit—just sayin'!

As for the rest of you—thank you for sticking around. You know I love you!!!

Until next time…
Much love,
Dyan xoxo

Seth, ten years old.

He sat buckled in the passenger seat of his father's old Chevy. Spice Girls playing on the radio. It reeked of cigarette smoke, whiskey, and cheap aftershave. Jarrid Black never smoked in the house. His congregation was blind to his fondness for the demon drink. Seth was more than well-acquainted with it, though.

They were on the way to Miss Catherine's. He hated going there and he didn't like her very much. She was surly to everyone, with the exception of his father. That didn't surprise him at all. Folks from church worshipped the preacher as if he were God himself. Sometimes Seth thought he actually believed he was.

His father lit up a Marlboro. Choking, Seth cracked the window open, letting the cold, damp March air rush in, and turned his face toward the glass.

"Seth." Jarrid glared sideways, taking a drag off his cancer stick. "Close it."

"But I can't breathe and it stinks."

Turning his head toward him, he exhaled. "Must I tell you again?"

"No, sir." He cranked the window back up.

Seth knew better than to disobey him. He was in a halfway decent mood this morning, and if he wanted permission to ride his bike with Jonathan to the arcade this afternoon, it had to stay that way. He'd deal with the stench.

The Dairy Queen rolled by. Closed for the winter, it wouldn't open again until the end of April. *Dumb.* Did they really think no one wanted ice cream when it snowed?

Then the car took an all-too-familiar turn at the next

corner. Lowering the window all the way down, his father flicked the cigarette out onto the street. It bounced a couple times, the embers creating a cascade of sparks before rolling into a puddle at the curb.

He left it down, in spite of the cold, waving his hand in the air around him. Then he spritzed on more of that nasty cologne. As if that smelled any better than his disgusting smoke.

It didn't.

At least with the window open, Seth could breathe.

They parked at the curb in front of the small two-story clapboard house. Catherine must have been waiting for them at the door. She opened it the moment they arrived.

Seth was sent to sit in the parlor, with the promise of a Coca-Cola that he knew would never come. Same as always. Glancing around the room he'd sat in a million times before, he twiddled his thumbs. A photo of Grace, when she was around his age, stood in a frame on the mantel. He liked her. She was nice. His father said she was his angel. When he was younger, she'd come to his house and stay with him while the preacher took care of church business. But he was too old for a babysitter now.

After what felt like an eternity, Jarrid and Catherine returned to the parlor. She carried a bundle wrapped in a fluffy white blanket. Grace stood by herself behind them. Hands balled into fists at her sides. Head hanging low, her pale-blonde hair covered her face.

"Son." His father stepped forward. "God has fulfilled his promise."

Miss Catherine put the baby in his arms. "She's for you, Seth Thomas."

He gazed in awe at her beautiful, precious face.

"Now, you must keep your promise to God, and everyone here, that you will love, cherish, and protect the gift that has been bestowed upon you..." Jarrid bent over and kissed the baby's head. "...every day of your life."

"I will. I promise."

She was given to him the day she was born.

God's promised gift.

He fell in love with her the moment she was placed in his arms.

And he'd loved her ever since.

Linnea. Was. His.

Books by

DYAN LAYNE

Red Door Series
Serenity
Affinity
Maelstrom
The Other Brother
Drummer Boy
Son of a Preacher Man (coming soon)
Rhythm Man (coming soon)

Standalones
Don't Speak
The Third Son
Whiteout (coming soon)

About the Author

Dyan Layne is a nurse boss by day and the writer of edgy sensual tales by night—and on weekends. She's never without her Kindle, and can usually be found tapping away at her keyboard with a hot latte *and* a cold Dasani Lime—and sometimes champagne. She can't sing a note, but often answers in song because isn't there a song for just about everything? Born and raised a Chicago girl, she currently lives in Tampa, Florida, and is the mother of four handsome sons and a beautiful daughter, who are all grown up now, but can still make her crazy—and she loves it that way! Because normal is just so boring.

One

'm going to fuck you. You may not know it yet, but I do. It's only a matter of time. I've been watching you. I swear that you've been watching me too, but maybe it's all in my head. No matter. Because I've seen you, I've talked to you and I've come to a conclusion: You are fucking beautiful. And I will make you lust me.

The words danced on crisp white paper. Her fingers trembled and her feet became unsteady, so she leaned against the wall of exposed brick to right herself, clutching the typewritten note in her hand. She read it again. A powerful longing surged through her body and her thighs clenched.

Who could have written it? She couldn't fathom a single soul who might be inspired to write such things to her. Maybe those words weren't meant for her? Maybe whoever had written the note slid it beneath the wrong doormat in his haste to deliver it undetected?

Linnea Martin, beautiful? Someone had to be pulling a prank. *Yeah. That's more likely.*

She sighed as she turned and closed the solid wood front door. She glanced up at the mirror that hung in the entry hall and eyes the color of moss blinked back at her. Long straight hair, the color of which she had never been able to put into a category—a dirty-blonde maybe—hung past her shoulders, resting close to where her nipples protruded against the fitted cotton shirt she wore. Her skin was fair, but not overly pale. She supposed some people might describe her as pretty, in an average sort of way, but not beautiful.

Not anything but ordinary.

Linnea slowly crumpled up the note in her hand. She clenched it tight and held it to her breast before tossing it into the wastebasket.

Deflated, she threw her tote bag on the coffee table and plopped down on the pale-turquoise-colored sofa that she'd purchased at that quaint secondhand store on First Avenue. She often stopped in there on her way home from the restaurant, carefully eyeing the eclectic array of items artfully displayed throughout the shop. Sometimes, on a good day when tips had been plentiful, she bought herself something nice. Something pretty. Like the pale-turquoise sofa.

Linnea grabbed the current novel she was engrossed in from the coffee table and adjusted herself into a comfortable position, attempting to read. But after she read the same page three times she knew she couldn't concentrate, one sentence blurred into the next, so she set it back down. She clicked on the television and scrolled through the channels, but there was nothing on that could hold her interest. The words replayed in her head.

I'm going to fuck you.

Damn him! Damn that fucker to hell for being so cruel to leave that note at her door, for making her feel…things. The words had thrilled her for a fleeting moment, but then the excitement quickly faded, replaced by a loneliness deep in her chest. Love may never be in the cards for her, or lust for that matter, as much as she might want it to be.

Once upon a time she had believed in fairy tales and dreamt of knights on white stallions and handsome princes, of castle turrets shrouded in mist, of strong yet gentle hands weaving wildflowers in her long honeyed locks—just like the alpha heroes in the tattered paperbacks she had kept hidden under her bed as a teenager. She thought if she was patient long enough, her happily-ever-after would come. She thought that one day, when she was all grown up, that a brave knight, a handsome prince, would rescue her from her grandmother's prison and make all her dreams come true.

Stupid girl.

Her dreams turned into nightmares, and 'one day' never came. She doubted it ever would now. It was her own fault anyway. She closed her eyelids tight, trying to stop the tears that threatened to escape, to keep the memories from flooding back. Linnea had spent years pushing them into an unused corner, a vacant place where they could be hidden away and never be thought of again.

It was dark. She must have been sitting there for quite a while, transfixed in her thoughts. The small living room was void of illumination, except for the blue luminescence that radiated from the unwatched television. Linnea dragged herself over to it and clicked it off. She stood there for a moment waiting for her eyes to adjust to the absence of light and went upstairs.

Steaming water flowed in a torrent from the brushed-nickel faucet, filling the old clawfoot tub. She poured a splash of almond oil into the swirling liquid. As the fragrance released, she bent over the tub to breathe in the sweet vapor that rose from the water and wafted through the room. Slipping the sleeves from her shoulders, the silky robe gave way and fell to a puddle on the floor.

Timorously, she tested the water with her toes, and finding it comfortably hot, she eased her body all the way in. For a time serenity could be found in the soothing water that enveloped her.

You may not know it yet, but I do. It's only a matter of time.

At once her pulse quickened, and without conscious thought her slick fingertips skimmed across her rosy nipples. They hardened at her touch. And a yearning flourished between the folds of flesh down below. Linnea clenched her thighs together, trying to make it go away, but with her attempt to squelch the pulsing there, she only exacerbated her budding desire. And she ached.

Ever so slowly, her hands eased across her flat belly to rest at the junction between her quivering thighs. She wanted so badly to touch herself there and alleviate the agony she found herself in. But as badly as she wanted to, needed to, Linnea would not allow herself the pleasure of her own touch. She sat up instead, the now-tepid water sloshing forward with the sudden movement, and reaching out in front of her she turned the water back on.

She knew it was wicked. Lying there with her legs spread wide and her feet propped on the edge of the tub, she allowed the violent stream of water to pound upon her swollen bud. It throbbed under the assault and her muscles quaked. She'd be tempted to pull on her nipples if she wasn't forced to brace her hands against the porcelain walls of the clawfoot tub for leverage.

Any second now. She was so close.

I'm going to fuck you.

And he did. With just his words, he did.

Her head tipped back as the sensations jolted through her body. The sounds of her own keening cries were muffled by the downpour from the faucet. Spent, she let the water drain from the tub and rested her cheek upon the cold porcelain.

Prologue

"Aidan, baby."

His mother took him by the hand and pulled him along behind her as she hurried out of the kitchen. He'd only eaten half of his grilled cheese sandwich and some grapes when the banging started. It startled him and he knocked over his juice. By the time she went to the front door to see who it was, the banging noise was coming from the other side of the house.

"You can't keep me out, bitch."

It was a man. He was yelling. He sounded angry. Aidan didn't recognize his voice.

His mother seemed to, though. Her eyes got real big and she covered her mouth with her hand. It was shaking.

There was a hutch in the living room that the television sat on. It had doors on the bottom. He hid in there sometimes. His mother opened one of the doors, and tossing the toys that were inside it to the floor, she kissed him on his head and urged him to crawl inside.

"We're going to play a game of hide and seek from the loud man outside, okay, baby?" his mother whispered.

Aidan nodded.

The banging got louder.

"You have to be very, very quiet so he doesn't know you're here."

It sounded like she was choking and tears leaked out of her eyes, but she smiled at him.

"Like at story time?"

Aidan's mother took him to story time at the library every Saturday, and afterwards if he'd been a good boy, she would let him get an ice cream.

"Yes, baby. Just like that." She nodded with tears running down her face. "Now stay very still and don't speak a word until I tell you to—no matter what, okay?"

He nodded again. "Okay, Mommy."

"I love you, Aidan."

"I love you, Mommy."

Everyone said the place was haunted. The kids at school. The people in town. It didn't look scary, but nobody ever went anywhere near the two-story white clapboard house that was set off by itself on the cove.

It was to be her home now.

Molly stood at the wrought-iron gate with her mother, holding onto her hand. She clutched her *Bear in the Big Blue House* backpack, that she'd had since she was four, with the other. A boy with sandy-blond hair sat on the porch steps. Aidan Fischer. He didn't pay them, or his father unloading their belongings from the U-Haul, any mind. He had a notebook in his lap and a pencil between his fingers. It looked like he was drawing.

The boy chewed on his lip as he moved the pencil over the paper. Even though he was in the fifth grade, and three years older than her, Molly knew who he was. Everybody did. He was the boy who didn't talk. And six days from today, when her mother married his father, that boy was going to be her brother.

Character Index

In alphabetical order by first name

Airdrie—Friesian mare

Amanda Jacoby Brooks (*deceased*)—wife to Matthew, mother to Kellan, younger sister to Heather

Arien Brogan—daughter to Jennifer, stepdaughter to Matthew Brooks

Benjamin Brooks—infant son of Matthew and Jennifer

Billy Gantry—younger brother of Jake

Cassandra "Cassie" Lewis—elder sister of Shiloh

Cayden Elijah Brooks—Harper's twin brother

Daisy—Arien's American quarter horse

Emily Keough—daughter of Kimberly, Timothy, and William (*deceased*)

Garrett Brooks (*deceased*)—father to Matthew and Kimberly, grandfather to Kellan, Tanner, Benjamin, and Emily

Griffin Archer—partner to Cassie and Shiloh

Gunner—Kellan's Friesian stallion

Harper Elizabeth Brooks—Cayden's twin sister

Heather Jacoby Brooks (*deceased*)—wife to Matthew, mother to Tanner, elder sister to Amanda

Jake Gantry—elder brother to Billy

Jennifer Brogan Brooks—mother to Arien and Benjamin, third wife to Matthew, stepmother to Kellan and Tanner

John Jacoby—father to Heather and Amanda, grandfather to Kellan and Tanner

Kellan Brooks—firstborn son of Matthew and Amanda *(deceased)*, half-brother to Tanner

Kimberly Brooks Keough—sister to Matthew, mother to Emily, aunt to Kellan, Tanner, and Benjamin

Lenny—the butcher

Levi Gantry *(deceased)*—one of the original settlers of Brookside, great-grandfather of Jake and Billy

Miss Lilly—dressmaker, sister to Victor, aunt to Jake and Billy

Maizie Jacoby—baker, wife to John, mother to Heather and Amanda

Matthew Brooks—father to Kellan, Tanner, and Benjamin, husband to Jennifer, stepfather to Arien, brother to Kimberly, uncle to Emily

Melinda Brooks—mother to Matthew and Kimberly, grandmother to Kellan, Tanner, Benjamin, and Emily

Noëlle—Airdrie's foal, sired by Gunner

Paul Brooks *(deceased)*—father to Matthew and Kimberly, grandfather to Kellan, Tanner, Benjamin, and Emily

Savannah Mason—classmate of Arien's in Denver

Shiloh Lewis—younger sister of Cassie

Sunday, Monday, Tuesday, Wednesday, Friday—Brooks Ranch border collies

Tanner Brooks—son of Matthew and Heather *(deceased)*, half-brother to Kellan

Timothy Keough *(deceased)*—elder brother to William, husband to Kimberly, father to Emily

Tux—Tanner's Shire stallion

Victor "Doc" Gantry—physician, father to Jake and Billy

William Keough *(deceased)*—younger brother of Timothy, husband to Kimberly, father to Emily

Made in the USA
Columbia, SC
24 September 2024

42285794R00164